D1706793

AUDRE

&

BASH

ARE

JUST

FRIENDS

BY TIA WILLIAMS

A LOVE SONG FOR RICKI WILDE

SEVEN DAYS IN JUNE

THE PERFECT FIND

THE ACCIDENTAL DIVA

IT CHICKS

IT CHICKS

IT CHICKS: SIXTEEN CANDLES

*For Carolina May, my favorite girl
in the world*

AUDRE

&

BASH

ARE

JUST

FRIENDS

Chapter 1

"Let's get back to your issue, Sparrow." Audre sat perched atop a toilet, resting her chin on her hand.

"Wait, which one?" asked Sparrow. She was splayed out in an empty bathtub, gulping vodka from a motivational water bottle. (STAY HYDRATED! NO EXCUSES! KEEP DRINKING!)

"Well . . . your love life," she reminded her gently.

"Oh. Right."

It was the last day of school, which always felt like a holiday. A day when all previous beefs and dramas were put to bed. No matter who they were—emo boys, anime girls, theater heads, full-glam baddies, fake thugs, K-pop queens, rich kids, scholarship kids, and people of all sexual preferences, genders, and astrological affiliations—everyone got along. It was only 4 PM, but almost every Cheshire Prep junior she knew was wasted, and hanging out at Reshma Wells's multimillion-dollar house. It was one of the bougiest brownstones in one of Brooklyn's bougiest neighborhoods, Park Slope.

As usual, Audre Mercy-Moore was *at* the party, but she wasn't *partying.* In fact, she only heard the muffled party sounds (Ice Spice and screechy laughter) through the walls. But she could imagine the rest. No doubt the air was thick with the scent of fruity vape smoke, Sol de Janeiro perfume, and pizza. Assorted sixteen- and seventeen-year-olds were hooking up all over Reshma's parents' furniture. Her classmates were wearing a copy-paste blur of Brandy Melville and white Air Force Ones. This party was identical to every other party.

Honestly, all Audre Mercy-Moore wanted to do was go home and pack for "Dadifornia"—that is, her annual summerlong stay with her dad and stepmom in Malibu Beach, California. The trip was her heaven, her summertime reward for busting her ass all year to be a model student. Her dad's cottage was so cozy, with its sun-faded teal exterior and seaside deck. Audre's bedroom window faced the beach, where the roar of the ocean lulled her to sleep every night.

Yes, she was a born-and-bred city girl. But Dadifornia was her happy place. For many reasons, she couldn't get there fast enough. But right now, she had a job to do.

Focus, thought Audre. *This is about Sparrow. Are you doing your "active listening" face?*

She snuck a quick glance in the floor-length wall mirror—doe eyes, dimples, a tousled tumble of gold-streaked goddess braids. Thrifted slip dress and Adidas. She was cute, and honestly? She'd earned it after years of acne treatments, braces, and a brutal keratin "treatment" that destroyed her natural curls in tenth grade. (On the bright side, without that keratin trauma, she wouldn't have started the Protective Styles Club, which was a hit among all five of the Black girls at Cheshire Prep.) Her only pieces of jewelry were gold hoops and a cameo ring—the good luck charm that had belonged to her great-great-grandma.

On a good day, she felt above average. But she would've killed to be dangerously sexy. Hot. Unfortunately, she landed just on the outskirts of hot. The suburbs of hot.

It's fine, she thought. *College is when my life will start. When my sexy chapter begins. Now focus on Sparrow!*

On any other day, Audre would've loved helping Sparrow through her latest mental health crisis. She was one of her favorite lifers. At Cheshire Prep, "lifers" were the kids who'd started Lower School in kindergarten. They'd witnessed every stage of each other's lives. Identities were established early, and they stuck like glue. Audre's identity? The person you hoped to run into in the school bathroom if you needed to cry, vomit, reapply lip gloss, anything.

She wasn't just junior class president, she was also the unofficial therapist of Cheshire Prep—a title she'd given herself back in middle school, when she used to charge classmates twenty-five dollars a session. (These days, she demanded forty-five. Cash only.) For as long as she could remember, people were drawn to her, dying to share their troubles. And Audre loved "therapizing" her friends. She had every intention of becoming a world-famous psychologist one day, so she needed the practice. Who better to study human behavior on than kids she'd literally grown up with?

Audre was everyone's rock.

The thing about rocks, though? They're hard on the outside *and* on the inside. They don't have insecurities. Or doubts. Or panic attacks, like the one she'd had earlier that day.

"Talk to me, Sparrow," said Audre in her kind-but-firm professional voice.

"So, I'm at the diner on Monday after school." As she spoke, Sparrow was peeling off her press-on nails and dropping them into the tub. "At the register, I realized I forgot my ATM card. And then this guy...this angel...shows up and pays for my bacon-egg-and-cheese."

Sparrow paused to sip her vodka. After a moment, Audre realized she wanted her to guess. "Who was the guy?"

"Bash Henry. That new senior at Hillcrest Prep? Moved to Brooklyn in February? Well, he's not a senior anymore—he must've graduated today. He's. So. Fine. Do you know him?"

Audre knew of Bash Henry. Hillcrest and Cheshire Prep were rival schools—and Black private school kids were always on each other's radar, since there weren't a ton of them. At most, they were friends. At the very least, they'd nod at each other in Silent African American Solidarity. But she hadn't met Bash yet. Rumor had it, he'd hooked up with three people at Rae Drake's Sweet Sixteen (with no official invite). And that some Hillcrest kid had a psychotic break in health class while tripping off mushrooms Bash gave him. For a new kid, he already had a wild reputation.

"He paid for your lunch?" continued Audre. "He's fine *and* generous."

"I know, right? Our eyes met and there was this COSMIC. SPARK. We both felt it."

"Love this. So what's the problem?"

Sparrow peeled off another nail. "Today, Marco told me he likes him, too. Look, Marco's my best friend, but you know how competitive I am. I'm an Aries moon—I go feral. It's why I had to quit the chess club."

Audre grimaced, remembering. "Hmm. So, do you know if Bash likes guys?"

"Unclear. It's more that he has this energy where everyone's attracted to him. He's just a vibe. He wears lots of rings and thrifted shit, and is floppy and lanky, and just seems, like, slutty but in a spiritual way?"

"Sounds like you really got to know him at the diner. How long did you talk?"

"About thirty seconds." Sparrow's face crumpled into a sob. "Fuck. I miss him."

"Good, good, just lean into the discomfort," said Audre, struggling to keep a straight face. "What do I always say?"

"It's not love, it's adrenaline."

"Did I say that? I don't remember that."

"Yeah, at my twelfth birthday party." Her voice was getting squeakier the more she drank. "I burst a nose capillary after crying for three hours over that Bieber doc. Remember, you left early cause your mom never let you go to sleepovers."

Audre stiffened at the mention of her mom. Nervously, she fidgeted with her cameo ring, twirling it around her finger. Once Audre's biggest fan and fiercest protector, these days her mom was practically a stranger. She didn't even come to the awards ceremony. She must've just...forgotten? Two, three, four years ago, that would've been unthinkable. Their relationship, once as cozy and impenetrable as a well-knit sweater, had been slowly unspooling all year.

Another reason why she couldn't wait to get to Dadifornia.

"Yes, but I also say, decenter boys. You're the star of your life. You're the prize."

"But Bash is so beautiful."

"He's beautiful, Sparrow, but he's also just a boy. Not to be gender normative, but have you met a boy? There's no reason to be intimidated by one." She lowered her voice to a stage whisper. "They barely have a coherent thought in their heads."

"That is . . . pretty gender normative."

"My point is, if you pursue Bash and he likes you back, cool! If not? His loss."

"But why would he like me? He could date anyone. I've heard that he has." She slumped down in the tub, walking her sneakers up the tiled wall. "Would I be hotter with highlights?"

"Sparrow, there's someone out there dying to love you. Don't 'fix' yourself before they get a chance to fall for the real you."

Damn. Audre wasn't even on her best game, and she gave herself chills with that one.

"My ex was into the real me. Dumping him was a mistake."

"Your ex was a cheater, Sparrow. He gave you and half our class mono."

"So it's a no?"

"*Yes.* Going back to him would be toxic settling."

"Toxic settling?" asked Sparrow, accidentally dropping a press-on nail into her vodka.

"It's when you return to a situation that's bad for you. If it was bad once, it'll always be bad. Think of it this way—if you see the same tree twice in the forest, it means you're lost."

Sparrow gasped. "You're so. Fucking. Wise."

Let's hope Stanford University thinks so, Audre thought, her mind accidentally wandering. College applications were due next fall, which was practically tomorrow. Stanford had the best psych program in the nation. And with her high school record—class president, debate team captain, AP everything, insane PSAT scores and extracurriculars—she should've been a no-brainer. But almost everyone applying would have her stats. It wasn't enough.

So, Audre had figured out how to wow the admissions board. Along with her application, she'd turn in a special project. *Extra* extra credit if you will. A self-published self-help book for teens. Rules for thriving based on her best advice! It was an excellent idea.

Well, it would be an excellent idea as soon as she figured out what to write. Unfortunately, brainstorming wasn't going well. Yet another reason she couldn't get to Dadifornia fast enough. In the laid-back paradise of Malibu, she could finish writing by summer's end—just in time for applications in the fall.

As Audre opened her mouth to answer Sparrow, Reshma Wells burst into the lavish bathroom. Hurricane Reshma.

Therapy session over.

Chapter 2

Reshma Wells was the party hostess. She was also Audre's best friend. Well, usually. At times, their extremely alpha personalities sort of clashed. When they were good, Reshma was her platonic soulmate. When they were bad, Reshma was her Regina George. But they were used to the ups and downs; they'd been friends since childhood.

"Audre!" she exclaimed in her British-inflected accent (she'd moved to New York City from London in fourth grade). Leaning in the doorway with her huge, smoky eyes, wild black waves, bralette, and slouchy jeans, she looked like an exquisite, haunted baby doll. "Bro. Ellery told me that Akilah knows who's responsible for Coco-Jean's pregnancy scare."

Sparrow gasped, sitting up poker-straight in the tub. "Tell us."

"We're in the middle of a session!" Audre loved Reshma to death, but she always did this. Showing up and sucking all the air out of the room.

"First of all, this is my house. Secondly, this is urgent." She draped herself over Sparrow like a blanket, entangling their feet together. Sparrow's eyes practically crossed, she was so mesmerized. Reshma had never spoken more than five words to her.

"You don't mind if I cut in, do you?" purred Reshma in her permanent rasp. She'd had bronchitis last October and kept the voice.

"I don't mind," gushed Sparrow, who had a nail stuck in her bangs.

"Great," sighed Audre. "To protect your confidentiality, let's finish tomorrow, okay?"

Audre knew when to pick her battles. And Reshma was a force of nature. They'd been besties since Reshma showed up in her fourth-grade class and Audre was assigned to be her "buddy." She was Indian by birth, adopted by British pop star parents, and was posh, beautiful, and five steps ahead of everyone. While most Cheshire girls were reading Dork Diaries, she was reading Mafia boss romances.

Though they were only nine at the time, Audre and Reshma were socially savvy enough to know they'd been buddied up because they were The Only Kids of Color in Mrs. Jones's Class. It didn't matter, though. Because they'd bonded in seconds! They both loved pink Simply Lemonade, poetry, and roller-skating. Reshma taught Audre how to eat with chopsticks and do winged eyeliner. Audre taught Reshma about horoscopes and horror movies. They decided they were a dynamic duo.

Their biggest trait in common? Both girls wore confidence as armor. The second-biggest one? They kept their deepest emotions to themselves.

If she were being honest, Audre wasn't sure she trusted Reshma with intimate secrets. Reshma was so self-centered (a result of her parents both spoiling *and* neglecting her), and Audre saw how she plowed through crushes, clothes, and interests. She didn't want to be discarded, too.

"Here's the story," continued Reshma. "Remember when Coco-Jean told us she missed her period? That same day, someone saw Bash Henry buying Plan B at CVS."

"My Bash Henry? Coco-Jean got to him first? They had actual sex?" Sparrow looked crushed. "God, why am I this upset about a boy I barely know? I'm so broken."

Before Audre could answer, Reshma jumped in.

"Everyone's broken, baby. It's about being *just* broken enough to seem sexy and interesting." She took Sparrow's hand. "Look. You're a bad bitch. You speak fluent Latvian..."

"Latin," corrected Audre.

"...and you're brilliant on the tambourine."

"Trombone," corrected Sparrow.

"...and it seems like pulling a cishet boy would be easy. Just be mean to them."

"Easy for you. But I'm not you." Clumsily, Sparrow disentangled herself from Reshma and climbed out of the tub. "Look at you! Perfect body. Perfect clothes. Your parents are goals. Mine hate each other and hate me. How am I supposed to understand functional relationships?"

Reshma snorted at this. "Goals? My father's fucking his plastic surgeon and wears violently skinny jeans. Mum's in a baby food weight loss cult and hasn't eaten anything solid since 2016." She pointed at Audre. "*Her* life is perfect. Fine-ass stepdad. Cool mom with the most incredible, random facts. One time, she told me that if you see a huge cluster of mushrooms out in the wild, it's growing over something dead."

"I hate mushrooms," sighed Audre, marveling at how quickly this conversation went left.

Sparrow was scowling. "Why am I talking to you two about boys, anyway? Reshma, you're extremely gay."

"I'm a child of God," she said.

"And Audre? I'm saying this as a friend, not a client.... You're anti-romance."

Audre gasped. "Not true! I'm just currently in my self-partnered era, that's all."

"I think I'm too drunk for this conversation," squeaked Sparrow, making her first reasonable statement of the night. "I'm going home, lighting my abundance candle, and doing my manifestation ritual. Bash will be mine by the summer solstice."

Audre and Reshma watched her stagger out of the room and then looked at each other with deadpan expressions. Reshma burst into throaty laughter.

"You really take that chaotic Swiftie seriously?"

"I support all women," said Audre. "Well, most. And secondly, stop interrupting my sessions! I love you, but advice is not your thing."

She giggled at this, knowing it was true. "Speaking of advice, how's your book going? What's the title?"

"*One, Two, Three, Four . . . THRIVE! A Teen's Rules for Flourishing on This Dying Planet.*"

Reshma paused. "Can I be honest with you?"

"No," said Audre quickly. "It's just a placeholder title! And I haven't started writing the book. Every time I brainstorm, I get all insecure. Like, am I even qualified to do this?"

"Oh, stop stressing." Reshma climbed out of the tub and linked her arm in Audre's. She led Audre out of the bathroom and into the rowdy crowd. "You don't have to write your book tonight. Wanna come with me to the after-party?"

"Where is it?" hollered Audre over the bass.

Reshma cackled. "Bash Henry's."

"Not this kid again."

"Right? I feel like if we say his name three times, he'll appear."

"Like Beetlejuice."

"Sparrow would immediately die."

"She better not—she owes me forty-five dollars."

As the girls zigzagged their way through the galaxy-light-spotted clusters of kids living, laughing, and loving all over Reshma's manse, Audre couldn't help but think that she had felt safer in the bathroom. In there, therapizing Sparrow, she was in control. At the height of her powers. But out here, surrounded by unselfconscious people giving in to Having a Good Time just for the sake of having a good time? She felt like an alien. Suddenly, she was too aware of her hands. She felt scrawny. Out of step. Exposed (one of her least favorite feelings).

Parties, drinking, flirting, small talk? Not her skill set. And what even was the point of liking somebody when most high school couples break up before college, anyway? Even tougher, how did you resist the urge to debate when someone lightheart-edly brought up a problematic conversation topic? Audre knew too much about human nature, was the thing. She knew why people acted the way they did, and what choices caused which outcomes. How do you let go and just ... live ... when you knew how every story ended?

Just then, she and Reshma stopped in their tracks. The hallway was blocked by Benji and Delia, two juniors high off edibles and hooking up on a beanbag. Benji was shirtless. Delia, a proud furry, had on bunny slippers and bunny ears.

"Ew! It's barely 5 PM, have some fucking decorum," Reshma hollered over the roaring bass.

Audre said nothing. She couldn't. She stood there, frozen, staring at her phone. An icy, ominous chill ran down her spine. She'd just received a text. It was a version of the same one she'd gotten several times over the past month.

> **Ellison:** pls answer. we deleted the video.
> pls don't tell anyone what happened. no
> one saw the vid. ok?

"What's wrong?" shouted Reshma.

Audre shook her head. Her chest was tightening; her throat was closing. A weird tingle stung her palms. Hot tears sprang to her eyes. She felt out of control.

She managed to holler, "Gotta run, I'll text later," and then hopped over the Delia-Benji pretzel, rushed downstairs, and ran out the back door into the late afternoon heat.

She didn't stop till she was a block away. Then she sat down on the stoop of someone's brownstone. With an anguished groan, she clenched her teeth and her fists, fighting off waves of nausea and rising hysteria.

No one saw it. No one saw it. No one saw it.

1, 2, 3, 4 … THRIVE!
A Teen's Rules for Flourishing on This Dying Planet

By Audre Mercy-Moore

Rule 1:
Always know when to leave a party.

CHAPTER 3

After several minutes, her breathing slowed to nor-
mal. With trembling hands, she deleted Ellison's text. She always
did.

And then she headed home. She lived a short ten-minute walk
from Reshma's—the same neighborhood—but today the walk
seemed to take forever. It felt like she was walking in quicksand.

I'm in denial, she thought. *A therapist in denial, so dumb. Do I
really believe that if I ignore Ellison, he'll go away? That if I delete the
texts, they never existed? That's not how life works.*

When Audre opened her apartment door, her stomach sank—
the same way it had for most of eleventh grade. There was barely
a trace of the tidy home of her childhood. Now, there were boxes
of books, bags of clothes, piles of kitchen tiles (why?), and baby
furniture crowded in the living room. The clutter spilled into
Audre's bedroom, which had been demolished.

The disorder drove her insane. Every time she opened the
door, she expected to walk into a home she recognized. The
home she grew up in. Before it smelled like sawdust and sweaty

construction guys. Before her bedroom had been demolished. Before The Goblin.

The Goblin was Audre's secret name for her year-old sister. Everyone else called her Baby Alice.

She knew it was a terrible nickname—after all, her sister was just a blob, as harmless as an amoeba—but facts were facts, and Audre could trace the disintegration of her life directly back to The Goblin's birth.

That's when her mom, Eva, and her stepdad, Shane, decided that instead of moving to a bigger place, they'd split Audre's bedroom in half and build a nursery ("since you'll be off to college in a few years, anyway"). That's when Audre became a displaced person, packing up her bedroom into plastic bags and moving to the couch. No door, no privacy, no good night's sleep.

That's also when Eva and Shane started planning a wedding. They'd already gotten hitched at city hall, but for some reason they decided they urgently wanted a big celebration.

Eva had a lifelong medical condition—daily migraines that sometimes required hospital stays. And Shane was a recovering alcoholic. He'd been sober for six years, but still. She'd read enough about alcoholism to know that sobriety was a daily battle.

They had real shit to deal with! So why complicate things with a baby, a wedding, and home repairs? Audre was glad her mom had found her person. It was a relief, not watching her juggle single parenthood, illness, and a big career alone. And Eva and Shane were both authors, so they "got" each other. Great, but sometimes Audre felt like the only adult in the family.

Maybe it's because they were high school sweethearts who broke up as teens and reunited as adults, thought Audre. *Maybe together, they slip back into adolescent behavior. Interesting theory. I'll research this on mentalhealth.org later.*

For the moment, Audre turned her attention to her mom, who was sitting on the living room rug. She was surrounded by toys, books, and bottles. Baby Alice was perched on her lap, taking turns nursing and shrieking.

(Their part-time nanny had just quit to become a nun. But that was a whole other story.)

"Oh, thank GOD you're home," wailed Eva. Baby Alice looked at Audre and shrieked.

"Same, kid," muttered Audre, flopping down on the couch. Aka, her bed.

Baby Alice had Shane's honey-brown eyes. And, like Audre, she'd inherited Eva's knuckle-deep dimples. Yes, she was cute. But she was irritating. Like a paper cut between your fingers that also smells like sour breastmilk.

"Shhh, sweetie. It's okay. You're fine," cooed Eva, rocking Baby Alice in her arms. After a moment, she settled down and Eva popped a paci in her mouth. As The Goblin lay wide-awake on Eva's chest, she glared at Audre with a side-eye so dramatic, it was almost funny.

"I know, the crying sucks," said Eva through a yawn. She was fully made-up, her coily curls swept into a half-up, half-down style. She was wearing chunky gold hoops, a Wu-Tang sweatshirt, cutoff shorts—and had an ice pack tied to her forehead.

Audre knew what that meant. "It's bad today?"

"Ehh. It's a four." Level four on the 1–10 pain scale. "Sorry Baby Alice is so intense today. She's stressed out from teething."

"I'm stressed out, too. But I have an inside voice."

Eva turned her way, her ice pack tilting to one side. "You're stressed? What about?"

Audre wanted to scream. Did her mom not realize that she, Shane, and Baby Alice had turned her life upside down—during the year when grades mattered most to colleges? It's not like she could explain her stressful family to Stanford. What would she even say?

Dear Stanford Admissions Board,

Hi, I'm Audre. My mom was my best friend. She was only twenty when she had me, so we sort of grew up together. When I was a baby, my parents divorced and Dad moved to Cali. It's weird, cause most moms are annoying, but mine was different. She never judged me or dismissed me. We lived in our happy little world, with its own rules and customs. Speaking in a French accent on Wednesday nights. Watching horror movies on Saturday nights. Attending drag-queen brunch every Easter.

When I had a bad day at school, she just knew and would order my favorite pizza without saying a word. And I could sense when her head was getting bad, the way old people know that it's going to rain. Codependent? I mean, yeah. But we were best friends. And then came Shane. Look, I'm not a hater. But you know when couples are so giddy it's like all self-awareness evaporates and they frolic around like they invented being in love? They do that. Imagine living with the gooiest couple in the cafeteria. It's so obnoxious. Hello? Some of us are single.

And I could handle it if my mom still noticed me. But little by little, we've grown apart. It's been a slow, painful untangling, but it's final. I've been replaced.

And now Mom, Shane, and Baby Alice live in their own happy little world. It's like the sun shines only on them. I'm fading away, Stanford. It's a classic case of Oldest Daughter Erasure, which is a term I invented. I've already registered the trademark.

Anyway, please accept me to your prestigious institution.

Love,
Audre Zora Maya Toni Mercy-Moore

For the zillionth time that day, she thanked the universe for Dadifornia. Two more weeks, just two more weeks.

For her sanity, Audre changed the subject. "Why are you wearing makeup?"

Baby Alice spit out her pacifier and blew a raspberry at her sister.

"I really can't take her negativity," muttered Audre.

"She's a *baby*," said Eva. "Is my makeup too much?"

"No, you look pretty."

"But do I look relatable? Like you'll want to be my best friend and buy my next book?"

"I guess? Why?"

"So, my next book comes out in September, right? *Back to Belle Fleur*."

Eva was famous for her fifteen-book Cursed series (about a nineteen-year-old witch in passionate love with a vampire). But she'd just finished writing a different book—a memoir about her Black Creole roots. For four years, she'd been researching the Louisiana bayou town of Belle Fleur, where her mom was born. *Back to Belle Fleur* would be a love letter to her maternal ancestors, all of whom were badass superheroes.

"I need to tell my IG followers about the release date. So I'm doing a reel. From the chest up, of course." She wiggled a fuzzy Christmas slipper–clad foot in Audre's direction and then grimaced. Today's migraine was clearly getting worse. "Can you help?"

Didn't she always? Audre popped the paci back in Baby Alice's mouth and then hoisted her up onto her hip. Then she set up Eva's ring light on a side table and aimed her phone at her mom.

Quickly, Eva slid off her ice pack and fluffed up her curls. "Hi, readers! It's Eva Mercy, here to introduce my upcoming book, *Back to Belle Fleur*! It traces the colorful lives of my Creole mother, grandmother, and great-grandmother in Belle Fleur, Louisiana. I'm uncovering all the secrets and lore that have shaped my identity." She beamed, her dimples popping. No one would know she was in pain. "But it's not just about *my* identity. Hellooo, Audreeee?"

Audre hated it when her mom put her on the spot. But the fans loved their mommy-daughter moments—which translated into book sales.

"Hi! I've grown up listening to Mom's stories about the powerful, inspiring sheroes in our family. As she always tells me, Mercy girls do what can't be done! Preorder at link in bio!"

Just then, Baby Alice sunk her two tiny, hard tooth nubs into her finger. Yelping, Audre stopped recording and dropped her phone onto the couch.

"Ow! Mom, take this Goblin . . . I mean, Baby Alice," she said, handing her over. "I hate it when you throw me in your videos like that, with no warning. I'm not even wearing lipstick! And I've had the worst day."

"But you're such a natural." Eva lifted her sweatshirt and resumed nursing. Back to business. "Don't be mad, okay? Just trying to sell books here. Tell me about your day."

"Well, it was the last day of school."

Eva gasped. "That's right, I forgot! Sorry, it's New Mom Brain."

Audre wanted to remind her that she wasn't a new mom. She'd been one for sixteen years. "And we got our yearbooks."

"I love yearbooks. Can I see? I never got one, thanks to my misspent youth." Just then, Shane, her stepdad, emerged from the bedroom. He was wearing gray joggers and a T-shirt that read FLIP IT AND REVERSE IT.

Shane Hall was a hotshot, award-winning novelist. Book reviewers had named him "the voice of a generation." But to Audre, he was like a fun uncle. The guy who, on her thirteenth birthday, had gotten them kicked out of the Museum of Ice Cream for eating the displays.

Shane fist-bumped Audre and then picked up Baby Alice, smothering her cheeks with kisses as she gurgled with glee. Eva looked at the two of them with a lovestruck gaze.

"Hi, honey," she cooed as if she hadn't been home with him all day.

"Hey, honey." He smiled, plopping down next to her.

Gross, thought Audre, handing Shane the yearbook.

"Your head's getting bad, isn't it? I watched a YouTube video saying that bone broth helps migraines," said Shane, jiggling Baby Alice on his knee. "Last night, after I fed Baby Alice around three AM, I deboned an entire chicken, per the tutorial. I'm gonna broth you, baby."

"You know you can buy bone broth," said Audre. "Like, at Whole Foods."

"Food tastes different when Shane cooks for me," sighed Eva. "It tastes like love."

They smiled at each other happily over their Goblin's head. Audre wanted to vomit.

"I'm sorry," she started, "don't y'all have a wedding to plan? And a house to finish? Why are you deliberately trying to make your lives harder?"

"Don't worry about adult things," said Eva. "Anyway, back to your day."

"Fine. So, after school I went to a party at Reshma's house...."

"Her parents were there, right?"

"Yep." She saw no reason to tell her that Reshma's parents (aka

Mr. and Mrs. Wells, aka the Well Well Wells, the Britpop duo responsible for some of the sappiest ballads of the '80s and '90s) were in London, recording an album. For all of Eva's "no-filter mom" energy, she was weirdly overprotective. Audre had a babysitter until eighth grade! So embarrassing.

Shane turned a page in the yearbook. "I'm sorry, but these aren't real teenagers. They look like adults who play teenagers on TV," he pointed out. "How was the party?"

"I had to talk Sparrow off the ledge." Sometimes, it was easier to talk to Shane than her mom. Less emotional baggage. "She falls for f-boys, and they become her entire identity."

"No one you date in high school should be that important in your life," said Shane.

"You literally dated Mom in twelfth grade."

"We dated *briefly*," he said.

"It took remeeting him fifteen years later for it to stick," said Eva, who had gingerly lain herself down on the rug and was re-attaching the ice pack to her forehead. She pulled two pills out of her pocket and dry-swallowed them.

"Audre, promise me you won't get hung up on an idiot," said Shane, looking disturbed.

Eva opened one eye. "This is Audre we're talking about. When has she ever made an irrational decision? Look at her prom date, Ellison. National Honor Society. Varsity basketball and wrestling. A little conceited, maybe, but nice manners."

Audre felt her chest tighten. *We erased the video. No one saw it.*

"I just don't like to picture my stepdaughter letting some clown throw her off course."

"No one's throwing me quote, unquote off course," said Audre, "let alone a clown."

Shane gave her a pound. "My girl."

"Whose trophies are those?" asked Eva.

"Mine. Who else's would they be?" Audre shrugged, annoyed. "The awards ceremony was today. I'm surprised you forgot, seeing how much you love accolades."

Audre gestured toward Eva and Shane's Shelf of Braggotry, which held all the awards, framed *New York Times* bestseller lists, and NAACP trophies between the two of them.

No pressure, thought Audre.

"Godddd," Eva groaned. "I'm failing you, I really am."

"Not important," lied Audre. She paused, waiting for Eva to ask her about it. Her daughter was class president, so she had to assume she was giving a speech, right? Nothing.

"We're so proud of you, honey," said Eva. But to Audre, it sounded like she was phoning it in. Her mom used to be in the front row of every recital, presentation, and debate team competition, cheering the loudest.

Almost immediately, Eva shifted her attention to Shane. "Why does your T-shirt say FLIP IT AND REVERSE IT? That's a Missy Elliott reference, right?"

He grinned, looking proud. "It's the name of the cover band I hired for our wedding. They specialize in 2000s R&B."

"But I told you, I want *you* to sing," said Eva. "Your voice is so smooth. Like Usher, but taller."

"What's a tall voice?" muttered Audre. She was fed up with their silly banter. Time to change the subject. "I have news. I'm writing a book."

Just then, two of America's most beloved authors gawked at Audre in absolute horror.

"But you're so young," protested Eva.

"I'm sixteen! You were nineteen when you published your first book." Audre knew Eva's biography by heart. At Princeton, she wrote the first book in the Cursed series, it won a fiction contest, she landed a publisher—and then she left college for New York. "Look, I need to be excellent for Stanford. I have a lot to live up to. Mercy girls do what can't be done, remember?"

"You're already excellent," said Eva.

"How would you know? You didn't even come to the awards ceremony."

Eva's head snapped up, her expression frozen between shame and hurt.

"Aaand this is my stop," said Shane, gathering up Baby Alice and attempting to escape.

"Sit down," ordered Eva. She faced Audre. "I'm sorry, I'm so overwhelmed right now."

"Doesn't matter," lied Audre. She wished she could tell her what happened earlier at the awards ceremony. That as she waited in the wings to give her speech, her phone buzzed. It was a text from Ellison, her prom date. The prom was two months ago, and they hadn't spoken since. But he texted constantly. Each time, it was a reminder of the worst day of her life.

Her brain froze, as if she'd bitten into a block of ice. She knew what was coming.

Audre fled to the bathroom. In the privacy of a stall, she had a panic attack. Shaking, sobbing, dry-heaving. She rode it out, then rinsed out her mouth in the sink. Dabbed her tears with paper towels, then ran back out to the stage and nailed the speech. No one could tell she was a mess. But Audre knew—and seeing her mom in the audience would've helped.

She was dying to tell Eva all of this. But Eva clearly had no room for her anymore.

"Audre, do you want a career as an author? Or is this just to get Stanford's attention?"

"Both. I'm going to self-publish this book in time for applications. After I graduate from Stanford, I'll get a three-book deal with a traditional publisher. And then become a world-famous self-help author. You know, when I'm not busy with my celebrity therapy practice."

Eva and Shane glanced at each other. Shane let out a weary chuckle.

"Honey," started Eva, "it sounds like a fun summer project. But it worries me that you're so career-focused right now. Be young! Yeah, I published at nineteen. But then I blinked, and at twenty-two, I had a huge career, a toddler, and divorce bills. I was stuck in grown-up land."

Audre flinched. "Oh. Okay, got it. Well, I'm so sorry you were stuck with me."

"That's not what I meant."

"Glad you have a chance for a do-over with Baby Alice. You know, the three of you sit there like the stars in your own movie while I'm off on the sidelines like...like...like..."

"An NPC?" offered Shane.

Eva cut her eyes at him, huffing.

"You made me stay!" he exclaimed.

His voice jolted Baby Alice awake, and she erupted in angry

sobs. Audre stormed off—forgetting she no longer had a bedroom to storm into. With an exasperated *UGH*, she rerouted to the fire escape at the back of the apartment. It was the only quiet place left. She climbed out and sat on the ledge, her legs dangling two stories above the backyard garden.

Just two more weeks in Brooklyn, she thought, like a mantra. *Just two more weeks.*

As if reading her mind, her phone buzzed. Her dad. She picked up so fast she accidentally knocked herself in the mouth with her phone.

"Audre?"

A veteran Pixar animator, Troy Moore was extremely good-natured. He had two settings: pleased and ecstatic. Audre couldn't imagine Troy and Eva in the same room, let alone married.

"Hi, Dad! I was just about to call you! Can I come out earlier? I just . . . I really miss the beach house. I feel like I'm losing it. I need to hear the ocean. Play with the puppy . . ."

"Donut's a year old now. But Audre . . ."

"I even miss Athena's decorating taste. I was wrong about her shell-shaped tub. It's not tacky at all."

"Audre. I, uh, have some news. I'll just come out and say it, okay?"

She froze. "Why do you sound so weird?"

"We're going to have to cancel Dadifornia this year. But it's for an exciting reason! Are you sitting down? We're pregnant. Can you believe it? It's been a difficult first trimester, and Athena's on bed rest. Don't worry, she'll be A-OK. But her mother moved in to help us, and . . . and she's staying in your bedroom. So, we just don't have room for you this summer."

Audre blinked several times. "But...but...I have an internship at a Malibu mental health clinic. They chose me over two hundred candidates."

"I know you're disappointed. But guess what? You're getting a baby brother!"

Audre didn't hear that last part. She'd turned to stone.

Chapter 4

Bash Henry's party was already out of control. Some kid had to be Ubered to the ER when a weed gummy got lodged in his ear canal. Two unknown girls were brawling on the kitchen floor over Chance Cross, who was in a corner sexting his camp girlfriend. Oddly, someone had stabbed a potted cactus with a huge steak knife—and left it sticking morbidly out of the plant. It was 6 PM. The sun hadn't even set yet.

Technically, it was Bash's party. But he wasn't there. He was outside of it. For the past thirty minutes, he'd been sitting on the stoop of his mom's luxury apartment building that overlooked Prospect Park. The party had become too rowdy for him. So now, he was leaning back on his elbows, disassociating, and trying not to doze off behind his sunglasses.

"You know what your problem is? You're stubborn as hell," said Clio Rhodes, who was perched next to him. "It'll be your downfall."

"My downfall already happened," Bash pointed out with a faint smile. He didn't feel like debating his stubbornness right now. But he also didn't want to be rude to Clio. He always tried to maintain an agreeable, friendly attitude—no matter how he was feeling on the inside.

"What happened to you wasn't a downfall," said Clio. "It was a setback."

"A setback suggests you still have options," reasoned Bash. "Like when you want chips but the bodega's closed. Sucks, but there's always DoorDash."

"But you *do* have options."

With a groan, Bash slid his sunglasses up into his overgrown curls. He began counting off his issues on his fingers. "My dad disowned me. So, I had to relocate to Brooklyn in February of my senior year. To live with my mother, a virtual stranger." He chuckled lightly, shaking his head. "There's no DoorDash to order a new past." He paused. "That'd be a fire app, though."

"You need to call your dad." Clio took a drag from her vape and offered it to Bash. He shook his head. He was high enough.

"I need a nap."

"If you don't make things right with him, you'll regret it. I know you, Bash. You're a softie. I know it's killing you."

This conversation was killing him.

How did I get here? he wondered to himself, hearing a loud crash through his mom's second-floor window. *Was that the vase or the chandelier? Who even are these rich-ass kids? What would make someone who has everything go to a stranger's house and stab a cactus? And am I perversely thrilled by this 'cause it's something I'd never do? At what point did I get uncomfortably high? When can I go home? Where even is home?*

That was the problem. He had no home. He was currently living in his *mom's* home, but it certainly wasn't *his* home.

Bash Henry didn't belong anywhere.

And right now, he really wanted to be alone. But if he had to be in the presence of anyone, he was glad it was Clio. His favorite person. She was eleven months older than Bash, but she'd always been light-years ahead of him, maturity-wise. They'd connected on Instagram years ago, and it was cool that they were finally in the same place. (She lived in Queens, and he'd lived on the West Coast, so they'd only spoken through FaceTime and texts before he moved to New York.) Clio was the only person who knew him before his life imploded. Before he had to leave everything behind. Before he'd become Brooklyn private school gossip fodder.

The kids upstairs at the party? They pretended to be cool with Bash but then turned around and spread over-the-top lies about him. The latest rumor was that he was a drug dealer. At the Nitehawk movie theater, he'd overheard some girl saying he'd sold shrooms to a Midwood High kid (Kyle? Kai?), which unfortunately led to him having a psychotic break on the B69 bus. Yes, Bash did sell him the shrooms, but not because he was a drug dealer. He worked at a novelty gift shop that had a license to sell shroom-infused chocolates!

No one bothered to ask his side of the story.

Rumors were annoying, but truthfully? There was a safety in realizing that no one knew the real him. It was like hiding in plain sight. So, he let the gossip fly. He had no intention of staying in Brooklyn past the summer.

Bash couldn't have stopped the rumors anyway. Without trying, he'd always pulled attention. In his experience, Black and brown kids always stood out at elite private schools. Especially when they were new. And especially when they were new, tall, tatted, and carried themselves with the "self-assured swagger and grace of a nationally ranked track star" (as *LA Times* sports reporter Jerome Radke had written about him back in November '23).

But no one in Brooklyn knew about his track and field stats. He never mentioned his past. He couldn't talk about it without mentioning his dad, Milton. And at the thought of Milton, a veil of darkness cloaked him. He was terrifying.

Good or bad, though, Milton was the only parent Bash knew. He had raised him since he was a baby. It was crazy to think about the turn his life had taken. Now, his sole guardian was a woman who gave him up when he was in diapers.

Sometimes, Bash felt like he was watching his life happen to someone else. Like he was the subject of a Hulu documentary about an Olympics-bound track star's harrowing fall from grace.

"Are you listening to me?" asked Clio, snapping her fingers in front of Bash's face.

"I'm sorry, I'm a little...fucked-up." He sat up and ran his hands over his face. Then he peered up at the window. "Do you think they'll go home soon?"

Clio laughed at this. Her smile was radiant, with an adorable gap between her front teeth. Micro-locs tumbled to her shoulders, a few decorated with gold cuffs. Her laughter was always contagious. Despite himself, Bash chuckled with her, shaking his head.

"Why'd you invite a bunch of high school kids to your house on the last day of school if you didn't want them to party?"

"High school kids, like you're so beyond this," he mocked with a sleepy grin. "You're a freshman at Cornell. This was you last year."

"This was never me. I wouldn't show up to somebody's house and break shit."

"You will show up and lecture me, though."

With a sigh, Clio drew her hand into a fist and gently pressed it against his jaw. "Stubborn."

"I know you're just worried about me," he admitted.

"I am. After everything that happened, the drama and the scandal...I just, well, I worry about your state of mind. You barely graduated. Your track plans are off the table. You used to be so driven. So ambitious." She pointed at him. "Now you're sitting outside your own party, high as fuck, feeling sorry for yourself."

"I don't feel sorry for myself," mumbled Bash, trying to hide his hurt feelings. "I don't really feel anything right now."

"Whatever," she sighed. "Call Milton. What he did to you? Unforgivable. But it's not about forgiving him. It's about getting closure so *you* can have peace. I don't want to hear you complain about your life until you've done it. I'm done."

She swung her canvas tote over her arm. It was embroidered with floral letters spelling out BLACK, BOOKISH, WITCHY.

"Wait, where are you going?"

"I have work early in the morning. Plus, this conversation's going nowhere." Clio was clearly annoyed. "I'll text later."

"Please stay. Just for, like, five minutes." He didn't want to be alone.

"Okay, but..."

Just then, Bash's phone buzzed. It was his mom on Face-Time. Unfortunately, in his altered state, he reflexively tapped the green button instead of the red one. He grimaced, whispered *fuck* through gritted teeth, and then quickly flashed a smile at the screen.

"Bash! Oh! Hi!"

Jennifer was the one who called, but she sounded so surprised to see him. It was as if she was startled simply by the fact that he existed.

To be honest? Bash wasn't used to her presence, either. This blond-haired, blue-eyed white lady was related to him? She was his mother? Surreal. Growing up, he didn't think of her a lot. It was hard to miss what he never had. But in his loneliest moments—late at night in a strange bed in a strange hotel in a strange track-meet city—he'd wonder what kind of mom would allow her ex-husband to move across the country with her baby. Rarely to be seen again.

Didn't she ever miss him? Did she ever feel sorry or sad about it? Bash didn't have the answers. But he didn't know how to ask the questions.

"How are you?" FaceTime-Jennifer trilled from his phone. "Having a quiet night?"

He glanced at Clio. She rolled her eyes.

"Quiet's probably not the word. But, uh, you're still coming back next week, right?"

Jennifer was independently wealthy. Rich, really. So, she didn't need to work. Instead, she spent her time volunteering at community centers for disadvantaged Black and brown kids. It took her all around the country. And she always stayed away long enough for Bash to throw a party—and then clean the apartment from top to bottom. Honestly, cleaning was the only fun part. After a messy, destructive rager, it was so satisfying to sweep, mop, and dust. Make everything look perfect again.

Maybe that's a metaphor, he wondered. *I can't put the pieces back together in my real life, so it feels good to repair a trashed apartment. Clio's right. I do need some fucking therapy.*

"I'm staying in Philly a few extra days," said Jennifer. "The UARYOC are especially in need of my time right now."

UARYOC, as in underprivileged at-risk youth of color. Jennifer had invented the term. It had yet to catch on in social justice circles, but not for her lack of trying.

"Working with underprivileged, at-risk youth of color really puts everything in perspective," she continued passionately. "But it's draining. Today, I was mediating a conflict between a fourteen-year-old kid and his mother, who was just released from prison after a decade. It's a bummer, the way the prison industrial complex rips mothers from children. That baby boy needed her. Can you imagine being abandoned by your mom?"

"Sounds traumatic," he said neutrally. Clio motioned shooting herself in the temple.

"Maybe you'd like to mentor one day, Bash. You'd have so much to teach these kids as a light-skinned, Black-presenting biracial."

"You mean a LSBPB?"

Jennifer breezed past his snark. "I've been meaning to ask you. Have you ever been unfairly targeted by police officers?"

"Me? Nah, I've got a clean record."

"Clean record," she repeated, nodding. "Well, you're one of the lucky ones. Being a Black man in America is a death sentence. I'd love you to volunteer with me sometime. You could connect with the kids far better than I." She lowered her voice to a whisper. "Sometimes I feel pointless. All talking points but no real authenticity. Like a white savior."

Bash squeezed his eyes shut, quietly losing his mind. There was so much he could say to this. But even though he barely knew her, she *was* his mother. And he didn't believe in being mean to moms. Or women in general. Or anyone, for that matter.

But Jennifer must've read his expression. "Your silence speaks volumes, Bash."

"What do you mean?"

She huffed out a sigh. "I wish you'd be nicer to me. I'm trying here. There's no guidebook on how to talk to your almost-adult son who showed up in your life out of the clear blue." Jennifer's voice broke, and her lip trembled. But her eyes were suspiciously dry. "Give me grace, my dear son. *Give me grace.* I'm doing the best I can."

It was quite a performance. To his left, Clio pretended to applaud.

"Okay, um, please don't cry. Grace is given," said Bash, deeply uncomfortable. "Listen, I gotta go. But have a good time, uh, uplifting Philadelphia's disadvantaged youth."

She beamed. All better. "Thank you. Goodbye!"

Bash dropped his phone in the pocket of his old-man pants. Jennifer was so melodramatic. So self-centered. And unable to see the irony of working with abandoned children—when she'd abandoned one of her own.

Bash felt the pull of darkness, of depression, on the outskirts of his brain. It pierced through the haze of his weed high, threatening to overtake him.

Blankly, he stared across the street at the park entrance. Prospect Park was a sprawling Brooklyn oasis with a zoo, lakes, a skating rink, playgrounds, concert stages, and tons of places to just...disappear. (It was like Central Park's less-crowded cousin.) And he had an idea.

"Wanna go for a jog?" asked Bash.

Clio looked at him like he was nuts. "You have an apartment full of people upstairs."

"I need to get outta here," he said.

Chapter 5

I need to get outta here, **thought Audre.**

The conversation with her dad had left her shell-shocked. Both of her families had replaced her with a newer model. A baby sister in Brooklyn, a baby brother in California. And now her summer was ruined.

Too stunned to cry, she zombie-walked back through the apartment, mumbling something to Eva and Shane about running an errand. And then she walked out the door.

It was that magical hour right before the sun set on the city. There was a zingy buzz in the air and the block was bustling with foot traffic from cafés and shops. Summer was here. But Audre was miserable. Aimlessly, she just followed one brownstone-lined street after another—until she reached the Prospect Park entrance.

Suddenly, Audre knew exactly where to go.

Inside the park, she wove through a volleyball game and some kid's sixth birthday party until she found her favorite spot—an old, gnarled tree set up on a small hill. Shoulders slumped in defeat, she sat down, hard, in the grass. For a while, she contorted her face and squeezed her eyes shut. Crying would've been a relief, but for some reason, the tears wouldn't come. Maybe she was in emotional shock.

She'd be stuck in Brooklyn all summer. Audre had never spent the summer in Brooklyn. What was that even like? Most of her Cheshire friends would be traveling, or "summering" at their fancy Hamptons houses (as Eva had once told Audre, her school tuition was their Hamptons house). And what about her summer job in Malibu? She'd volunteered sixty hours at a bleak suicide call center to gain the experience needed to land that gig!

And forget about her book. There was no way she could finish her manuscript by the end of summer. How could she, living in the wilds of that apartment?

Surely, Eva and Shane didn't want her here. She'd be an afterthought . . . an annoyance who was supposed to leave for the summer. To make room for the real family.

No one wanted her in Dadifornia, either.

Both of Audre's families had replaced her. She didn't belong anywhere.

*   *   *

The sun was finally starting to set. Feeling wrung-out, she leaned her head back against the tree and tried to just zone out. Life was happening all around her. Dads throwing Frisbees with toddlers, kids climbing trees. Tweens shooting TikToks. Dogs frolicking. Lovers reclining on Mexican serape blankets. And Audre was on the outside of it all. It was like that at the party, too.

Always watching, assessing, observing—rarely joining in. But that required spontaneity, didn't it? Audre wasn't a fly-by-the-seat-of-her-pants girl. She was a planner.

That's the thing, though. She'd *had* a plan for her summer. And now it had gone awry, and she didn't know what the hell to do with herself.

Don't think about the disappointment, she thought. *Eye on the prize. Just write. If Eva and Shane can write in that house, you can, too.*

With a weary exhale, she stared off into the distance, beyond the grassy hills to the running path. Joggers of all ages, sizes, and shorts lengths ran together in sweaty harmony. And then her eyes zoomed in on one specific jogger.

A guy. Her age, or maybe older? He was so tall it was a thing, and also a bit gangly. With his long legs and arms, his form should've been awkward, but he moved gracefully. Like a pro, even. A mop of dark curls with blondish tips framed his face. His hair was lighter than his deep bronzy-brown complexion—which was disorienting. In a hot way.

Breathing hard, sweat glistening, chest pumping...he was mesmerizing. It was nice, having something to focus on as her world fell apart. Like in elementary school when her mom was hospitalized for migraines. Audre would be left at home with a sitter, and she'd gaze at her sparkly malachite collection on the nightstand till she felt relaxed. Watching the pretty shapes move and morph was soothing.

He kept running along the path, until Audre got a closer look at him.

Wait.

Was he running in pink Crocs?

"Stop!"

Audre heard a girl call after him, from the grass. At the sound of her voice, Pink Crocs peered over his shoulder. He stopped, almost causing a ten-person pileup. Quickly, he ran off the loop into the grass where she stood.

Audre squinted, her drama radar going off. She didn't look familiar. And she'd remember a girl this stylish. Shoulder-length micro-locs, a few decorated with gold cuffs. A tote reading BLACK, BOOKISH, WITCHY. Whoever she was, she wasn't used to running, as she was breathing heavily and clutching her heart.

Uh-oh. They were having a contentious conversation. As every good therapist knew, body language often revealed more about emotions than words did. Witchy Tote was passionately gesturing at his pants pocket. Finally, she yanked his phone out of the pocket.

Oh shit, thought Audre, relieved to be distracted from her life. *What did he do to her? Probably cheated. More than likely, she'd caught him texting some other girl. Typical. Most Brooklyn boys were allergic to being faithful.*

Pink Crocs watched as Witchy Tote punched something into his phone's keypad. Then she shoved the phone back in his face. He grabbed his phone back. Glanced in Audre's direction briefly. Did a double take. Paused. And then, after a huge exhale, he walked away.

The girl just stood there, looking after him. It was impossible to read her expression. Finally, she shouted his name.

"Bash! Come back! BASH HENRY!"

Audre gasped. It was him. Bash Henry. Damn. Maybe he *had* appeared because she said his name three times today.

Bash turned to face Witchy Tote. Head hanging a bit, he walked back to her and pulled her into a hug. She leaned in, rising up on her tippy-toes. Then he whispered something to her and she smiled. Interesting. Apparently, she was too blinded by his coppery skin and sculpted, tall frame to stay mad at him.

Too easy, thought Audre. *Make him work for your forgiveness, sis. You're teaching him how to treat you.*

She hated to see a girl down bad. But it was guys like Bash who kept Audre in business. Poor Witchy Tote, poor Sparrow, and poor Coco-Jean with her pregnancy scare. Their only fault was trusting the wrong guy with their heart.

She does look happy, though, thought Audre. *Maybe ignorance actually is bliss. After all, I've pretty much figured out the teenage brain, and look at me. I'm miserable.*

Wait.

Bash was walking over to her now.

Oh no.

Why was he approaching her? Did he realize she was spying on him? Audre sat up straight against the tree and attempted a neutral expression. It was officially dusk now, but she wished she had sunglasses.

Three breaths later, Bash was standing over her, impossibly tall and peering down into her face. He was even more . . . overwhelming . . . up close.

"Uhh . . . hi?"

"Hi?" she said, matching his questioning tone.

"Not to be rude, but are you staring at me?"

1, 2, 3, 4 … THRIVE!
A Teen's Rules for Flourishing on This Dying Planet

By Audre Mercy-Moore

Rule 2:
If you see tall, curly-haired boys in the wild, avoid looking directly into their eyes. Their retinas have special powers that turn smart girls stupid. This is science.

Chapter 6

His voice was deeper than she'd expected, which threw her off. Also, how was she supposed to explain that, yes, she was staring at him? Don't mind me, I'm a professional eavesdropper?

To kill time, she stood up and made a big thing of brushing nonexistent dirt off her short slip dress. Unconsciously, she tucked her braids behind her ears.

"I wasn't staring at you," she said.

The corner of his mouth quirked a bit. "You sure?"

She straightened her posture. "I mean, it's kinda presumptuous of you to think I was staring. It's a park—there are people everywhere. I was looking in your direction, that's all."

"All good," he said with an easy sigh. Then he stuck out his hand. Audre looked down at it like she'd never seen a hand before. She shook it quickly.

"Hi, I'm Bash."

"I know. I'm Audre."

"I know."

She arched a brow, instantly suspicious.

"Everybody knows who you are," he said with a little smile. "Should I pay you thirty-five dollars now or later?"

She couldn't tell from his tone if he was making fun of her therapy fee, or if he actually wanted her services. Just in case, she said, "It's forty-five. But I'm off the clock."

"Good, I don't have the best track record with therapists. No offense."

"None taken. Though," she said under her breath, "it explains a lot."

He tilted his head. "You said what?"

"Oh nothing," she said. "You were new at Hillcrest Prep this year, right? A senior?"

"Yeah, I just moved to Brooklyn in Feb. I graduated today."

"I see. You were the talk of my friend Reshma's party earlier today."

"Reshma." He frowned a little, looking away. "Do I know a Reshma? Oh wait, she's @mtreshma on IG, right? Yeah, she's cool as hell. Her accent goes hard." He paused. "Was I at her party?"

Bash asked this with the privilege of someone whose presence was so in demand that his social calendar was a blur. Like he was juggling too many girls, parties, and people to remember names. But before she could formulate a response—or properly pinpoint why exactly this guy was getting under her skin—Witchy Tote breezed over to them.

Casually, she stepped between them and linked arms with Bash. Up close, Audre saw that her nose was sprinkled with freckles and she had a cute gap between her front teeth. "Remember what I told you, okay?"

He nodded. And then smiled at Witchy Tote, just as easily as he'd smiled at Audre. Then she squeezed Bash's shoulder, wiggled her fingers at Audre, and left.

Audre stared after her, mouth open. Was she marking her territory? Did Witchy Tote think she and Bash were flirting or something? Suddenly, Audre was *so* done with this conversation.

Hands on her hips, she took a step closer to Bash. "Do you realize that this afternoon I sat in the bathroom for an hour comforting a girl who was in tears over you?"

"Tears?" Bash's brows pinched together. He looked confused by this information. "Over me? Nah, man, couldn't be me. What girl?"

"You know who."

"I don't, though."

"Oh, I think you do."

"I don't make girls, or anybody, cry."

Audre chuckled wryly. "Oh, Bash. If you believe it, I believe it. Go forth and break hearts. Just do me a favor, okay? Be gentle. Because I'm the one who has to rehabilitate the girls of Greater Park Slope after you're done with them."

Bash took a step back from her, raising his palms up in surrender. For the first time, she noticed his outfit. A clearly thrifted Sunkist T-shirt, loose old-man pants, and a thousand rings. He'd really gone running in that?

Bash blinked several times, seemingly baffled. "I . . . you really must be thinking of some other dude."

She was dying to bring up the pregnancy scare but held back. She was nosy—but not tacky. "You're not seeing anyone?"

"I mean, I dabble. But generally? I keep things chill. And I don't believe in being mean." He paused and thought about this for a moment, fingering his thin, silver necklace. "Meanness is too easy. People think being mean makes them seem edgy or unique. Kindness is more radical."

Was this guy for real?

"Mm-hmm," said Audre, nodding in the direction of Witchy Tote, almost out of sight now. As if on cue, the girl looked over her shoulder at them. Bash waved at her and then crossed his (sinewy, sculpted) arms over his chest. For the first time, Audre noticed the intricate, black-and-white sleeve tattoo swirling over his arm. The ink was breathtaking. Distracted, Audre tore her eyes away from his arms and peered up at his face.

Also distracting.

"You got it all wrong about her," Bash was saying. "That's Clio. And, umm, we were just vibing on some design shit. I'm drawing her a tattoo."

Audre noticed that Bash had given her an explanation—without questioning why he owed her one. She had that effect on people. Something about her energy was disarming; she made people want to spill everything. "You're a tattoo artist?"

Bash's eyes followed Audre's gaze to the sleeve tattoo on his arm. "Yeah, I tattooed and designed this myself."

"Don't you need to be eighteen to get a license?" Audre knew this, because her sixth-grade art teacher was a tattoo artist. As a kid, she was obsessed with painting and collage, but she'd given it up before high school. She couldn't help but be impressed by Bash's work. His shading, dimension, and detail were so intricate.

If she were honest, she was a little bit jealous. Why had she given up art, anyway?

"I'll be eighteen soon."

"It's nice work. You're talented."

"You interested? I start at seventy-five dollars. That's hella cheap, considering my experience."

No one in Brooklyn said "hella." In fact, his voice didn't sound New York–y at all. His words were slow, drawn out. Laid-back. He took his time. If she knew her accents, Bash Henry was definitely from the West Coast. He sounded like every boy she knew in California.

Dadifornia. Audre's throat clenched up.

"No, thank you," she managed to croak out. "No, tattoos aren't for me. I don't like needles. And, anyway, how do you commit to one? They last forever."

"That's the point," said Bash with a small shrug. Suddenly, he moved closer to the tree, where she was standing. The air seemed to go electric. Without warning, he slowly reached his hand toward Audre's face. She sucked in her breath, backing up against the trunk and going rigid. He was close enough for her to take in his scent, something coconutty, beachy, and familiar. Gently, he plucked a tiny wildflower growing from a low branch just above her head. With a grin, he stuck it behind his ear.

What was this flower child hippie shit? Was he being an f-boy menace, or did he simply enjoy nature? Audre exhaled slowly—but shakily—and hoped Bash didn't realize that his closeness had made her go all tingly.

Don't feel silly for being affected by his antics, she told herself. *He's objectively hot, and you're raw and vulnerable right now. It's hormones. It's science.*

And that's when she remembered.

"Wait. Aren't you hosting a party right now? Reshma said some Cheshire kids were going to your house tonight."

"Oh," he said, the corners of his mouth drawing downward. "Yeah. Generally, I like to show up late and leave early. Skip the boring parts."

"But...the party's at your house."

"It's not *my* house," he corrected. "It's my mom's house, where I'm temporarily staying. She's right on Prospect Park West, like two minutes away. I'm not far. Anyway, yeah. I'm staying there till I save enough to get my own apartment."

Audre wondered why he needed his own place. Wasn't he going to college in September? Most colleges didn't allow freshmen to live off campus. Maybe he needed financial aid for housing but didn't qualify. It was impossible to get a read on this guy. Which was weird. It usually took a good five minutes before she had most people figured out.

"Let me get this straight. You left a bunch of people at your mom's to go for a run?"

"Umm...no? It was a light jog." He eyed Audre like she was the ridiculous one.

Audre blinked at him. Again, she wondered if this dude was for real. "How high are you right now?"

"Not high enough, to be honest."

"Listen, Bash," she started carefully. "You're new in town. But I grew up with the kids at your house. They're rowdy. If your mom has any interesting prescriptions in her medicine cabinet, they're gone now. You should go back."

"They all seem pretty chill," he said, waving his hand. "Besides, my mom doesn't believe in Western medicine."

"Mmm. Does she have any traumas due to America's broken health care system?"

He huffed out a laugh. "Like I said. I've heard about you. You're not gonna get me."

"Just a matter of time," she said, and she wasn't joking.

"I know it sounds weird that I left my own party. But I get claustrophobic after a while. I don't like, love, how it feels when hella people are in your space. It's just..." He scrunched his pretty features into a mask of disgust and clenched his fists at his chest (which automatically flexed his biceps). "I needed some air."

The sight of him flexing was a little much for Audre this evening. Did he do that on purpose? Bash Henry's wide-eyed-earth-angel act was wearing thin. She knew his type. He was addicted to making everyone fall in love with him—but was impossible to pin down.

"I don't know, man, my time is valuable," he continued. "And every moment counts. I only want to have good moments. If the vibe is off, I'm out."

Every moment did count. She wished she could be like Bash, feeling free enough to walk out of any situation he didn't love. How had he learned to do that?

Suddenly, irrationally, Audre wondered if he was going to ask her to the party. After her dad had uninvited her from his house, a part of her yearned to be wanted somewhere right now. Besides, it would've been the polite thing to do. Nervously, she shifted her weight from foot to foot and employed her favorite nervous tic—collecting her braids in one hand and sweeping them over one shoulder.

The invitation never came. In fact, Bash started to look preoccupied, chewing on the inside of his cheek distractedly.

Wait. Why was she standing in the park, straining to understand the psyche of some airhead who was such a textbook player it was almost funny—especially when his was one of the only personality types she didn't even like therapizing (too easy)? She should've been packing her bags for Malibu Beach! How did she get here?

All of Audre's feelings from the day—upset, crushed, rejected by everyone she loved—began to bubble up. But she had nowhere to put these emotions. So, she made the terrible decision to unleash it all on a virtual stranger.

"So, if the vibe is off, you're out," said Audre, repeating his words with a slight edge.

"Pretty much, yeah."

"Interesting. I know your type. Everything works out for you. You don't take anyone you hook up with seriously. You have a little lover's spat with some girl in Prospect Park..."

Bash flinched, shaking his head. "Lover's spat? No."

"... in the middle of your party while hearts are breaking all over town. And I'm left picking up the pieces while sitting on a self-heating toilet comforting Sparrow Lipsitch and her press-on nails."

Bash blinked in confusion with his absurdly long lashes. "Sparrow? A self-heating toilet? And wait, I'm ... not a type."

"Neither am I!"

"I feel like I'm in trouble. And why am I justifying my life to an eleventh grader?"

"Twelfth, as of today."

"Exactly, so why are you even out here? You should be party-ing instead of worrying about what I'm doing." He tilted his head to one side, studying her. "You have narc energy."

Audre flinched. "Narc energy?"

"Yeah, like you're pretending to go to Cheshire but you're an undercover cop."

"I *know* what a narc is. Look, I'm just looking out for my girl-friends. Maybe I've just had it up to here with guys making my friends cry."

"Or are you just nosy?" Bash's tone was jokey, as if trying to defuse the tension.

Audre didn't skip a beat. "Boys who call girls nosy generally have something to hide."

This caught Bash off guard. He glanced away. "I don't have anything to hide."

"Okay, well. You should get back to your party before Gideon Mathison pillages your mom's panty drawer. He's famous for it. Have a great summer."

Aware that this conversation made her look unhinged—and that her life was over, anyway, so it didn't matter—she realized she had to get away from Bash, immediately. So, she gave Bash a quick wave goodbye and began to walk away.

But then he called out to her.

"Audre."

She whipped around so fast, her braids almost smacked her in the face.

"You want to know how I commit? I don't overthink it," he said.

Confusion flashed over Audre's face. "Overthink what?"

"My tattoos. Sometimes, when people's aesthetics or interests change, they hate their old ink. Not me." He shrugged. "Everything changes. Nothing'll be the same a year from now. But my tats will. They're like reminders of things I loved once. Even just for a day."

She nodded but couldn't say anything because, inexplicably, she felt near tears. Bash's words had hit her somewhere—some melancholy, yearning place that longed for things not to change. For everything to go back to the way it used to be.

In a move that would embarrass her every time she thought about it for the rest of the summer, she ran off. She ran before the tears spilled. Before she revealed anything about herself that she'd regret.

1, 2, 3, 4 … THRIVE!
A Teen's Rules for Flourishing on This Dying Planet

By Audre Mercy-Moore

Rule 3:
Stay alert around suspiciously hot joggers in the park. For safety reasons, first and foremost — but also because they sometimes drop pearls of wisdom.

Chapter 7

A week later, Audre's Dadifornia devastation had worn off—a little. Eva and Shane, of course, weren't sympathetic. Quite the contrary. They were thrilled they'd have extra hands while they searched for a new nanny. Which was why she was spending her Saturday grumpily babysitting Baby Alice while her mom and stepdad were out at book signings in Manhattan.

Audre was so lost without her planned summer. It was the only time she had unobstructed, IRL access to her dad. Maybe he would've tried harder to make room for her if they had a closer relationship. If he wasn't her "vacation" parent.

Audre was trying to accept her new summer reality. But she hated change. What had Bash said to her? *Everything changes. Nothing'll be the same a year from now.*

Bash Henry, the accidental philosopher. Audre stiffened, remembering how nuts she must've looked to him that evening in the park. Without hearing his side of the story, Audre believed all the rumors about Bash—and had been judgmental and rigid.

Two things she prided herself on not being. Besides, who he chose to hook up with (and why) was absolutely none of her business. No matter what sketchy insider details had been revealed to her in confidence.

That was another thing! In her race to put him in his place, she committed a cardinal therapy sin. She revealed the secrets of a client.

I'm trash, she thought, groaning out loud and disturbing Baby Alice, who was finally dozing off. Baby Alice jerked upright, spit out her pacifier, and began scream-crying.

"Why are you even mad?" Audre complained, carrying Baby Alice over to her vibrating baby rocker. "You have no problems. No homework. No acting a fool in front of a popular guy who's done nothing to you. No divorced parents who are sick of raising you. What kind of person shrieks for no reason?"

Audre strapped her into the chair, covered her with a thin blanket, and sat on the hardwood floor next to her. She copied what she'd seen Eva do a million times and placed her hand on Baby Alice's thigh and lightly jiggled her. Her sister grabbed her index finger in her chubby fist and squeezed hard, her baby nails digging into her skin. Audre grimaced, gulping down a yelp. The assault was worth it, though. The baby was asleep in under five minutes.

A relief. Audre grabbed the baby monitor walkie-talkie and zigzagged her way through the construction materials piled throughout the apartment till she reached the back window. She climbed out and sat on the fire escape. With a soul-clearing sigh, she texted her best friend.

Forty-five minutes later, they were both sitting on the fire escape in crop tops and cutoffs, their flip-flopped feet dangling through the iron bars. Two floors below them was the owner of the garden apartment, a short, round, older gentleman named Barry Carroll. He spent every summer barbecuing in the garden in Hawaiian-print swim trunks. At the moment, he was grilling hot dogs and listening to early Madonna. He was a generous, helpful, friendly neighbor—but, curiously, he never spoke.

"I wonder how old Barry is," said Reshma, peering at him over her glam white sunnies.

"Unclear. I feel like he's beyond age."

"Like he's immortal?"

"Maybe he regenerates, like a starfish. Or Groot." Audre sighed, her shoulders slumping.

Reshma adjusted her position so she was facing Audre. "Talk to me, baby. Which part upsets you the most? Losing your internship? Not seeing your dad? Or spending the summer babysitting and continuing to live on the couch?"

"Yes," responded Audre.

"Look, it might be fun to stay here for the summer. The city will be empty. Brooklyn will be your playground. You think I want to go to Argentina and 'assist' my parents in making yet another album full of dentist office bangers?"

"I mean, yeah. It's Argentina."

"But music is their thing. They're dying for me to follow in their footsteps." She shook her head. "I'm not trying to be a nepo flop. I wanna be radically different from them."

"But it'll still be fun. You'll meet some hot Argentinean girl who'll make you happy for exactly forty-eight hours. Watch."

"You think I enjoy hopping indiscriminately from hookup to hookup?" She tilted her head back, exhaling up to the sky. "It's exhausting. Try it, you'll see. Maybe this'll be your slut summer."

"Me? You know I'd never," said Audre, leaning her forehead against the iron bars. "Besides, I've gotta focus on my book. I'm struggling to come up with advice that isn't cliché."

"How hard can it be?"

The thing was, nothing was hard in Reshma's life. She didn't have to obsess about college, her future. Her parents were sixty-five. They'd been pop stars in the UK since the '80s. They'd been rich for a long, long time, and once Reshma turned twenty-one, she'd inherit millions.

"Well, what would be your advice for living your best teen life?" asked Audre.

Reshma nibbled a cuticle, thinking about this for a moment.

"Number one, keep a daily planner. Two? Always smell good. Three, don't take drugs from anyone you've known less than three months. Four, learn how to give yourself an orgasm."

"And if you can't make yourself come," added Audre, "your antidepressant might be making you numb."

Reshma raised a luscious eyebrow. "And how would you know?"

"All therapists know that. It's in every psychology book I've ever read."

"Just what I thought! You know it *intellectually*, but not from experience. You need to live a little." Reshma ran her pointy acrylics through her long, thick waves.

"What do you mean?" asked Audre.

"Listen, you give the best advice of anyone I know. But it's all from psychology books and mental health podcasts. So. Many. Podcasts." Reshma grimaced. "My point is, your book will be even more meaningful if you lived a little. If your advice came from IRL experience. Would you go to a dermatologist who'd never had a pimple?"

Audre's fingers flew up to her cheeks, where the shadow of her eighth- and ninth-grade acne still haunted her. "Do I have a pimple?"

"Are you listening? You have writer's block because you're lacking authentic inspiration. Especially when it comes to boys." She took a drag of her cigarette and then whipped her head around to face Audre. "That reminds me. What happened with that kid from prom?"

"Ellison," said Audre, who'd been dreading this conversation for a month. During prom weekend, Reshma and her ex-girlfriend, a swimsuit model, had been canoodling at her shoot in Hawaii. Since then, every time Reshma brought up the dance, Audre smoothly changed the subject by asking a million questions about Hawaii.

Audre wished she could press a button and erase that mortifying night. It was damn near impossible, considering Ellison kept texting her the same empty, pleading messages.

> No one saw it. i promise. pls
> don't tell anyone

Ellison went to St. Francis Academy, a castle-like private school nestled underneath the Brooklyn Bridge. The good-looking son of a Wall Street business titan, Ellison was the definition of prep school arrogance. (His Snapchat name was, unironically, @KingEllisontheFirst.) Earlier this year, she had debated abolishing the death penalty against him at the citywide debate team championship—and lost. When Ellison won, he actually fist-pumped the air. Annoying. But then . . . he asked her for a slice of pizza after the meet. A date? She never went on dates. Who had the time? Plus, she was such an overthinker that a casual date was excruciating. But he sprung it on her so fast that *yes!* flew out of her mouth before her brain caught up.

They had some grandma pepperoni slices. Gossiped about people they knew in their schools' Black student affairs clubs. He showed her shots of himself "crushing it" on St. Francis's varsity basketball IG page. And just like that, Audre and Ellison were sort of . . . talking? Audre wasn't sure she liked him, but being liked was nice. In quiet moments, though, she had to ask herself—was she so hungry for male attention that she'd force a crush on a guy who texted her weight lifting selfies every morning?

After two movie dates, one dinner date, and an awkward night cheering Ellison on at a basketball game (Audre didn't know basketball rules and clapped at the wrong times), she asked him to prom.

And her life had been unraveling ever since.

"Prom sucked," she said after a weighty sigh. "It was so bad, and . . . and I was too embarrassed to tell you. I mean, I've counseled tons of people on prom drama. I'm the person who has all the answers. And my first prom blows up in my face?

"Everything was normal, at first. I wore that teal halter mini-dress, remember? I actually felt pretty. We took pictures at the pre-party. Danced a little at the actual dance. But halfway through it, I noticed that he was getting *drunk* drunk. And I wasn't drinking. He was just, like, overly touchy and kept pulling me up to dance, and I was trying to laugh it off, because I didn't want to be lame. Like, maybe he's being fun and I'm just boring?" Audre lowered her voice to a whisper. "The truth is, I'm sixteen years old and don't know how to act at a dance with a boy. Like, are we supposed to be all over each other? Is it okay if I blow him off? I asked him, so I can't be rude, right? Plus, he goes to a different school, so it's my job to be a good host. Right?"

Reshma's brow furrowed in split-second fury. "I'm gonna refrain from speaking till you're done. Continue."

"Afterward we went to Nu Hotel. Someone rented a duplex suite with a bunch of rooms."

Reshma flinched with her entire body. "Oh my God, oh my God..."

"Stop, it's not what you're thinking," said Audre. "Just listen. We go into a bedroom. I'm exhausted, but I know he wants to hook up. And a part of me wants to, too. Not because I'm attracted to him, but because I want the *experience*."

"But you've hooked up before. Sort of. What about Kenji James at the Young Business Leaders of America retreat?"

"Does he count? It was a quick peck."

"Well, you kissed my cousin Silas when he flew in for my birthday cruise."

"But he'd eaten shellfish, remember? I'm allergic! My mouth blew up."

"Oh riiight." Reshma nodded. "Back to prom. What happened in the room?"

"Somehow, we ended up on the bed. And we start kissing. And it's sloppy and not great, and my dress feels too tight, and he's too grope-y. So, I pushed him off me. And I started hyperventilating! I couldn't get enough air, and I was just crying. My chest got tight. I was pouring sweat. I thought I was dying." Audre looked down at her feet, dangling in the air. "Since then, I've had a few more panic attacks. Please don't tell anyone. My mom doesn't even know."

"Why not? You of all people know that it's a side effect of anxiety. She could help you!"

"I don't need help," Audre said, fast. "I mean, I already know all the therapy techniques, deep breathing and everything. Honestly, I just need to . . . relax."

"You don't have to act perfect all the time, babe," said Reshma in a whisper.

"Yes, I do."

Mercy girls do what can't be done.

"Anyway," Audre continued, "I was scared. I kept getting more hysterical. Finally, I curled up in a ball and I remember begging him to get help. And he laughed at me." She paused. "My eyes were squeezed shut, and I'm just rocking back and forth, wailing and shaking and freaking out. He's still laughing. Then I heard the door open and close. And whispering. When I opened my eyes, there were three more boys standing over the bed. Not Cheshire guys. I didn't recognize them. But . . . they were laughing, too. And one was recording me on his phone."

Abruptly, Reshma untangled her legs from the fire escape bars and hopped up.

"Reshma! Where are you going?"

"To fucking chop his dick off," she shouted. "He thinks he can get away with that?"

"Sit down," whispered Audre, dragging her back down. "Don't upset Barry."

Barry glanced up from the grill, his brow cloudy with concern. As Madonna's "Into the Groove" softly streamed from his phone, he pierced a hamburger with a fork and silently raised it up to the girls.

"I'm good." Audre smiled.

"No, thank you, doll, I'm plant-based," said Reshma. Gently, she took Audre's hand in hers. "What happened after that?"

"Nothing. I jumped up, pushed the guys out of the way, and ran out. I got in an Uber. And I haven't spoken to Ellison since then. He keeps texting me, telling me he deleted the video. But I won't respond."

She couldn't. Every time she thought about it, her stomach went queasy. She got a sense memory flash of feeling so vulnerable, as naked as if she were actually nude, losing control and weeping in front of four assholes who were using her as entertainment. And then the desperate, raging fear she'd felt every day since that night—what if that video ended up online somewhere? What if Ellison was lying, and it had been shared all around St. Francis? Had it been passed on to Cheshire people? Was everyone secretly laughing at her? When she gave her speech at the awards ceremony, was the audience snickering at the girl who pretended to have it all together but was a mess?

"Is this just my reality? Having panic attacks in the middle of making out?"

"You weren't attracted to him! And he ruined the vibe by being gross all night."

"I guess. Maybe I'm just too in-my-head about it. I just wish I was braver. Less anxious. Fearless."

Reshma stared off into the distance for a moment, lost in thought. Then she uttered a small yelp of excitement and whipped out her phone. "Fuck Ellison. We're moving forward."

Reshma started typing in her notes app. After a moment, she announced, "I just wrote you a list of dares to complete this summer. This is your Experience Challenge."

Audre stared at her. "You mean like ding-dong ditch?"

"What are you, seven?" Reshma rolled her eyes.

"What I'm not gonna do is let you get me in trouble *right* before senior year."

"No, it's nothing illegal or weird. Here, just read the list."

Audre took the phone and began to scroll.

1. Try a risky new physical activity.
2. Buy a dildo.
3. Stay out at a party past 10 PM.
4. Hook up with someone you have *ACTUAL* chemistry with.
5. Face a major fear.

Audre cackled with laughter. "Buying a dildo isn't weird? Why do I need to do that?"

"Babe, if I have to explain why..."

"And you know my bedtime is nine thirty PM. Justice for sleepy girlies."

"Think of it this way. Your new experiences are gonna make your book so good."

Audre reread the list, slowly coming around to the idea. She *did* love a challenge. And what else was she doing this summer, anyway? Maybe this insane Experience Challenge would take her mind off her troubles. Plus, Reshma was right—how was she supposed to write a book about living your best life without, well, living her own?

"Every moment of this summer counts, Audre. Don't waste it in bed. Well, in bed alone."

"That's what Bash said," said Audre. "The part about making every moment count."

Reshma ripped off her sunnies. "Bash Henry? When did you talk to him?"

"I saw him in Prospect Park the other night. I was in a horrible mood and I said some wild shit to him. Ugh, I'm so embarrassed."

"I doubt anything you did seemed wild to *that* guy. You've heard the rumors, right? The girlies say he went down on his girlfriend's mom back wherever he comes from. Also, I heard he's in a gang," said Reshma. "That, I can't see. He looks too soft for that life."

Audre was barely listening. "I ran into Bash right after I found out Dadifornia was canceled. Dad didn't even seem sad about it. You should've heard him 'consoling' me. It was like he was giving me a pep talk after losing a Little League game."

"People get weird when they get pregnant. Remember *Lady and the Tramp*? When Jim Dear and Darling got pregnant, they forgot Lady existed. But by the end, they were one big happy family."

"That's a terrible example," answered Audre. "Lady ran off

with Tramp, a naughty dog who, thanks to his antics, got her thrown in the pound."

"Lady had the time of her life with Tramp. And so will you, when you get through my list. But, wait—with me going to Argentina, who's gonna hold you accountable? You need a partner."

"My own Tramp to show me a good time," said Audre, half joking.

"Brilliant idea! Who do we know that's adventurous? That's down for whatever?"

They both gasped. The answer was obvious.

Chapter 8

Audre wasn't the only one with a well-known side hustle. It was a thing at her school. Most kids had wealthy families and didn't need the money—but earning dollars in sneaky ways gave them a perverse thrill. Asher Janus hired a bouncer to let his friends into bars in the city, charging kids fifty dollars a head. Paloma Wood charged one hundred and fifty dollars to make a fake ID. For sixty dollars, Tessie Maxwell allowed people to steal vintage designer pieces from her mom's closet.

As a longtime entrepreneur, Audre appreciated this. You provide a service, you collect a fee. It was a clean, straightforward exchange. Everyone knew what to expect. In a world where everything was confusing, sometimes good old American capitalism was a comfort.

And Audre was ready to get comfortable.

Reshma made an extremely good point the other day. Audre did need some real-life experience to write an excellent book. And now that Reshma was in Argentina, she'd need a Fun Person to help her loosen up. So Audre was going to flex her businesswoman muscle—and hire Bash Henry to be her consultant.

Bash seemed perfect for the job, based on his reputation. But since Audre didn't personally know anything about him, she did some research. That night, at dusk, she headed to "The Turf"—a city block of fake grass behind a neighborhood elementary school that turned into a rowdy high school party most nights after sundown.

Audre casually worked her way from friend group to friend group. After a few moments of small talk, she dove in. "Wait, random question—do you know Bash Henry? I have a friend who thinks he's cute. Just doing a little research."

The responses varied wildly.

Oliver Franks: "I for real heard he was kicked out of his last school for breaking up the principal's marriage."

Harper Yao: "He works part-time at Just Because, that random gift shop on Degraw? I've never seen anyone there. It cannot be profitable."

Jagger O'Mally: "And he does tattoos out of the stockroom. You need a secret password, though. Don't get a tat, Audre, it's sophomoric."

Callie Verchinski: "Somebody said he bleaches the tips of his curls with L'Oréal box dye. Honestly? I'm about to ask him to do mine."

Lulu Watson: "I heard they call him Bash 'cause he parties."

Georgia Mayo: "No, Calder told me his name's short for bashful. But don't believe that shit. I hooked up with him two Saturdays ago. If he's shy, I'm Lily Rose Depp."

The reviews were mixed. And, it must be noted, everyone she'd spoken to was on various mind-altering substances. But the reports painted a picture.

The next day, she threw on a tank, a low-waist maxiskirt, and nonprescription glasses (they made her look professional). And then she walked the twenty minutes to Just Because.

It was a scorching-hot day, the sun glinting off strollers and cars. Folks were moving slower than usual, and so was Audre. After twenty sweaty minutes, she saw the shop just ahead of her on Degraw Street. The dusty gray awning read JUST BECAUSE in old-timey typewriter font. She'd passed it a million times on walks, but she'd never been inside. It was the kind of store that sold zany home decor that you couldn't imagine anyone buying. Like oven mitts embroidered with I WILL CUT A BITCH. A soap dispenser reading YOU KNOW WHAT YOU TOUCHED. Meghan and Harry salt and pepper shakers. Novelty canvas totes, hammered silver rings, a disco ball vase.

Standing outside of the store, Audre started to rethink her mission. What was she going to say to Bash? She'd acted like such a maniac at Prospect Park— Bash would be well within his rights to kick her out of this goofy store. If he was even working there today.

You're confident, she reminded herself. *You're accomplished. You were interviewed for the National Honor Society newsletter last fall! He's just some boy.*

On a deep inhale, Audre pulled open the glass door, rattling the bell hanging from the doorknob. And then she strode in like she owned the place.

Through the rows of merchandise, she could see Bash sitting on a stool behind the register. His elbows rested on the counter, and one hand propped up his chin. He was slumped over a bit as he scrolled on his phone. His posture was terrible.

A skinny stretchy headband held back his curls, which were

popping out all over. He was wearing a white tee with a slouchy mesh shirt over it, joggers, and, again, so many rings. The mismatched ensemble would look nuts on anyone but him.

Bash looked up, locking eyes with Audre. She shot him a wide smile. He didn't return it.

Which, fair. If she were Bash, she wouldn't be thrilled to see her, either. But she didn't let him throw her off. Audre had a job to do. Left to her own devices, she'd never complete the Experience Challenge alone.

"Me again. Hi!" Audre stood at the entrance, waving like a fool.

Bash put on a friendly, neutral expression. "Hi. Umm... you're letting out the AC."

"Whoops. My bad." Quickly, she shut the door and then made a show of browsing the aisles of nonsense. "So, what's up?"

"Just working." He held up his phone. "Reading."

"What are you reading? A book?"

"An essay called 'Punks, Freaks, OutKasts, and ATLiens.' It's about Afrofuturism."

Pasting on a smile, she headed up the aisle to the register. He watched her cautiously.

"Cool, cool. Outkast, huh? They're iconic."

Duh. Of course they were. This was so awkward, she could die.

"Yep. Iconic," he said. "So, can I help you?"

"Yes, you can! I'm looking for, uh, something to decorate my room. It's being renovated. Oh, this is cute." She grabbed an embroidered throw pillow off a small display table. It read: ASK ME ABOUT MY CAT.

Bash glanced over at the pillow. "What's your cat's name?"

Audre didn't have a cat. She was violently allergic. Desperate, her eyes scanned the wall shelves behind Bash for inspiration. She landed on a glow-in-the-dark birdhouse.

"Bird. His name's Bird."

"Bird the Cat, huh?" Some of the tension went out of his expression. He bit his lip, looking like he was holding back a laugh. Maybe he was softening up! "What's the breed?"

Buying time, Audre asked, "Why? Are you a cat guy?"

"Huge cat guy. In preschool, I got bit by a feral kitten and for years after I thought I was half-feline. I found out I wasn't when I jumped out of a second-floor window and didn't land on my feet."

"Tough lesson," said Audre. What a thing to come out and say. Bash Henry had an odd, unfiltered way about him. It was kind of endearing.

"So, what's the breed?" he repeated, the ice slowly melting.

"He's a mutt," she blurted out. Wait, was *mutt* a term exclusively used for dogs, not cats? Audre didn't know anything about animals. In a panic, she picked up a tote that read I'M CRYING MY BEST. She grasped its handles in both hands, needing something to hold on to.

"A mutt, huh?" Bash smiled. "I used to have a ginger guy named Channel Orange."

"For the Frank Ocean album? A cat with taste."

"Yeah, he was my little buddy. But then he got his head stuck in a Doritos bag and suffocated."

Audre burst out laughing. "They do say orange male cats are the least intelligent."

Bash's eyes widened. His mouth went slack.

"Wait. Oh no." She clasped her palms against her cheeks. "Did . . . did that really happen?"

"Yes, it really happened. The fuck?" His eyebrows furrowed in hurt surprise.

"Bash, I'm so sorry. I'm a monster. What a horrible thing to say."

"Also, it's objectively untrue! Orange cats aren't dumb. Garfield's legendary."

One-on-one, Bash Henry was practically wholesome and she felt . . . horrible for hurting his feelings. His wild reputation wasn't matching her experience with him. Was this really the same guy who was breaking hearts all over Brooklyn?

"You're right. I was way out of line with that orange cat comment. It was unforgivable."

"I just don't get it." His voice was slow and careful, like he was trying to work at the mystery of Audre as he was talking. "I feel like you're targeting me. I mean, I'm just minding my business." He paused. "I'm kinda disappointed."

"Disappointed?"

"Cause I figured you came in here to apologize. For being weird to me in the park. But it kinda seems like you showed up just to be mean again, and I'm just like . . . why?"

Bash dropped his phone on the counter, crossed his arms over his broad chest, and looked at her, his gaze unwavering. His skin was a rich, burnished golden brown—like he'd just returned from some Caribbean island. He looked like he was from some Caribbean island. The tip of his nose and his forehead were sunburned, eraser pink, and his cupid's bow mouth? Poetic. This was why he had people talking. Normal people weren't this striking.

He had a dreamy look to him, like an indie softboy visiting from a different planet.

Audre was stunned by his looks for a moment. And then she pulled it together.

"I was going through family stuff the other night. I wasn't myself. I have no right to criticize what you do or don't do with girls. I apologize."

He flashed a small, tentative smile. "Nah, you good. I figured whatever that was, wasn't about me. And I'm sorry for calling you a narc. That wasn't cool."

"Wow. Such an emotionally healthy response."

"That's me, the picture of emotional health."

Just then, a girl breezed out of the stockroom, her forearm shiny with ointment. A periwinkle-blue tattoo of a dolphin was a bit bloodied underneath. Audre recognized her—Olivia, she graduated from Cheshire two years before. She breezed through the store and to the door, nodding hi to Audre. To Bash, she said, "Thanks again. I love it!"

"Fosho!" he called out with a friendly wave.

Fosho? Again, a very not-Brooklyn thing to say.

"Bye, Olivia." Audre waved (to show how cool she was). Then she whispered, "The owner's okay with a seventeen-year-old running an unlicensed tattoo parlor in the stockroom?"

"The owner's my mom," he whispered back. "If you find her, you can ask her."

Just then, Audre's eye was unconsciously drawn to a framed portrait on the far-right wall. It was of a blond woman in a white shift dress, posing with former NYC mayor Bill de Blasio. "Is that her? She looks like Lindsay Lohan's mom in *Parent Trap*."

"So I constantly hear," he said.

"Does your dad own the store with her?"

Bash stared at the photo for a beat. "No, he lives in California. And they've been divorced since I was a baby."

"I *knew* you were from California. Your accent! San Fran?"

His eyes widened a bit, clearly impressed. "Close. Bay Area. Oakland."

"I spend summers in Malibu with my dad. We both have West Coast fathers, so funny."

"Hilarious," he said wryly. "Umm. Not to be rude, but I... don't like talking about myself."

"Force of habit." Audre fidgeted with her braids, worried that the melting ice between them was freezing again.

"Nah, you good." Bash scratched the back of his neck. "So. Why are you here?"

"Here, in Brooklyn? Well, my dad and his wife are pregnant, so I couldn't visit..."

"No, why are you *here*. You want something, and I doubt it's a fried egg wall clock."

Trying to buy time, she turned around and walked over to a display of kitschy socks with celebs embroidered on them. When she turned back around to face him, they locked eyes.

"You seem like a guy who likes adventure. Right?"

"Depends on the adventure."

"I mean, your reputation is... colorful. And you seem to just take life by the horns. I'm wondering if you can help me." She dove in. "I'm writing a book."

"Yeah? What's it called."

"*One, Two, Three, Four... Thrive! A Teen's Rules for Flourishing on This Dying Planet.*"

Bash drew his mouth to one side. "Are you accepting feedback?"

"No," she said. "Anyway, as you know, people pay me to give them advice. I'm good at it, and I think I can write an incredible self-help book. But the thing is, I'm...kind of...socially stiff. And you seem like a person who doesn't have as many hang-ups as I do. You seem fun."

Bash looked helplessly intrigued. "I am fun. But what are you asking me?"

"Will you show me how to have fun? Be my fun consultant? I'll pay you. And no strings attached, by the way. This is business only. Hook up with whoever, I won't ask questions."

He chuckled a little and paused, fingertips trailing the side of his jaw. "I don't get it. I know you have friends. You don't need to hire me to hang out with you."

"This isn't about friendship. I'm looking at it like an internship. A learning opportunity."

"Bro, you know nothing about me. I could be a liability."

"I need to get into Stanford," she blurted out, desperate. "This book'll help me stand out to the admissions board. I'm not exceptional enough on my own."

Bash stuck his bottom lip out in a mock pout. "Aww. But you're crying your best."

"I'm serious. You're saving up to get your own place. What's your price?"

Now he laughed outright, shaking his head. "I can't be bought. I have integrity."

"Please! My friend and I came up with five things I should do. Wanna see?"

Bash attempted to look nonchalant. But his eyes were sparkling when Audre handed over her phone. He cleared his throat and began to read out loud:

1. Try a risky new physical activity.
2. Buy a dildo.
3. Stay out at a party past 10 PM.
4. Hook up with someone you have *ACTUAL* chemistry with.
5. Face a major fear.

Bash couldn't hide his fascination. His expression screamed "challenge accepted." Or maybe it was just "I'm bored and I have nothing better to do." Either way, Audre would take it.

"Well, what do you think?" she said as he handed her phone back to her. She slipped it into her pocket.

"I think you got too much time on your hands."

"Time is what I don't have. I've given myself a book deadline of August fifteenth."

Desperately, Audre thought of what Reshma would do in this situation. She changed her stance, tossing her braids to one side and popping out her hip seductively. Unfortunately, her long hair hit a shelf of bobblehead dolls, knocking them to the floor. Quickly, she scrambled to pick up the dolls, her phone slipping out of her pocket. With a groan, Bash rushed over and bent down next to her, collecting the dolls into a shopping cart.

"If I say yes," he started, "will you go? Please?"

They both stood up, and Audre's mouth went dry. He towered over her. He smelled like coconut, beachy stuff. She nodded and said, "Yes."

"Thank you." He grinned. "I'll do it. Gimme your number—we'll link on Friday."

Audre could hardly believe his response. She'd gone way out on a limb, hiring a stranger to help her learn how to loosen up. He could've rejected her, easily. Which made her wonder . . .

"Why did you say yes?" she asked.

He looked down at her, biting back a smile. She could tell he loved this challenge. " 'Cause these days I rarely say no."

These days? As opposed to when?

Just then, she realized he'd picked up her phone. She reached for it, but Bash held it above her head, out of reach.

"I have one condition, though."

"I'm listening." Audre planted her fists on her hips.

"Please don't ask me anything too personal."

"Virgo?"

"And I ain't on that astrological shit."

"Ugh, fine."

Bash handed her back her phone. Audre straightened her spine, all business.

"So, how much will you charge?" She slid her glasses up her nose.

"Can't I just do it for free? An actual cash payment makes me feel . . . whorish."

"Embrace it," she said. "I need to pay you so we're clear about where we stand. What'll it be? Two hundred dollars?"

"I hate this," he groaned. "Okay, let's say seventy-five. I'll do it for seventy-five."

Audre grinned. "We have a deal, sir."

Bash stuck out his right hand. She slid her palm into his. To exert power, she squeezed as she shook his hand. His eyebrow quirked, and he squeezed harder. And then they both let go.

He's competitive, she thought. *Not a Virgo, then. Aries maybe?*

"One more thing," said Bash. "I wanna meet your cat."

"B-but we already shook on it!"

"Let's shake on it again," he said, reaching for her hand. She shook it, already wondering if she knew someone with a cat she could borrow for an afternoon.

1, 2, 3, 4 ... THRIVE!
A Teen's Rules for Flourishing on This Dying Planet

By Audre Mercy-Moore

Rule 4:
Be smart about lies or you might tell one that exacerbates your allergies.

Chapter 9

Bash collapsed flat on his back on the wet sand, waves foaming and dissipating over his feet. His surfboard, Nick (named for Nick Gabaldon, the most famous Black surfer in history), stood next to him in the sand, nose-first.

These New York waves are gonna kill me, he thought, struggling to catch his breath.

He'd spent all morning surfing Rockaway Beach in Queens, which had zero in common with the beaches back home. At Half Moon Bay, his favorite beach on the San Francisco Peninsula, the waves were smooth and mellow. Perfectly chill barrels you could ride forever. The sand breaks here in New York, at Rockaway, made the waves fast and unpredictable. Like the city itself.

It didn't matter how rough the waves were, though. What mattered was that, out here, Bash Henry had the freedom to do his second-favorite thing in the world (after tattoo design): surfing to absolute physical exhaustion. For the first time, he could do it without sneaking around! Without fearing that his dad would somehow catch him breaking the rules—indulging in an "unmanly non-sport for white boys with meth addictions and slutty girlfriends." His dad loved an extremely descriptive put-down.

Drying off in the unrelenting sun, he sucked in a huge gulp of beachy, salty sea air and held his breath, letting it make him dizzy before exhaling. Bash savored the taste of the sea. The feel, the smell. But nothing tasted better than the freedom to be here, worry-free, in the first place. Six months ago, it wasn't possible.

Bash had come out to the beach alone, which was fine. To him, surfing didn't feel like a group activity. It was meditation. And besides, he hadn't met anyone here he wanted to share this with. Or anything about his former life at all.

Especially his track and field life. He never mentioned his athlete past. No one had searchable info about him. Bash Henry wasn't even his actual government name.

If everything had gone right, twelfth grade was supposed to be a year of triumph. Athletic scholarships. Olympic trials. Trophies, accolades, applause. Instead, when he landed in Brooklyn, he was friendless, fatherless, and too burned out to even consider running for Hillcrest Prep—despite the coach aggressively recruiting him.

No, Bash was done with coaches. He was done with the pressure. The expectations. The ruthlessness. Coaches had ruled his life since he was five years old. And his dad was the worst one of all. As the director of track and field at California University, Milton had an entire Division I team to manage. But his greatest obsession was his son.

Bash was a once-in-a-generation talent. Everyone said so. And Milton expected him to follow in his golden footsteps. His son would be a better athlete than even him.

Turns out, Bash *was* a better athlete than his father. But now, he was also dead to him.

And it had only taken seven minutes for Milton to strike him from his life.

Yes, he knew the exact time. He'd been at the California University track, getting ready to do a practice session under the watchful gaze of his dad. A regular Saturday, no different than the rest. A bright, clear day. He'd just called Nadia Robertson and told her that he couldn't take her to homecoming after all, because his dad banned him from attending a dance the night before a meet. (Milton also didn't approve of Nadia's short skirts. No "tramps" for his son.) Later that afternoon, Bash was meeting a track and field recruiter from University of Arizona. His muscles were on fire from that morning's workout, but when didn't his muscles ache? Everything was the way it always was.

Bash remembered getting in position at the starting block, glancing down at his watch, and setting the timer.

00:00

And then, with propulsive force, he sprinted. One circle around the track later, Milton walked down from the stands.

"I want you out of the house. You've got till tomorrow. After that, you're no longer my son," he said, turning on his heel. As Milton walked away, he added, "And you know why."

(At the moment, Bash didn't know why. But he found out later.)

The wind had been knocked out of him. Desperate for

something, anything, to ground him, his eyes traveled down to his watch.

Seven minutes had passed since he set the timer. In seven minutes, his whole world had changed. In seven minutes, he had lost everything. The timing of it was always in the back of his mind. In the shower. On the subway. At school.

School. Thank God high school was over. It was funny—he didn't mind it back home. He had a respectable average (low Bs), star athlete status, and teachers generally liked him. But every day at Hillcrest had felt like he was moving through a vague, unsettling dream. He felt both too visible and invisible at the same time.

Now that Track Star Bash was gone, he wasn't all the way sure who he was, anyway. One thing was for sure—he certainly wasn't into probing questions or heart-to-hearts, to try to figure it out. He just wanted to forget why he was in Brooklyn in the first place. He wanted to forget everything. He'd gone from having everything planned out for him—every meal, every race, every training session, every sports agent dinner—to having a wide-open future with absolutely nothing on the horizon.

It was a twisting tornado in his stomach. The thing he'd do almost anything to ignore.

His latest "almost anything"? Letting a pretty girl hire him to do . . . what, exactly? Unclear. It wouldn't be the first time he'd done something stupid because a pretty girl asked. But this might be the stupidest thing. And she was the prettiest girl. Upsettingly pretty.

When Bash saw Audre sitting by herself in the park, it was like all the cells in his body started buzzing. He knew who she was: Audre Zora Maya Toni Mercy-Moore. She was brainy and confident, and had a wild best friend, an adorable set of dimples, and was a rising senior. She was earnest as hell and square in an adorable way. And extremely out of his league. She was the kind of girl who thought guys like him were a cautionary tale. He wondered what she would've thought if she'd met him in Cali. He looked like a different person then. Low fade, uninked skin, no piercings, no jewelry. He was a squeaky-clean, all-American jock. Bursting at the seams.

But that wasn't really me, he thought. *She met the real me. The person my dad wouldn't let me be.*

When he first got to Hillcrest Prep, the guidance counselor demanded a meeting with him, to find out his plans for senior year and beyond. It was the strangest interview. For the first time in his school career, he told the truth. He just unloaded everything that had been pent up for years. Stuff he'd never uttered out loud.

Where do you see yourself in five years?

No idea.

Ten years?

Even less of an idea.

You don't have the slightest idea? No interests, or...

You know what? I do know. So, I'm just gonna say it. I want to be a tattoo artist. I love art and design, and I've always been into ink. My heroes are tattoo artists—I know all the greats and I've memorized their designs. I close my eyes and see them in the dark. Ever since I could hold a pen, I've been sketching designs. Before I even knew what a tattoo was. But I always kept it a secret. A few years ago, I went to a meet in Oklahoma City. And, it seems random, but one of the sickest artists in the country lives there. Keith Littlefeather. I had to meet him. So, I snuck away from practice one afternoon and found his studio. I had to dodge the coaches 'cause they spied on me for my dad. Anyway, this artist was so chill, like he looked at my designs, gave me advice, told me who I should apprentice with in Oakland. And he gave me an old tattoo gun. Ever since then, every chance I got, I'd practice on . . . umm . . . on fruit.

Fruit.

Grapefruits, mostly.

Really?

Really.

You don't find that odd?

Maybe it is. I guess that's one of the reasons I kept it secret. I even rented a locker at a gym two towns over and kept the gun there so my dad could never find it. So, um, yeah. Long story short, that's what I see myself doing.

You do realize that pursuing such a . . . low-status career would be an unfortunate waste of your track and field record. Plus, you've received a top-notch education! Greater Oakland High School and Hillcrest Prep are two of the finest institutions in America. Do you really want to throw away everything you've worked for?

I do. Pretty badly.

Let's move on to the next question. What are three adjectives that best describe you?

Creative. Curious. And, I guess, low-status.

Joke all you want, young man, but tattoo artistry is not a respectable profession.

Maybe I'm not a respectable person. Respectfully.

Audre seemed like the kind of girl who had it all together. It was surprising, learning that she, of all people, needed his help. That she didn't think she was fun. Or didn't know how to have fun.

The thing was: Bash could relate to this in ways she couldn't imagine. He was brand-new to being an impulsive, "adventurous" teenager. He wished he could tell her how regimented his life used to be. He'd never even eaten a meal that wasn't planned by his coaches (who were in cahoots with his dad). His dad approved all his clothes—Republican-coded Polo shirts and khakis because college recruiters and sponsors liked it. He knew how it felt to drown under everyone's expectations. To feel like a list of accomplishments instead of a real person.

When Audre asked him to be her "fun consultant," there was no other answer but yes. Bash was all in before she finished asking the question. Audre and her slightly unpredictable energy were exactly the kind of shit he could get into. In her, he recognized a stifled person, dying to break free. Like him.

Besides, the unreal combination of her beauty, boldness, and (accidental?) meanness turned him into an idiot. His anecdote about being half cat? What was that? He was so embarrassing. He said so many dumb things yesterday. But Audre had walked out in a cloud of delicious perfume before he could redeem himself.

When Bash moved to Brooklyn, he'd decided that he was saying "yes" to everything put in front of him, everything he'd always wanted to do. Nothing was off-limits anymore. He tatted up his arm. Wore whatever the fuck felt right. Pierced things. Stopped buzzing his hair. Made out with whoever he wanted to. Partied. Woke up at 4 AM on the weekends and took the train over an hour to Rockaway Beach.

Plus? There was just something about Audre, wasn't there? It was excruciating, trying not to stare at her at the shop. His eyes were magnetized to her.

But he chased the idea of her out of his mind. This was the exact worst time for him to get a crush. He had nothing to offer.

Just then, the alarm on Bash's watch went off. Seven minutes were up. He'd given himself that much time to catch his breath after surfing all morning. Time to get up.

Seven minutes, he thought, *grabbing his towel and wiping the sand off his skin. That's all the time it took for Dad to get rid of me.*

That's where his mind went when he was still. Ever since Milton said that he was no longer his son, Bash had been obsessed with timing things, with figuring out what could be done in seven minutes. He timed everything. He'd discovered that he could whip up an edible pan of chicken stir-fry in seven minutes. He could bike half of the Park Slope loop in seven minutes. He could tolerate four highball shots in seven minutes.

And, because there were a zillion clocks in Just Because, and he watched them obsessively—he knew that it had taken seven minutes to say yes to Audre.

●　　●　　●

Much later, back at his mom's sparklingly clean apartment, he was slouched down in the only place he felt comfortable—a window nook in the guest room. It made sense that he liked being in the guest room rather than his own hastily furnished bedroom. Bash felt like a guest. He was a guest.

The sun had set. It was just him and Jennifer's three toy

poodles in the cavernous condo. Everything was quiet. He was slouched in the window seat, meditating (i.e., scrolling through the tattoo art on his For You page). The only sound was the occasional firework coming from Prospect Park, across the street.

Suddenly, his phone buzzed through the silence. Spiritually, he jumped five feet in the air. And then he checked his phone. Unknown number.

Bash lowered his already deep voice to sound intimidating. "Hello?"

"Hi, this is Mack Rhodes. You Bash Henry?"

Bash sat up, poker-straight. Mack Rhodes owned Fifth Angel Ink Designs in Myrtle Beach, South Carolina. *The* Fifth Angel Ink Designs—one of the most experimental, cutting-edge tattoo shops in the country.

During spring break, when most of classmates were skiing in Aspen, Bash was organizing and editing photos of his best work. Painstakingly, he designed a portfolio. And, holding his breath, he sent it off to his twenty-five favorite shops across the country. The actual city didn't much matter. Wherever he got a job, he would go. After all, he had no home base. His only criteria? The shop had to be near a beach. With waves.

Myrtle Beach had it all. Extremely surfable waves, and Fifth Angel Ink. He'd do anything to work there. His ambition to make it as a tattoo artist was the only thing keeping his heart beating these days.

"Yes? Yeah, man, I...I'm Bash Henry. It's a pleasure to meet your acquaintanceship...I mean, to be introduced to you."

Grimacing, he buried his face in his hands.

Mack Rhodes chuckled through the phone. "Cool. Cool.

Yeah, so we had a few artists relocate, and I'm on the lookout for fresh talent. Yo, your work is clean, kid. You're good. Real good. Where are you based again?"

Bash was so stunned and honored, he could barely find his voice. "In Brooklyn. I'm in Brooklyn right now, but I'd move, like, tomorrow. I just graduated high school and I'm a massive fan, man, I know all your stuff. I used to trace it on fruit."

"Oranges or grapefruits?"

Bash's mouth fell open a little, and then a shy smile lit up his face. A warm, sunny feeling flooded through him. This was what it felt like to find your people.

"Grapefruits," he said.

"I did that, too. I used to tape one of my mom's sewing needles to a highlighter and use it as a tattoo gun," he said with a short chuckle. "Look. I can't promise you anything, but I'd love you to come down to the shop. We'll have you do some test art, see if you vibe with the team."

Bash went silent. He was too thunderstruck to respond. After a few seconds, he jolted himself back to life. "Cool. Yeah, I'm there. But I should tell you. I'm a minor. I won't be eighteen till August. So, I don't have a license."

He held his breath. This was a once-in-a-lifetime opportunity. He couldn't lose it.

"All good. If we like you, we'll pay licensing fees, train you, all that. Just let me know when you can come down in August, after your birthday. Cool? Talk soon."

With that, Mack Rhodes clicked off. And Bash exhaled until his whole body went limp.

For the first time in ages, he forgot to check the time.

Chapter 10

It was Thursday. Audre just had one more day before she met up with Bash. And she was counting the milliseconds.

Since she barged into Just Because early that week, she'd been filling up her days with a bunch of random activities to pass the time. She chatted on FaceTime with Reshma in Argentina. She sat in various cafés rereading Evelyn Hugo. She swam laps at the YMCA.

Anything to swallow her growing nervousness at meeting Bash for her first challenge. What if she bored him? What if he thought she was too cerebral? What if he was actually a serial killer and drowned her in the Gowanus Canal? And, even worse, what if the girl from Prospect Park, Clio, really was his girlfriend? And what if, when she found out about their little project, she thought Audre was trying to steal her man? Audre hated cheating and cheaters. And she prided herself on being a girl's girl. The last thing she wanted to do was disrupt someone's relationship.

Oh no, she thought, opening the apartment door after a busy day of doing nothing memorable. *Was this a bad idea?*

Too late. Bash had just texted her, confirming their nondate.

Bash: wyd? we still on for tmr?

Audre: YES. i'm relieved, thought you'd cancel

Bash: why would I do that tho

Audre: cause I made that terrible comment about your cat who passed away

Bash: suffocated tragically, you mean

Audre: ugghhhghgh…

Bash: lol I told you, you good

Audre: sometimes my sense of humor is weird and I just blurt out nonsense

Bash: nah, I'm the weird one. it was our second convo & I brought up my dead cat

Audre: ok you have a pnt

Bash: so how's noon

Audre: perf, i'll meet you at Just Because

Bash: bet

Audre: what should I bring?

Bash: just yourself

Audre: nothing else?

Bash: an open mind

His last text had been running through her mind all day. An open mind. They were following Reshma's list, right? Or was he planning to go rogue? Should she be scared? What was she gonna wear? Should her look be Casual Downtown Girl or Coquette Core? Why did she care? Should she pack mace?

Her brain was absolutely scrambled. So much so that when she stepped into the apartment and accidentally stomped on Baby Alice's squeaky teething giraffe toy, she screamed in surprise. In response, Sophie let out a sad, flattened sound into the darkness.

It was around 6 PM. *The Exorcist*, her mom's comfort movie, was streaming on the living room TV. Audre heard a faint rustle coming from Eva and Shane's bedroom. Then a loud, annoyed sigh. Finally, her mom emerged, wearing a tee and Shane's sweatpants, rolled at the waist. Tortoiseshell frames almost masked the dark circles under her eyes. She looked both blissed out and bone-tired. Ever since the baby was born, her personality was split into those two halves: lovestruck and sleepy as hell.

Also, sprouting from the top of her head was a floor-sweeping, Italian lace veil.

"Your grandmother's gonna be the death of me, Audre, I swear," she said, storming into the kitchen and grabbing a La Croix from the fridge. The veil trailed dramatically behind her. Standing at the island, she tilted her head back and downed the entire thing. Then she slammed the empty can on the counter. And, in response, grabbed her temples.

"Excuse me, why are you wearing your veil?" asked Audre, curling up on her bed, aka the couch.

"Grandma Lizette wanted to see it. So, I took a pic and sent it to her." Eva shook her head, a rueful smirk on her face.

"Uh-oh. What'd she say?"

"About the veil? Oh, nothing. But she did tell me I needed a facial."

Such savagery was on-brand for Grandma Lizette. Audre's grandma lived in Houston and was terrified of flying—and they were always busy with school and work—so she barely ever saw her. But they all FaceTimed on holidays and birthdays.

Audre couldn't help but adore Grandma Lizette. After all, Eva's stories about growing up with her were divine. Lizette was a beautiful, talented unicorn brimming with power. She'd won a

trillion titles in the notoriously racist, misogynist pageant indus-
try and, with a tenth-grade education, she had launched a successful modeling career. And had traveled the world with Baby
Eva. And had found the resources to send Eva to Princeton. These
days, when most women her age were retired, Grandma Lizette
ran an elite pageant training academy in Texas.

She was a superhero. The definition of "Mercy girls do what
can't be done."

"The facial thing is harsh," admitted Audre, who always
jumped to her grandmother's defense. "But she was a pageant
queen, so she's naturally beauty-focused."

"That's a long-winded way to say she's vain." Eva joined Audre
on the couch—and then attempted to hug her. Stiffly, Audre
leaned in with her shoulder. It was weird—they used to hug all
the time. But lately, every attempt felt so stilted. Both feeling
awkward, they pulled away and sat side by side. With their faraway expressions and one leg tucked under the other, they were
mirrors of each other.

After a lengthy yawn, Eva said, "Thank God my book's almost
done and I can sleep without stressing out."

"How are your edits going?"

And then, an odd shadow seemed to pass over Eva's face. In a
blink-and-you'll-miss-it moment, her expression went dark. "It's
fine. Revisiting certain parts is hard."

"Which parts?"

"My childhood. Going back in time can be tricky. And, um,
draining." She was choosing her words extra carefully.

"What happened . . ."

Eva cut her off. "I know you want to ask me a million questions right now. But I'm exhausted. I promise I'll fill you in before the book comes out later this fall, okay?"

Her mom was right. Audre did want to ask questions. What was it like growing up with Lizette? Who was Eva's childhood best friend? When she met Shane in twelfth grade, did she know immediately that he was her true love? Her mom talked about the past in unemotional, vague terms. *Lizette did what she had to do for us to survive. We lived all over. I was in pain every day as a kid, but I was used to it. Mercy girls do what can't be done.*

Eva's history was Audre's history, too. So was Lizette's and Great-Grandma Clothilde's, and Great-Great-Grandma Delphine's. She couldn't help but be curious. Judging from Eva's stiff posture and rigid shoulders, Audre could tell her mom was stressed. So, she let it go. Plus, Audre had her own shit to deal with.

"...Shane missed his book deadline and couldn't care less. He just left for his mentorship class with Baby Alice." Twice a week, Shane led a support group for Black teen boys. He loved it almost as much as cooking aggressively healthy meals. "Imagine being so unbothered! So, where were you all day?"

"Nowhere. Reading in the park." Audre rested her foot on a pile of carpet swatches. "These swatches have been here for months, Mom. Is the contractor ever gonna finish this renovation? We can't keep living like this. Isn't it driving you crazy?"

"Of course it's driving me crazy." Distractedly, Eva ran her fingers along the delicate lace of her veil. "Everything is chaotic in our lives right now. But I take it as it comes."

That may be fine for Eva, but Audre craved *order*. Rules, logic, sense. Especially when it came to family. Quietly, it bothered her that her family wasn't tied in a bow like everyone else's. She had two sets of parents. Two homes on two different coasts, with different lives in each place. "Brooklyn Audre" was driven. "Malibu Audre" was relaxed. Eva, Audre, Shane, and Baby Alice all lived in the same house but had different last names. On their Christmas cards, for example, they couldn't sign off with *Happy Holidays from the Walker Family*. Instead, it was *Happy Holidays from the Hall, Mercy, Mercy-Moore, and Hall-Mercy Family*.

Baby Alice was her *half* sister. Which sounded fake, like it didn't count. Audre wished she was her *full* sister. It felt cleaner. Easier. Why did her life require so much explanation?

A year after Baby Alice's birth, Audre still couldn't believe there was another Mercy girl in the world. Her little sister had so much to learn—especially about the feats of power and magic their lineage was supposed to pull off. As her big sister, it'd be her job to teach her all about how their family worked. What would she tell Baby Alice about their mom?

Unclear. Audre was raised by a very different Eva than she was now. Audre's Eva was a stressed-out single mom—writing books and raising a daughter alone despite her painful disease. Shane's love changed her mom. Baby Alice's Eva was lighter. Happier.

Audre would love to trade places with her sister. Once, she'd read that babies have bad eyesight to protect them from overstimulation. Must be nice.

"When is Grandma Lizette coming to meet Baby Alice?"

"Not sure. It's hard for her to travel."

"Maybe she'll come now that I'm here all summer?" Audre said this with a hopeful lilt.

Eva picked up the endless veil in one hand and faced Audre. "Honey, I know this isn't how you wanted to spend your summer. But there *is* an upside. You'll have time to bond with your sister!"

"We've bonded. I'm not a monster."

"I didn't say you were," sighed Eva. "Though I know you call her The Goblin."

Audre grimaced guiltily.

"Also, you can help me with wedding stuff. You love planning events at school."

"I have my own life, Mom," said Audre, her voice rising. "I'm too busy to be your event planner, okay? Who wants to spend their summer planning their mom's wedding?"

Any other summer, she thought, *I wouldn't even be here. Technically, I'm not even supposed to see Summertime Mom in person.*

"Fine, but you *will* have time to do an original art piece for our wedding gift, right?"

"You know I don't paint anymore," muttered Audre.

Eva made an exasperated sound. Annoyed, she grabbed the remote and muted *The Exorcist*. "*Jesus*. Why are you so cranky all the time?"

"I'm the easiest kid ever. You're lucky! Other kids are on drugs right now."

"But you're not. Obviously." Eva squinted, peering into Audre's eyes.

"Well, maybe I just haven't been brave enough to engage with that side of my personality. Who knows what scandalous activities I'll get into this summer?"

"Don't even joke about that. I'd have to sell this veil to make bail."

Audre nibbled on a nail, suddenly itching to bring up an issue that had been gnawing at the corners of her mind. "If I asked you something weird, would you tell me the truth?"

"Always. What is it?"

"If you were a boy, would you think I'm . . . cute?"

"Of course! You're adorable. You're beautiful."

"But I don't want to be adorable. I want to be dangerous."

Eva frowned. "Dangerous."

"You know," said Audre, wiggling her shoulders seductively. "Hot. Like, sexy."

Eva almost launched out of her seat. "Sexy? Why are you asking me that, out of the clear blue? Are you . . . do you . . . are you having sex?"

"Mom. Relax."

"Jesus Christ, who are you having sex with? Was it Ellison at prom? Did you use protection? How could you not TELL me? Jesus. Oh, Jesus."

"Mom! Relax!"

"Just tell me this. Did you get on top? Both me and your grandmother have tilted uteruses, so you might, too. And getting on top is most comfortable."

"MOM, PLEASE."

"WHY ARE YOU YELLING, AUDRE?"

Audre was overwhelmed. "I'm going to erase the last two minutes, okay?"

Slowly, Eva pulled the veil over her face. "Sorry, that was a lot. I'm not emotionally prepared for Elder Teen Audre."

"I'm not emotionally prepared to hear about your tilted uterus.

And what girl gets on top the first time they do it?" Audre let out a long-suffering sigh. "I've just...I don't really have experience with guys, and sometimes I feel so behind."

"Oh. Okay, this I can talk about," breathed Eva. "With sex, everyone your age is on their own timetable."

"But Reshma..."

"Don't compare yourself to Reshma, come on. You two are very different girls, with different lives. She needs a lot of attention to sustain her. Those self-absorbed parents who stay away most of the year? She's sexually advanced because she's looking for love and affection, any way she can get it. But then, she shuts down when the girls fall for her. It's as if she can't trust anyone who claims to love her."

Eva was right. Audre nodded in full agreement. And gratefulness. In the middle of the turmoil that was her life, it felt good—safe—knowing that she could talk to her mom about sex, boys, all of it. Most moms weren't this transparent or understanding.

Audre missed being close to her mom like this.

"You're not behind anyone," continued Eva. "You're moving at your own pace. Whatever happened with Ellison, anyway?"

"I don't know what I was thinking. Not my type, at all. Whatever that is."

Audre could never tell her mom what really happened. That night, the panic attack—it made her feel like something was wrong with her. That she was different from other girls, who could flirt and hook up and go with the flow. And underneath that fear was shame. Mercy girls were supposed to be strong. Not sobbing, shaking, scared train wrecks.

"What was it like dating Shane in high school?" Audre asked softly.

Eva gave her daughter an unreadable smile. "Tumultuous. It's probably why we broke up so soon. We weren't ready for each other yet. I made so many mistakes when I was your age. Believe me, it's better to wait."

No specifics, as per usual. Just vague statements. No real information that Audre could hang on to.

"I wonder if Grandma Lizette had high school boyfriends. Boys probably loved her."

Did Audre see Eva flinch? Did her expression go tight all of a sudden? Odd.

"Oh, I don't know," she said, gingerly removing the veil from her head. She took her time folding it, carefully, on her lap. "I don't know about her history with men. All I know is that when I was growing up, she focused on moving mountains for me. Men were secondary, if they were around at all." Suddenly activated, Eva placed her hand on Audre's shoulder. "Listen. We pull greatness out of our asses. Through all sorts of nonsense. Mom raised me despite enormous obstacles. I've raised you despite enormous obstacles. And you will get into Stanford, if that's what you want. Like Public Enemy said, it took a nation of millions to hold us back."

"Who's Public Enemy?"

"Seriously? I've failed you." Eva shook her head. "Listen, I hate you feeling insecure. I'm so proud of you! You're the one thing in my life that I don't have to worry about."

Amazing, thought Audre. *So glad I can make your life easier. Ever heard of golden child syndrome, Mom? How about parentified child syndrome? Well, I have both. It's an adultlike need to always be perfect. To never be a problem. To not cause chaos. To parent your actual parents. And guess what, Mom? When kids live under that kind of pressure, they usually end up suffering a mental breakdown, an ulcer, or both. So, thanks for that.*

Audre wanted to scream. She wanted her to worry about her sometimes. She wanted to ask Eva for help with her book. She wanted to tell her about how she was entrusting her summer to a stranger, hoping it would bring some light into her eyes. How she was fading and lost, and how everyone seemed to have the answers but her. How she was humiliated on prom night. Not as bad as Carrie, but still . . . bad. She wanted to lay in her mom's lap and cry.

"What are you doing tomorrow? Think you'll have time to watch Baby Alice in the evening? We should be finalizing the new nanny soon, God willing."

Audre quickly thought about this. She was meeting Bash at noon, so she'd be home by the evening.

"Sure, I can babysit. I have plans during the day."

"Oh? What are you doing?"

"Meeting up with this guy named Bash. He graduated from Hillcrest. We're just hanging out at his house, or whatever."

"Will his parents be there?"

"I'm not a child."

"Until you leave this house, you're a child. I don't know this boy. So there should be a parent in the house."

What Eva didn't know was that "parents in the house" didn't

mean anything. When Audre went to Nola Stone's house for her fourteenth birthday party, Nola's parents had been just upstairs. And yet, half the guests were making out within forty-five minutes.

"I know the rules, Mom," she said, peeling herself off the couch and heading to the bathroom. This conversation was over. "There'll be parents in the house. Trust me."

CHAPTER 11

I am simply a girl asking a boy for help in reaching a *goal*, thought Audre as she strode toward Just Because. *Nerves? None to see here.*

She told herself that Bash was just a guy she hired to perform a service. A means to an end. She was being proactive! Instead of sitting around, wallowing in self-pity because her life was in shambles, she was wrestling her personal drama to the ground! As she headed down the bustling sidewalk, she felt lifted by a powerful surge of confidence.

But then, flashing across her brain, was a picture of his sculpted biceps flexing as he crossed his arms. And his sparkly-eyed, megawatt smile. And she remembered that his (apparent) kindness felt weirdly at odds with his reputation. Hello, nerves.

Something about him made her feel things—which was embarrassingly cliché. It's like he was AI designed to be crush-worthy. When Sparrow said he looked at her and she felt a cosmic spark? For once, that girl wasn't being dramatic. Audre had felt the same thing. When his soulful gaze fell on her, she went all gooey. Clearly, he was cosmic with everyone. Maybe it was a trait he couldn't help, like freckles or a super-long second toe. He'd probably have sexual tension with a potted plant.

No. Audre was too practical to let this meaningless attraction spiral into a Whole Thing. And, she reminded herself, he was almost certainly dating that Prospect Park girl. Besides, she suspected he only had two brain cells in his head. He could go from super engaged to checked out in seconds. Was he fried? Was she boring? Hard to say. But he could help with her book.

Besides, feeling attraction wasn't the same as acting on it. And maybe it wasn't even attraction. Maybe it was just appreciation. Like admiring good art.

Audre turned the corner on Degraw. And there was Bash. He was standing under the Just Because awning wearing striped swim trunks, a short-sleeve button-down (the buttons were pointless since the first three were undone), a rope necklace, and Nike slides. The top of his hair was tied into a knot. He looked like a person who lost their luggage on a tropical vacation.

And yet he made Audre's stomach flip-flop. She swallowed hard and then tugged at her short smocked sundress. Was she too dressed up? Were the platform sandals too much?

"Hey!" she called out.

Bash looked up from his phone and saw her. His eyes widened and, from her vantage point, he seemed to freeze. Just for a moment, though. Then his face softened, and he flashed Audre a small, hesitant grin. It was a symphony of expressions.

"Hey you," he said. "What's going on?"

"Nothing much!" Her voice sounded strained.

"That's wassup."

They stood silent for a bit, fidgeting and looking at their feet. Finally, Bash spoke up.

"Let's just start over. Like we're meeting for the first time."

"Great idea!"

"Are you a hugger? I'm a hugger."

"Let's hug!" They embraced stiffly while managing to keep their actual bodies far from each other. She did note that the top of her head fit nicely under his chin.

Bash pulled away, thrusting his hands in his pockets. "You look nice."

"You too. Um...this isn't a date," she blurted out. Immediately, she wished for death.

"Um...I know," he said, his eyes widening. "Damn. You're hella direct."

"I don't know why I said that. I'm sorry. I just think boundaries are super important."

"I'm aware it's not a date. I'm your fun consultant. Your funsultant."

"You're funny." She lightly punched him on the shoulder and immediately felt like an idiot. "So. I'm excited to get started."

"Me too, but I just wanna manage your expectations. I'm not as interesting as you think."

Audre's face fell. "Please don't back out. You already agreed to help me. On this mortal plane, all we have is our word, Bash."

"On this mortal plane." He tilted his head, mulling it over. "Bars."

"Well, in third grade I won a citywide poetry contest," she offered awkwardly.

He grinned. "Don't worry, Audre, I'm not backing out. I kinda feel like you're nervous."

"Fuck," she said quickly. "Does it show?"

"It's okay if you are. This situation is weird," he said. "I get nervous all the time. In ninth grade I drank, like, nine Mountain Dews to get the courage to ask this girl out to Applebee's. I was awake for two days."

"Did she say yes?"

At this, his face went a little blank, as if he didn't understand the question.

"Right, of course she said yes," she said under her breath.

Just then, two moms pushing double-wide strollers came barreling down the sidewalk in a full sprint. Bumper stickers reading MARATHON MOMS decorated their strollers. Protectively, Bash's arm shot out across Audre's chest, and he backed them both up against the front door of Just Because. He held her against the door until they passed.

"Be careful, ladies!" he called out, dropping his arm from her chest. "Those moms almost took you out."

Audre blinked up at him, breathless. She nodded in silence.

"You good?"

"Yeah. Yeah, uh, thank you for stroller-saving me." She felt an anxiety flush coming on. Suddenly sweaty, she swept her heavy braids over one shoulder. She needed to reclaim her power, and fast. "I'm thinking...maybe we should do some icebreakers? When I led the orientation for new juniors at the beginning of last year, I did icebreakers."

"What, like trust falls? I'm six four. You can't catch me."

She raised her brows. "First of all, I have enormous upper body strength."

"Do you?" He stepped back, taking a good look at her frame. "Is that based on blind confidence or an actual unit of measure?"

"Confidence. Secondly, no. I meant like Two Truths and a Lie. Would You Rather."

"I'd rather do a trust fall."

"Okay, we'll skip the icebreaker," she said. "So. What do we have planned for today? I'm along for the ride. Following your lead."

"Cool. Cool." Bash clapped his hands together. "So, yeah, I've been thinking this over for the past few days. Your first challenge is to do something physical and risky, right? I wrote them all in my notes app." He held up his phone as proof. "I was thinking it should be something you're not used to, right?"

"Honestly, I'm not used to any physical activity. I'm pretty much a stationary object. So whatever we do will be a stretch for me."

"Cool. We're going out to Rockaway!"

"Rockaway Beach in Queens? To swim?"

"No, to surf," he said brightly.

Audre laughed, positively certain that he was joking.

"Wait. You can't be serious."

"In general, no, I'm not serious. But about surfing, I am."

"You don't look like a surfer."

"No? What's a surfer look like?"

She thought this over. "Ken."

He chuckled. "*We* surf, too, Audre. Expand your mind."

"No, I meant . . ."

"I heard enough of that back home," he said mildly. "My dad

wasn't feeling it. He was . . . what's the word? Strict. He never saw surfing as a real sport."

Audre wondered why he was speaking about his father in the past tense. She tried to hold herself back from digging deeper, because she wanted to respect his rule. No therapizing.

She tried for a full ten seconds. But she was dying to learn more about Bash's background. Good thing she knew how to get people to open up without asking intrusive questions. She'd figure him out. Bash was no different than any other stubborn kid she'd convinced to open up.

"I bet you have a basketball dad, right? With your height, he wanted you to be LeBron."

"Nah. My dad's a track coach. He qualified for the Olympics for Jamaica, where he was born, but got injured. I never had a choice but to run." He paused. "Sometimes parents see talent in you before you see it, I guess."

Bash sounded stilted. Like he was reciting lines he'd heard before a thousand times.

"So," she said, "I'm in the presence of a bona fide track star."

He shrugged, shifting his weight from foot to foot. "Something like that."

"What track star runs in Crocs?"

"You don't miss anything, huh?"

"Be careful," she whispered. "It's my superpower."

"The Crocs were *intentional*. I'm not a competitive sprinter anymore. Bad memories. But sometimes I'll go on a half-assed jog to clear my mind. And if I'm wearing Crocs, it's a reminder that it's not serious. Helps me relax." He grinned. "Happy?"

"Happy," she confirmed. "You know, I could tell you were

from the Bay Area the first time I heard you talk. 'Hella' this, 'fosho' that. It made me miss Cali. I spend the summers with my dad and stepmom in Malibu."

"Hold up. You spent summers in Malibu and never surfed? Illegal behavior," he said, shaking his head. "Malibu surfing is elite."

"So, you're really a hang-ten, gnarly-dude, life's-a-beach surfer."

"You sound like a kook," he said, striking a goofy surf pose. " 'Kook' means beginner."

"Wait. The blond tips are natural, then. From the sun! The streets are saying you dye your hair with L'Oréal bleach."

"Whaattt? Do I look like a person who'd do that?"

"Well..."

"Don't answer that." He fingered an errant curl and sighed. He'd been offended, but now he dialed it back. "Nothing against those drugstore box dye joints. Mostly old ladies use them, right? Elders deserve to look and feel their best. I'm not ageist. It's just that, if I was gonna color my hair I'd get a professional to do it. My homegirl in Oakland worked at a salon on weekends, right? She said my texture is fragile. So it isn't something I'd do by myself."

Audre's mouth dropped open, and she dissolved into giggles. She couldn't help it.

"What?" he asked, dead serious. "I respect the natural hair journey."

"As you should. We must protect our texture at all costs." There was something so earnest and innocent about Bash. Guys that looked like him, with the floppy hair, thrifted aesthetic, and ungendered jewelry—they were usually putting on a softboy cool act. But Bash seemed so...pure. Nice. Like he was one of Santa's helpers.

Acknowledge the crush, she told herself. *Make peace with it, and let it go.*

"I'm just, like...why is my hair a topic of conversation, though? Of all things." Bash shrugged in confusion.

"You can't fault people for being curious about you," said Audre. "New kid. Blank slate. Interesting dating life. And a part of you encourages rumors because you never clear anything up. Never complain, never explain, right?"

Bash shoved his hands in his pockets, thinking this over. After a moment, he glanced at her with an amused expression. "Why do you like therapizing so much?"

"I guess I'm fascinated by what lies beneath. Some philosopher said that unless you deal with your unconscious mind, it'll direct your life and you'll call it destiny."

He chuckled. "Great answer. Okay, I'm going to the beach. You can come and chill or stay here and explore your unconscious."

"But I want to explore *your* unconscious."

"It'll never happen. You won't break me." He tugged on her tote bag and set off toward the subway. "Come on, let's go."

"Wait! I can't go surfing without a bathing suit."

Over his shoulder, he called out, "You can rent a wetsuit at the Surf Shop. I'm renting a surfboard. Let's gooo."

Audre stood there for a moment, watching him disappear into the bustling sidewalk. She was actually dying to go to the beach. But the idea of being half-naked in front of Bash with zero preparation or warning? That was a no. No. Reshma wouldn't approve of her backing down, but learning to embrace spontaneity didn't happen overnight.

Still, Audre could watch him surf. Maybe book ideas would strike her on the beach. It was, after all, her happy place.

Before she could talk herself out of it, she hurried to catch up with him.

•　　•　　•

Ninety minutes, two trains, and one bus ride later, Bash and Audre had made it to Rockaway Beach. During any other summer, she would've been chilling on Malibu Beach—and the differences between the two were drastic. The water was cloudy and the sand was...interesting. (A few feet from them, a sequined thong and a discarded lash strip were half-buried in the sand.)

Bash had rented a surfboard and two towels, and Audre sat on one of them while he replaced his T-shirt with a rash guard.

It was a struggle, trying not to stare. His chest was strong. His shoulders were broad. Her gaze traveled along his chest, all that nut-brown, sun-kissed skin dipping down into a perfect V. Quickly, she looked away, feeling a little dizzy. She was grateful for her sunglasses, which hid the fact that she was outright ogling her paid funsultant.

"I'm gonna go in," he said, raising his voice to combat the windy sea air. "You coming?"

She did rent a wet suit. But she needed a moment to work up the courage for a Surf Lesson L'Bash. In response, she pulled a notebook out of her tote. "I'm just gonna vibe, take some notes. But you go! Hang ten, friend. I'll get in soon."

With a nod, he jogged down to the water and dove in easily. The water was his second home. God, she did want to go swimming. Memories of Dadifornia flooded her... the seafood shacks with her dad, slumber parties with cousins, the roar of the ocean lulling her to sleep. The scent of salty air and coconut oil clinging to her for two and a half months every year. Yoga with her weird-ass stepmom. Audre would've done anything to be there right now.

But instead, she was stuck. Staring at Bash hopping on a surfboard with a nimble quickness, making yet another thing look incredibly easy. He took wave after wave, smoothly and with a balletic grace. And for a moment, she felt like she was back in California. She let herself feel transported. And at some point, her eyelids fluttered closed. When she opened them, Bash was gone.

Audre frowned. What happened? His surfboard bobbed on the surface, but he was nowhere to be seen. He probably just wiped out. That was a part of surfing, wasn't it? She waited a few heartbeats, but still, he hadn't surfaced.

Then Bash's phone lit up from where he'd left it on his towel. Audre didn't intend to be nosy, but she couldn't help but see the caller's photo. It was Clio, the Prospect Park girl. Audre stared at the phone with rising anxiety as Clio called two more times. She hoped Bash told her that they were hanging out, extremely platonically. She wouldn't want her to get the wrong idea.

Audre switched her focus back out to the ocean. Bash still hadn't resurfaced. And suddenly, all of her panic sensors flared. She stood up, fast. Her notebook flew off her lap and landed in the sand.

"Bash!" she hollered. No response. With a gasp, she ran down to the edge of the water. "Bash! Bash, where are you? Are you okay?"

Frantically, she whipped her head from left to right, looking around for a lifeguard. There wasn't one. She didn't have a choice. It was time for action.

Audre tore off her sunglasses, kicked off her platforms, tossed her phone onto the sand—and ran into the water. She swam out to Bash's surfboard, using the clean strokes she'd learned from her California cousins. When she reached the board, she attempted to stand and realized her feet didn't touch the bottom. Taking a deep breath, she dove in with wide-open eyes. Her vision was blurry in the murky water, but she spotted Bash instantly. He was down at the sea floor holding on to something she couldn't make out. Was he tangled in seaweed? Was he drowning?

Thinking fast, Audre popped back up to get air and then dove down to Bash. She tugged on his arm. In dreamlike slow motion, he turned toward her. Blurry surprise registered on his face—and then they both kicked back up to the surface. They popped up at the same time, sputtering, coughing, and frantically treading water.

"ARE YOU OKAY?" he yelled at her. "YOU DROWNING?"

"ME? I THOUGHT YOU..."

Before Audre could finish, he hooked an arm around her waist and swam over to his board. In one smooth motion, he hoisted her onto his surfboard and then, lightning-fast, he paddled back to shore. Once on dry land, Bash tossed Audre over his shoulder, superhero-style, and sprinted over to their towels. With careful urgency, he laid her down and knelt next to her, salty water droplets rolling from his face onto hers. Stunned from being tossed around like a rag doll, her heartbeat roared in her ears, and she was breathless and too overwhelmed to speak.

"You're fine!" hollered Bash. "I got you. I know CPR."

Before he lowered his face to hers, she pushed him away, shouting, "I don't need CPR, Bash! I was rescuing you."

"Me?" He drew back from her, frowning. "I don't need rescuing. I never need rescuing."

(Audre's therapist radar perked up at this. She tucked it away for safekeeping, almost certain it meant something.)

"You disappeared, Bash." She paused to cough her face off. "You... you were underwater forever! What are you, a merman?"

"Sort of? I've been learning how to be a free diver, on YouTube! Free divers hold their breath for insane amounts of time. I'm up to two minutes. I was fine!"

"Why didn't you tell me that? You disappeared. I was terrified."

"You're right, that was so stupid."

"What were you doing down there, anyway?"

"Ugh. It's so embarrassing." With a massive exhale, he stood up and started pacing back and forth in front of their towels. "Fuck, you scared me to death. What if something had happened? What if you'd gotten hurt and I was responsible..."

Audre stood up, grabbing his arm to get his attention. Bash stopped pacing, stumbling a bit on the uneven sand. They stood facing each other, practically vibrating with adrenaline. Her eyes got tangled in his. As briskly as if she'd touched open fire, she dropped her hand.

And then, time stopped. Audre suddenly felt uber-aware of everything—that her short, thin dress was drenched and clinging to her body. That her skin was tingly. That the sunrays were making her dizzy. Or was it him? His soaked, sculpted skin glistening in the sun? His lanky, outrageously tall frame? The fact that he'd just rescued her like Superman? (No, Aquaman.) Wet Bash was more than she was prepared to handle.

Audre feared she was five seconds from swooning into his arms. But it wasn't in the movie kind of way, with flawless lighting and perfectly written lines. No, she wanted to back up a few feet and then take a running leap onto him, knocking him to the ground, spread eagle.

But that was ridiculous. She was paying him for a service. This was just sixteen-year-old hormones and adrenaline from the botched rescue. Right?

Maybe. But she didn't know how to handle all of the . . . hormones and adrenaline.

And then, accidentally, her eyes found his—and she caught him, for a millisecond, absolutely gawking. He was staring at her with open fascination. Like he'd never seen a girl before.

"Audre—" he started.

"No," she interrupted nonsensically.

No? What was she saying no to? The electric surge crackling between them? The expectation? The pressure? Suddenly, she felt unsteady. Her hands were shaking, and her chest went tight. Her palms started to sweat. A feverish heat flushed over her chest. She started to tremble, her breath coming in tortured gasps. The panic attack was threatening to explode.

Audre grabbed her shoes and tote. And ran.

Chapter 12

Reshma's Argentinean trip ended before it had really started. A mere week and a half after she arrived, her parents sent her ass packing.

Much like her bestie's situation, Brooklyn was not her plan for the summer. Unlike her bestie's situation, the change in plans was entirely her fault.

She'd been back home for half a day, but she hadn't told Audre yet. Instead of texting her the news (boring), she planned on showing up at her apartment as soon as she slept off the jet lag. A dramatic reveal! Who wouldn't love that? Such antics were expected of Reshma. She knew her role, and it was to surprise and delight.

As disappointed as she was to be back in town, it was cool that she and Audre would experience their first Brooklyn summer together. Maybe it wouldn't be so bad. Plus, she was dying to get all the details about her experiment with Bash. Over Face-Time, Audre told her that they were tackling the "physical activity" challenge today. If she knew her friend, she was probably using her time with him as a psychological study rather than an "experience."

Hopefully she was being bold and hadn't chickened out.

With an indulgent yawn, Reshma rolled over on her side and curled into a snuggly ball. She'd only been home for a few hours, but she was already bored. This was a problem. Being left to her own devices was historically not a good idea.

That's pretty much what happened in Argentina. Reshma got into *huge* trouble at her parents' recording studio. She was there to be a music production intern. But after two days, she caught a terrible cold—and was bedridden at the Four Seasons Hotel. Too busy to deal with Reshma, her parents had the production assistant deliver cold medicine. Kiki Silva was Afro-Brazilian, a music theory major at University of Buenos Aires—and looked like the long-lost sister of Chloe and Halle Bailey.

Reshma decided to act sicker than she really was.

The first day Kiki stopped by Reshma's hotel room, she didn't come out for two hours. The next day, it was three hours. And so forth, until the day Kiki was late for an important meeting with record label execs.

Not good. Even worse? Kiki was twenty, and Reshma was sixteen and a half—an age-gap scandal punishable by jail time. So, they agreed to part before they were caught. But not before Reshma convinced Kiki to break into the studio after hours, so they could record an original song, "For You I'd Catch the Flu." Fatal mistake. That night, Reshma accidentally spilled champagne all over the mixer. The damages added up to $21,000—and the couple was caught.

Without hearing Reshma's side, the Wells were certain that

their daughter was the instigator in this scenario. (They were correct, of course. But their lack of faith hurt Reshma's feelings!) That day, they sent their troublemaking kid back home.

Which is where she was now—curled up in her massive bed. Her room was so good: twinkly lights, a 1950s record player, a heart-shaped red guitar (she didn't play). On the far wall hung a poster of a toothless, six-year-old Reshma posing with Robert Pattinson on a red carpet. During a goth phase in 2021, she'd burned out his eyes with cigarette butts. Sometimes, she wished she could stay in this room forever. Whenever she left, trouble found her.

And when she was in trouble? That was the only time her parents noticed her. She wondered why they adopted her, anyway. Her mom had been forty-five, her dad fifty-five. They were too old to decide to be parents! Deep down, Reshma suspected they were following the "white celebs adopting kids of color" model that was so trendy at the time. Maybe their careers were fading and they needed a publicity boost. Whatever it was, by the time she'd aged out of being the little brown cutie-pie they could flaunt on red carpets, they got bored.

Relatable. Nothing held Reshma's attention for long, either.

When I get what I want I never want it again. That old Courtney Love lyric described her perfectly. It was from a song Eva played all the time, "Violet." She had such eclectic music taste. Audre was lucky. Her mom was strict, but she was a normal person. Reshma wouldn't have minded if her parents were a bit overprotective at times, like Eva was. At least she'd know they gave a shit. They never knew where she was, and they didn't care.

Ugh, she was so jet-lagged. Too wired to sleep, she padded

over to the mirror in her lace bralette and men's pajama pants. She examined the dark circles under her huge, expressive eyes and decided they looked badass. Quickly, she blew out the Boy Smells Woodphoria candle simmering on her vintage vanity and rubbed on a matte red lipstick. Time to go. She was taking herself on a picnic in Prospect Park.

Reshma headed up Third Street with a picnic basket, a bottle of Malbec from her parents' wine cellar, and her comfort book, *A Thing of Beauty*. It was a biography about the heroin-addicted '70s supermodel and proud lesbian Gia. (Years ago, she'd watched the Angelina Jolie–starring biopic on a burner phone at sleepaway camp and fell in love.) Gia was tough. Naughty. She wore *wrecked* eyeliner. Relatable!

Also relatable? Gia's desperation for love and attention, which no amount of glamour could satisfy.

Lost in thought, Reshma walked deep into the park, past the swan pond. If she met her at a party forty years ago, would she have caught Gia's eye? Saved her from drugs? No, she'd probably just accidentally set Gia's hair on fire with a lighter (which is what Reshma did to her last girlfriend, a far less famous model). No doubt, they would've been too similar to date. They'd eclipse each other, like the sun and the moon, a force too bright for human eyes to take in. At least, not without those eclipse glasses you buy off Amazon.

Reshma was so lost in her fantasy that she barely heard the squawking behind her. She kept walking, her AirPods playing old Summer Walker. And then, she felt an energy shift. She froze and whipped her head around. A huge swan was a few feet behind her. It looked *mad*.

With a shriek, she spun around and bolted. The swan ran after her, squawking and flapping its wings. Clutching the picnic basket to her chest, she ran and ran until she tripped and fell, like some pathetic Last Girl in a bad thriller. Just then, someone leapt over her and ran toward the swan.

"Darlene! Darlene, what are you doing? You calm down right now, young lady."

Darlene the Swan let out one more squawk, but this one sounded far less aggressive. Frozen on the ground, Reshma opened her eyes and saw a girl bend down and hug the swan around the neck. She whispered something close to her head (did birds have ears?!) and then pointed back at the pond. Darlene rubbed her beak against the girl's cheek and then waddled off, leaving a trail of ivory feathers behind her.

The girl was wearing a green vest that read PROSPECT PARKS & REC. She was so earthy-baddie cute, Reshma was thunderstruck. Micro-locs tumbling to her shoulders, a few decorated with gold cuffs. Radiant complexion the color of Reshma's favorite flower, the toffee rose. Freckles across her nose. And, oh, a blinding smile with an adorable gap between her two front teeth.

"I'm Clio," she said, stretching out her hand to Reshma. She grabbed it and stood up.

"Reshma," she mouthed, but no sound came out. She cleared her throat. "I'm Reshma. Are you a Disney princess?"

Clio let out a twinkly giggle. "No, I'm a Prospect Park Alliance teen volunteer. I know all the swans. Darlene's a fighter. You must've walked near one of her babies. She's so aggressive, the city tried to put her down, but that won't happen on my watch." Her voice was silky and soothing, like ASMR. It didn't match what she was saying, which was that Reshma was almost slain by America's Most-Wanted Swan.

"You just saved my life," said Reshma. She felt curiously weightless. Floaty. No one had ever saved her before. She felt like the protagonist of a cheesy old rom-com. She wanted to fall again so Clio could catch her. "You said you're a teen volunteer?"

"I am!" Clio smiled at her brightly. "Are you interested in volunteering?"

"No, no, I just... how old are you, exactly?"

"Eighteen and a half."

A respectable age gap, thought Reshma. *Definitely not punishable by jail time.*

And then, Reshma's smile matched Clio's.

Chapter 13

Audre ran and ran, until she made it to the board-
walk. And then she kept running, dodging bicyclists and families
with small children, until she tired out. Tears helplessly streaming down her cheeks, she staggered to a bench and sat down,
hard. There she stayed, dripping wet and folded over at the waist.

After a while, her heart rate settled. The tears began to dry
up, but her cheeks still felt raw and hot. Her chest was pounding.
Her hands were trembling.

And, outside of the prom disaster, Audre had never been more
humiliated.

If she'd had the strength to get up and continue running, she
would've—straight for the bus and home, never to speak to Bash
Henry again. He must've thought she was batshit. Shaking like
that? Blurting out NO without even hearing what he had to say?
And worse, hyperventilating. She could only imagine what he
must be thinking of her right now. How unhinged she must've
looked.

It was Day 1 of her Experience Challenge and she'd already

failed. Reshma would be so disappointed. Audre was someone who couldn't be in any risky situation with a boy—without getting a panic attack. Who was she to ever advise a client on anything? Let alone write a self-help book.

Audre leaned against the back of the bench. As she came back to earth, she focused on regulating her breathing. She soon became aware of how heavy her braids felt, soaked with sea water. Eyes still closed, she slid the scrunchy off her wrist and swept her hair up in a high ponytail. Slowly, she let her eyelids flutter open. And then she shrieked.

Bash was sitting on the boardwalk, at her feet. Legs crossed and grasping four grape Gatorade bottles. The line of his jaw clenched with stress and worry. When she screamed, he scrambled to his feet and sat next to her on the bench.

"Bash! You scared the shit out of me."

"You scared the shit out of me!"

"Why were you sitting down there?"

"I thought you were gonna pass out. I wanted to be here to catch you, just in case. Like a trust fall."

Bash smiled but she didn't. She couldn't even look at him directly.

"Here, drink this. You need electrolytes. It's over ninety degrees today. I know all about overexerting yourself in the heat—it fucks with you."

Shielding her eyes with her palm, she gratefully accepted the Gatorade, downing half of it in three gulps. Then she handed it back to him and dropped her face into her hands.

"Are you okay?" he asked, nudging her with his shoulder. "What happened back there?"

Audre kept her face in her hands. She felt so exposed, so thoroughly embarrassed. Her mind kept going back to prom night, the way Ellison and those faceless boys had laughed at her. If she could've disappeared between the slats of the bench, she would've.

Just my luck that Bash did track, she thought, mortified. *Why did I think I could outrun him?*

"Did I do something wrong?" Bash was saying.

"No, you're fine. It's me. I don't want to talk about it."

"And yet you want me to reveal my deepest, darkest thoughts, huh?"

"I know, I'm a hypocrite," she said, her voice muffled behind her hands. "I just . . . I don't think this is a good idea."

"What isn't?"

"This." Audre dropped her hands and looked over at Bash. "My experiment. I thought I was ready to be adventurous, but maybe I'm not. I'm not used to being out of control. I don't think I like it."

"Understood." He nodded, his brow knitted with concern. "You were hyperventilating. Has that happened before?"

"It was . . . it was . . . ," she started haltingly. She couldn't get the laughter from prom night out of her mind. Ellison left her in the bed and went out and grabbed his friends. To record her. He made her a joke, a punch line—and at her most vulnerable moment. The shame curdled in her stomach.

Bash waited patiently, his expression open and encouraging.

"It was a panic attack," she whispered. "I get them sometimes. It's not a big deal, though. So let's just . . . forget it, okay? I'm good." She stood up, felt unsteady, and plopped back down.

"Back in Oakland, I knew someone who had panic attacks," he said, a shadow of something flashing in his eyes.

"Who?"

"No one," he said quickly. "Anyway, panic attacks fucking suck, man."

"Understatement," she said, clutching her stomach. "God, the world is moving but I'm sitting still."

"You're dizzy. You need more Gatorade," he said, handing her another bottle.

Gratefully, she finished the first bottle, and downed the second. "Thanks. But I should take myself home now."

"You can't get on the bus alone like this. I'll take you home. Where do you live in Park Slope?"

In a daze, she gave him her address and he typed it into his notes app.

"Cool. But let's sit here till you feel better. I don't have anywhere to be. Do you?"

She didn't. So, Bash sat in silence with Audre while she sipped Gatorade and slowly floated back to life. Their clothes dried in the blazing sun. The squawking of the seagulls and steady hum of the crowded boardwalk lulled Audre into something close to calm.

After a million years, Audre spoke up. "Hey."

He perked up. "Hey."

"Question. Did you take any pictures of me freaking out back there?"

"Pictures? Why would I do that?"

"I had to ask. You never know," she said with a strained smile, trying to lighten the mood. "But can you do me a favor? Please, please, promise to never tell anyone about this."

"I'd never do that. It's your private business. You can trust me."

Shyly, Audre cast her eyes in his direction. "Will you promise? Just say it."

His eyes met hers. "I promise."

She let out the tiniest, smallest exhale of relief. An effusive "thank you" was on the tip of her tongue, but just then she got distracted by his phone, lighting up in his palm. Clio's face flashed on the screen. Again? Was this the fourth time in the past hour? Why wasn't he answering her? Bash peered down at his phone, shook his head, and then slid it in his pocket.

She had to ask. She *had* to.

"Did you tell your girlfriend that I hired you to help me? I don't want her to get the wrong idea."

"I don't have a girlfriend." He put up air quotes around "girlfriend."

"Convincing. Are you one of those 'I don't believe in labels' guys?"

"No, I know that labels mean things. Which is why I'm telling you, Clio isn't my girlfriend. She's an acquaintance. And, yeah, she knows about you. And your Experience Challenge."

She chewed the inside of her cheek, digesting what he was saying. If Clio was just an acquaintance, then why did Bash tell her about the challenge? Audre felt a nagging sense of doubt. But in that moment, she pushed it away and chose to believe him.

It was easier to believe him.

Audre tried to think of things in a clinical way. It made sense that tensions were high back there on the beach. Bash was beautiful. He'd just rescued her from the actual Atlantic Ocean. He almost pressed his lips against hers. For CPR, not a kiss, but still. The last time she was that close to a guy, she almost vomited in his mouth (shellfish allergy be damned). It made sense that she panicked.

Get it together, Audre told herself. *Think of the advice you gave Sparrow. Decenter men and remember you're the star of your story. Bash Henry is your conduit to great writing. Nothing more.*

Bash must've sensed that she was in emotional turmoil, so he made a suggestion. "Let's walk. Are you ready to walk?"

She nodded with a grateful smile. And then, just as the sun was starting to set, they headed down the boardwalk—Audre on legs that were still a bit trembly. After a block or so of silence, Bash asked, "How about an icebreaker?"

"Ha. You're using my tactics against me?"

"I am." He grinned. "What are three things that make you happy?"

Audre answered right away. "Making class president. Promoting mental health. And public speaking."

He chuckled. "Nahh, bro. Those are all resume-type things. Goals and shit."

"But that is my shit. I set a series of incremental goals and crush them all."

"Okay, but what makes you *happy* happy. What gets you excited?"

Audre had never thought about this before. "My brain's a jumbled mix of nonsense. TV? *Shameless. Sex Education. American Horror Story*, seasons one through four. Sausage pizza. Civil War trivia. Rare Beauty blush. Crispy winter grass. Old Lil Wayne.

New Tyler, the Creator. Watching movies with my mom. I used to love hanging out with her, but we don't anymore."

"Why, what happened?"

"My little sister happened. Baby Alice. She's the new-and-improved me. I've been replaced." She walked another block, thinking. "My mom was my best friend. Is that weird?"

"No, you're lucky. All I know about mine is that she looks like the *Parent Trap* mom."

"Why did you grow up with your dad instead of your mom?"

Bash took a breath. Was he deciding how to answer, or if he was going to answer?

"You owe me a secret," said Audre. "You just saw me melt down on a public beach."

Bash smiled down at her. "That's fair. On one of my first nights in town, my mom took me to dinner. This awkward-ass, get-to-know-you dinner. I said maybe two words. But she talked the whole time. Like she was confessing, almost. She told me about meeting my dad at a track meet, back when he was a Brooklyn high school coach. Her brother was competing. Anyway, they liked each other and got married too fast. Right after I was born, California University recruited my dad to be a coach. So, Milton divorced Jennifer. Gained custody of me. And then moved to California to start a new life."

"But why didn't she fight for you?"

Bash shrugged. "You don't know my dad. He's, like, not a dude you argue with. And he had big plans, you know? I guess he was waiting for a son that he could mold into a superstar. And he *meant* that shit. I had sponsorships and national press when I was in sixth grade. I was profiled on ESPN in tenth. If I was still living with him, I'd be in a training camp right now." He nibbled on his bottom lip, pausing a beat. "My dad wanted total control, so my mom gave me up. The other thing? Maybe she didn't want me in the first place. I'll never know."

Bash sounded curiously removed from his explanation, almost robotic. Audre wondered how often he even allowed himself to think about it. To her ears, it was heartbreaking. Bash just dropped so much information on her, she wasn't sure how to respond. That was a new feeling.

"What's that expression on your face?" he asked with slight amusement. "You just got all frowny."

"Oh sorry, this is my 'active listening' face," she said, massaging her brows with her fingertips. "Why's your mom so busy? Managing Just Because?"

"Nah, she has a manager. My mom's the owner. She owns hundreds of stores, all over Manhattan, Queens, and Brooklyn. Her great-great-grandfather was a retail tycoon."

"She's an heiress? Glamorous."

"I don't know about all that. I don't really know her at all."

"It sounds like you're not that close. Can I ask? Why'd you move here?"

Bash shrugged, scratched his forearm. His shoulders slumped a little. It was as if the question depleted his energy.

"Family drama," he finally said. And then he changed the subject. "Long story short, it's cool that you're close to your mom. Or, at least, you used to be."

"The other day I gave a speech to the whole student body. Everyone was there—staff, parents, everyone. And she forgot to go. I had a panic attack right before, worse than this one, but

I got it together in the bathroom, came back out, and I did the speech anyway. And I was good. It just would've been nice to have someone in the audience be proud of me."

Bash handed her another Gatorade. He'd been carrying the last two under his arm as they walked. She took a swig and handed it back.

"What do you think the panic attacks are about? What are you anxious about?"

"Don't know. Everything? It's funny, when I was younger, I wasn't scared of anything."

Just then, Bash's pocket lit up. Without knowing, Audre knew who it was. And she had to address it.

"Not to jump to conclusions . . ."

"Oh God."

". . . but are you gonna call Clio back?"

Bash aimed his index finger at her. "You are jumping to conclusions."

"Do you realize that when you point your finger at me, you're also pointing three fingers at yourself?"

Bash drew back in surprise. He examined his fingers and saw that, yes, his last three fingers were aimed at himself. "*Crazy.* Who are you?"

She answered with a grin. "But back to you. Why do you juggle so many girls?"

"Who says I'm juggling girls?"

"Well, everyone's heard about Coco-Jean. People saw you buying her Plan B at CVS."

"It's not the way it sounds. I was vaping with her over by that pizza place Peppino's. She said she needed to buy Plan B for a friend but was scared someone might see her. I could tell that wasn't the truth, and she needed help. So I picked it up for her. That's all."

"Hmm. And Sparrow? She said you had a cosmic connection at Little Purity. She was weeping about your unspoken lust for each other."

"The girl I bought lunch for? She was out of cash. I had cash. No more, no less. I didn't even know her name was Sparrow. What's up with y'all's names out here?"

"Aging hipster parents." Audre sighed. "You're guilty of being too nice, Bash. Buying hopeless romantics bacon-egg-and-cheeses. Letting strangers party in your house when you're not there. Breaking hearts all over town."

"There are worse things to be, right?" His expression brightened, and he grinned at her. She smiled back. "Hey. Can I hear your speech?"

"You're changing the subject."

"Maybe. But also, I really want to hear your speech. You need someone to be proud of you. I'll be proud."

Audre thought about this for three-point-five seconds. And then she cleared her throat and launched into her speech with such gusto, Bash was startled.

Welcome to the Cheshire Prep Junior Class Awards Ceremony, friends, parents, and caregivers. We're almost at the finish line, folks. And we've been through so much together in these past eleven years. Living in Brooklyn is such a specific experience. It's like the world slowly gets bigger, in itty-bitty increments. Remember the first time you were allowed on the stoop by yourself as a kid? The next step is hanging out on the block alone. Then walking to school. Taking the bus to the Brooklyn

Museum. Taking the train to the city—most likely, the Soho Sephora!
{Pause for laughter.}

    Growing up here happens in these clean-cut stages. Even so, we some-
times don't notice growth as it happens. It can just feel like waiting. But
those stages are important. Because they're the ones that prepare us for Us
2.0. So, my fellow lifers, I leave you with this. Yes, we're facing climate
change, war, diminishing reproductive rights, the recession. Yes, being a
teenager today can feel like mopping up a flood with a paper towel. But
when we come out on the other side, no one will deny our power. Eff it, we
ball. Go, Cheshire Tigers!

Audre stopped. Shyly, she glanced at Bash through her lashes.
He looked like he'd just seen his first natural rainbow—all twinkly eyes and a wide, delighted smile. With a wild yelp, he started
vigorously clapping.

"Did you like it? Was it good?"

"It was excellent. You're a genius. You should give speeches
professionally! Is that a profession?"

Audre bit her lip to stop herself from beaming. She'd impressed
Bash, who'd never seen her do public speaking before. She was
standing there in a salty, rapidly-drying-but-wrinkled-as-hell
dress and smeared mascara—not presidential at all—and he was
still mesmerized. It meant a lot.

It wasn't until this moment that she realized she might've
gone too far with him today. She never showed her cards and she
barely knew Bash. What would he do with this information?

"Hey, don't tell anybody what I told you today. Okay?"

"I'd never. And same. Please keep it between us, the stuff
about my parents and track."

"I will. This is a circle of trust."

"You're dangerous—you make me want to talk."

"Last fall, I was the most-requested peer helper on the Teens in Crisis app," she said, by way of explanation. "East Coast only."

They smiled brightly at each other, with clear delight at finding a new friendship. They were bonded after this day. And that was that.

· · ·

An hour and a half later, Audre floated into her apartment, feeling happier than she had in ages. Until she heard Eva's panicked fury.

"WHERE THE HELL WERE YOU?"

1, 2, 3, 4 ... THRIVE!
A Teen's Rules for Flourishing on This Dying Planet

By Audre Mercy-Moore

Rule 5:

Wearing a light-colored summer dress? Any chance you'll jump in the ocean? Wear nude-colored underwear. That way, if you get wet, no one will see your orange panties.

CHAPTER 14

Audre should've never let herself have fun.

She and Bash had strolled along the boardwalk for hours, just talking, talking, talking. Like learning about each other was their new favorite pastime. It was a thrill, stumbling across a kindred spirit in the most unlikely person. She hadn't made a new friend in years.

Yes, she had fallen to pieces in front of him. But being so emotionally raw had created an instant bond between them—and then Bash let his guard down, too. Outside of Reshma, Audre had never had such an instant, I-get-you connection with anyone. It was no wonder she had lost track of time. Unfortunately, she didn't realize that she'd lost her phone, too...until she was face-to-face with her mad-as-hell mom.

"Where were you?" shouted Eva. "I've been calling you for hours!"

"I—"

"Where WERE you?"

"I—"

"What the hell, Audre?" Eva stormed over to her, raging and all dressed up in an off-the-shoulder jumpsuit. "I was supposed to have a dinner meeting with my editor tonight! To go over publicity plans for my new book. It's launching in September. One month after the wedding, Audre. It's crunch time! You were supposed to watch Baby Alice!"

Audre gasped. She'd totally forgotten she was supposed to babysit until now. How did this happen? "Flaky" wasn't even in Audre's chemical makeup.

"Oh no, Mom. Oh no . . ."

"It's on our joint Google calendar. We talked about this! Shane's at a speaking engagement, upstate! What's going on with you? I was depending on you!"

"I'm so sorry, Mom." Audre stood in the doorway, feeling utterly useless in her wrinkled, sun-dried dress and salty skin. "It just slipped my mind."

"I've been calling all day!"

From her playpen, Baby Alice the Hypewoman repeated, "Ahhl ayyy!"

"I know, I know. It was so irresponsible. I forgot my phone on the beach! It's all my fault."

Eva stormed over to the couch and sat down. She took a deep breath, exhaled, and rubbed her left temple with two fingers. "Jesus Christ."

Stunned by the onslaught of her mom's fury, which happened next to never, Audre gingerly walked over to the kitchen and leaned against the island. Whenever there was strife in the family, the accused party hovered near the island. It felt like a no-fly zone.

"I'll make it up to you, Mom. I'm really sorry. But don't overreact."

"Overreact? Excuse me? I have one major rule. Always tell me where you are. You know how scared I get when I can't find you."

"But why? I literally never do anything wrong. I've never given you a reason to worry about me. You said it yourself the other day. I do everything right!"

Eva glared at her. "You ran away from home two years ago."

"This again." Audre threw up her hands. "Mom, you know I didn't run away."

"You were missing! I called the police!"

"I fell asleep at the twenty-four-hour McDonald's on Fulton," she said. "I was studying for the PSATs. I got *tired*. I can't believe this is still a thing."

"A thing?" Eva's eyebrow arched. "Snap at me again and you can move into that McDonald's."

To solidify the point, Baby Alice picked up a toy tambourine and, with the aim and precision of a major league pitcher—plus truly theatrical timing—hurled it directly at Audre's midsection. She yelped, doubling over and clutching her stomach.

"OWWW! Mom! Do you see how your baby abuses me? This violent behavior doesn't worry you? You're raising a demon!"

"Audre."

"Is everyone in this house against me?"

"She's not just my baby, she's your sister," Eva reminded Audre. "And back to the McDonald's episode. Hell yes, it's still a thing. Wait until you're a mother and your child disappears into thin air. It sucks."

Audre stood upright again, still holding her stomach.

"Listen, Audre. I know you're not used to summers here. We don't have a summertime rhythm and everything's hectic in our house with the wedding, and my book, and the babysitter quitting, and the construction. I'm sorry it's a mess, and I'm sorry you don't get to hang with your dad and his wife, Alina."

"Athena."

Eva waved this off dismissively. "I'm sorry this summer isn't what you hoped for. You're my favorite oldest daughter, okay? I love you. I want your life to be perfect. But that's not realistic, kid. I know everything feels hard right now, but life's what you make it. You can't forget responsibilities 'cause you feel inconvenienced." Eva took a breath and then narrowed her eyes at Audre. "Is your rebellious era starting? If so, can you postpone it? We have a wedding and a book launch to get through."

What about what I want, thought Audre. *Or what I need? I'm a whole person with a life, not an extension of you or one of the problems you have to juggle.*

It would be out of line to say this to Mom. But apparently today she was out of line.

"It's always about you," said Audre. "Isn't it?"

Eva stared straight ahead, too stunned to even breathe.

"You have a book to promote. You have to meet your editor. You decided to make another daughter, you decided to renovate. What about me? I didn't decide any of those things!"

When she saw the fury in her mom's expression, she knew she'd gone too far.

Eva cut her eyes at Audre from the couch. "First of all, watch your tone. Secondly, we're trying to finalize a babysitter. It's not that easy. Obviously, I know Baby Alice is my responsibility.

You're not her mother. But you are her sister, and we're family. We help each other when we need it. Got it?"

"Got it," said Audre. She was tired of arguing. She was stressed out that her phone was all the way out in Rockaway. And she was drained from the emotional roller coaster of her day.

"I feel like all we do is disagree these days," said Eva softly.

"I disagree."

"Let's please move on. I'm too tired to do this." Eva slid her tortoiseshell glasses up her nose, squinting over at Audre. "Are your braids wet? Why is your mascara smeared? Where were you?"

"I just...I was...I went to the beach."

"I thought you were going to that new boy's house? Who'd you go to the beach with?"

"Reshma." She knew she was going to lie before she said it. Later, she'd wonder why it was her first instinct.

"Come on, Audre. Reshma left for Argentina over a week ago. Why are you lying? You never lie."

"I...I don't know. I'm sorry. I don't know what's going on with me."

Now Eva didn't just look angry, she looked hurt. "If we don't have trust, we don't have anything. I've always trusted you."

"You still can, Mom. I'm just off today. I think I'm getting my period."

"I'm once again asking who you were with."

Audre fidgeted with the hem of her dress. "The new guy. Bash."

"Huh. Okay. So, why are you sneaking around? Are you dating him?"

"No, definitely not. I'm pretty sure he has a girlfriend." How was she going to explain this? "Bash is just . . . he's a guy I hired."

Eva's jaw dropped. She glanced over at Baby Alice, who'd gone completely silent and was now staring from her mom to her sister and back again, grasping her giraffe teether.

"A guy you hired? Audre, help me understand. I know you want to lose your virginity, but this ain't the way."

"MOM!" Audre clapped her palms on her cheeks almost comically. "Be for real right now. You really think I hired a sex worker? How? From where?" She paused, raising up her index finger. "Not that there's anything wrong with sex work."

"Of course there's nothing wrong with sex work. A job's a job. Maya Angelou was a sex worker. And I take pole classes!"

"Those are fitness classes, Mom. You're not a stripper."

"The point is, it's not appropriate for my sixteen-year-old daughter to hire a sex worker!"

"I obviously didn't do that," groaned Audre, rolling her eyes to the ceiling. Her mom was the most embarrassing person in New York. And possibly the entire United States. "I told you I'm writing a self-help book to turn in with my Stanford application. And I realized that I can't authentically write about teen life if I haven't experienced anything myself. So I hired a guy to teach me how to have platonic fun. You know, spread my wings."

Eva narrowed her eyes at Audre. "You better keep your wings closed."

"Oh God," she groaned.

"Please," begged Eva. "Please, just be normal. Stop saying and doing weird things. I can't take it."

"You're being weird. I'm the normal one."

"Then why are you wearing orange panties with a white dress?"

"I'm throwing myself out the window, I swear to God."

"Listen, I get that I'm putting pressure on you to step up, but, well, you have no choice. I need you right now. I show up for you, you show up for me. That's who we are."

Audre nodded sadly. That was who they were.

"When you were growing up, I think I treated you more like a best friend than a daughter. I depended on you more than I should've. I regret this every day." She paused. "I've made mistakes. But I've always trusted you to make good decisions and be safe. In a year, you'll be off to college and you can do whatever you want, within reason. But right now? Under my roof? I need to know where you are. That's all I ask."

But that's not all Eva asked. It never was. It was bizarre—she was both the most easygoing and the most overprotective mom of anyone she knew. How could those two things coexist in the same person? Why was she so weird about boys, and being unchaperoned in people's houses? It was so unfair. And unnecessary. Audre worked her ass off to be a model student, person, all of it. How could she prove herself more?

Maybe she would never be good enough.

"I'm sorry I messed up today. It won't happen again."

"Better not," she said, and motioned for Audre to come sit next to her. "You're grounded for the weekend."

Audre sighed. "Yeah, I figured. But can I go to the Rockaway lost and found tomorrow? Try to get my phone back?"

"Nope. You're trapped here for the weekend, gorgeous. But you can use my phone to call lost and found, and tell them you'll stop by in a few days." Eva squeezed Audre's hand and let go, picking up a horrific-looking bowl of green, leafy soup resting on the coffee table. "You hungry?"

"I'm extremely opposed to whatever that is. Not to yuck your yum."

"Shane made me kale-turnip stew! It's supposed to help with energy and focus. He went out and bought little food containers, and packages healthy, homemade meals for me every day of the week. I don't have to worry about what to eat anymore. Remember how we used to have tater tots and chicken nuggets every night?"

Audre never minded that her mom was too sick to cook real meals. In fact, Eva would tell her stories about how she and Grandma Lizette would eat Baby Ruths with a side of rice for dinner sometimes when Lizette was too single-mom tired. But Shane took care of the meals now. He'd taught himself to cook for his new family, which was thoughtful. But . . . were things so bad before? Audre would rather order pizza than eat kale-turnip anything.

It was so weird to think that they dated as teenagers, lost touch, and then found each other again as grown-ups. How could her mother be so protective of her when Grandma Lizette had obviously given Eva the space to have a life in high school? To have a serious boyfriend? It was unfair—no, it was hypocritical.

And grounded or not, Audre decided that the Experience Challenge was not over.

•　•　•

Three hours later, everyone was asleep but Audre. How could she sleep while Shane's, Eva's, and Baby Alice's snores blared from the primary bedroom? Also, being phone-less felt bizarre and uncomfortable. She usually scrolled before sleeping, but tonight she was curled up on the couch, rereading one of her comfort books: *Soothe Your Nerves: The Black Woman's Guide to Understanding and Overcoming Anxiety, Panic, and Fear.*

It was an epic read. But she couldn't concentrate. She had an itchy need to text Bash. Something. Anything. Just a sign of life. She wondered if he'd texted her already. Did he think she was rude for not answering? Maybe he wasn't thinking of her at all.

It's just that they'd experienced something emotional together. When Audre had the panic attack, an invisible barrier had been broken. It felt like they were being real friends now. Bash had hidden depths. And she was still reeling from the careful, considerate, sweet way he took care of her after her episode. She wasn't expecting to relate to him on any level, but so much of their lives were surprisingly similar.

I wish I could text him, thought Audre, laying the book face down on her chest. She wished she could send up a smoke signal to let him know that she hadn't disappeared, she'd simply gotten grounded and the Experience Challenge would be postponed for a few days. And she wanted to make sure, just one more time, that what happened earlier would stay between the two of them.

Restless, she hopped off the couch and wandered into the kitchen. Maybe eating would soothe her nerves. Some crackers? Ritz and Nutella? (It was her comfort snack.) With a yawn, she opened the snack drawer. Her eyes were immediately drawn to her mom's box of Reese's Pieces (Eva's comfort snack) in the back of the drawer. An oversized fuchsia Post-it was stuck to the back, her mom's recognizable cursive scrawled across the paper.

Her whole life, Audre had seen her mom jot down notes on neon Post-its while she was writing. But Eva never let her read them. And she always tucked them away somewhere private. Eva did not play about keeping her creative process secret and sacred. But these days, her mom was overtired, overstretched, and over-burdened. Hence leaving this note . . . in the snack drawer, of all places.

Audre looked over her shoulder in the direction of her mom and Shane's bedroom. No sign of them. Quickly, she grabbed the Post-it.

LIZETTE: WHERE'S THE LINE BETWEEN TELLING THE TRUTH . . . AND SHAMING YOUR MOTHER?

GRANDMA DELPHINE: PASSING FOR WHITE IN THE JIM CROW SOUTH = A MEANS OF SURVIVAL. DO NOT DEMONIZE.

GREAT-GRANDMA CLOTHILDE: FACT-CHECK 1930S EXORCISM PRACTICES WITH CATHOLIC CHURCH.

Audre read this over a million times before sticking the Reese's Pieces exactly where she'd found them. What the entire hell did any of it mean? Had Grandma Lizette done something so horrible that Eva was afraid to mention it? Passing? Exorcism? What? Whatever these notes meant, it sounded like fiction, not the golden, aspirational reality of the Mercy girls. But *Back to Belle Fleur* was a memoir. Nonfiction. What did it all mean?

Who were the Mercy girls, really?

Before she had a chance to take the thought further, she heard a soft knock on the door. Who'd be knocking at this hour? It had to be a neighbor from one of the building's four apartments—an outside visitor would ring the outside doorbell.

She climbed off the couch, too drained to change out of her bedtime topknot, sports shorts, and old Renaissance tour T-shirt. Yawning, she peered through the peephole.

It was Barry, her downstairs neighbor. What did he want at eleven thirty? Also, he didn't speak, so she couldn't imagine how this was going to go.

"Hey, Barry," she said as she opened the door. "Is everything okay?"

He smiled and gave her a thumbs-up, and then handed her a reusable tote from a nearby supermarket.

"What's this?"

With a shrug and a goodbye wave, Barry padded back downstairs in his slippers.

Audre watched after him for a moment, confused. Then, still standing in the doorway, she opened the bag. It was her phone! And a note, handwritten with gloopy blue pen in half-uppercase, half-lowercase letters. It looked like a serial killer's scrawl. And it seemed to start in the middle of a thought.

Hey Audre,

So, yeah, I texted you a couple times tonight. And after I didn't hear from you, it hit me. You left your phone on the sand. And it was my fault. I felt bad b/c I brought you out to Rockaway and maybe pushed you too far. I'm sorry if I did. I just thought you'd have fun surfing, being half-Malibuian (not a word). Anyway, I went back and got it from the Rockaway lost and found. They know me there. I'm a serial forgetter of keys.
    —Bash

PS: After you charge your phone? Ignore my thirsty texts. I was worried.
PPS: Barry's that dude. Have you had his hamburgers?

Chapter 15

Audre wanted to squeal. She wanted to cartwheel around the room. She wanted to run downstairs and high-five Barry. She really wanted to call Reshma, until she remembered she was probably asleep in an Argentinean five-star hotel.

She couldn't believe that Bash had smuggled her phone in from the beach. When they got back to Park Slope, it was almost sunset. Which meant that after he realized that Audre's phone was missing, he got back on the train and traveled ninety minutes back to the beach—in the dark. He wasted a Friday night! It was so thoughtful and selfless, and no one had ever done anything like that for her.

(Out of nowhere, Audre had a vision of an outrageously muscle-bound Bash machete-chopping his way through a wild, overgrown rainforest, leaping over an alligator-infested swamp, and double-barrel-rolling down a waterfall to capture her phone from the jaws of a mighty tiger. A hero and a legend.)

She scrambled back to the couch and plugged in her phone. The second her charge light came on, she pulled up her text messages. She had three missed calls from Reshma, five from Eva, and four missed texts from Bash.

The first thing she did was call Reshma. A part of her was putting off reading Bash's texts. She didn't like how excited she was. Her heart was thumping a little too fast, and she felt a little too invigorated. She had nowhere to put this feeling.

Don't get ahead of yourself, she thought. *Fine, Bash Henry might not be the person everyone says he is. He might, indeed, be a misunderstood cinnamon roll. Okay...and? It doesn't mean you have any business liking him. And you'd be smart not to forget it. Decenter this boy.*

Reshma wasn't answering her phone. So Audre had no choice but to face Bash's texts—the very ones he told her to ignore.

8:20

> u get home ok?

8:31

> wassup, u home

8:46

> hope we're good. I liked being ur funsultant

9:02

> lol just realized I'm texting into the void.
> u left your phone on the beach 🤚. don't
> worry, I got u

10:30

figured your parents wouldn't like some strange guy showing up hella late @ ur house. so, I left your phone w my good buddy Barry. funny guy. we talked for like 30 min before I realized it was only me talking. is he a warlock

Audre let out a chirpy yelp of a laugh into the dark, quiet apartment. Then she held her breath, listening to hear if she had woken up The Goblin. When she decided she was safe, she exhaled and texted Bash back.

Audre: BASH! THANK YOU! u saved my life

Bash: nah, i didn't do anything

Audre: yes u did

Bash: it was the least I could do. I'm the one who dragged you out to Rockaway

Audre: but i made you

Bash: nobody makes me do anything

Audre: barry MADE you talk to him for half an hour

Bash: true but we have a lot in common!!

Audre: lol

Bash: wyd

Audre: i'm grounded for the entire weekend. forgot I was supposed to babysit The Goblin

Bash: Who?

Audre: Baby Alice

Bash: u call your sister the goblin? diabolical behavior

Audre: i know, it's so bad. anyway, my mom couldn't reach me all day b/c my phone was missing

Bash: honest mistake, tho. who hasn't lost their phone? Or lost track of time?

Audre: i haven't. no one's more responsible than me

Bash: u wanted to experience being messy. happy to be of service

Audre: almost forgot, u owe me an explanation

Bash: i already spilled my guts to you. There's nothing left

Audre: yes there is. what were you diving for?

Bash: it's gonna sound crazy

Audre: just tell me

Bash: i was going after a smurf lunch box from the '80s

Audre: WTF

Bash: this is gonna be a long text, kk? it's a rockaway urban legend. no one knows why, but sometimes these old Smurf lunch boxes wash up on shore. they're collectibles now, they sell for hundreds

Audre: i can't tell if you're fucking w me

Bash: on mamas, I'm not fucking w u

Audre: on mamas?

Bash: it's the bay area version of "on god"

Audre: wait, I need to google this smurf thing later. i'm sorry it doesn't seem real

Bash: lol not only is it a real thing, if u ever find a smurf lunch box at the beach, you owe me. I missed my chance for clout b/c you decided I was drowning

Audre: my diving days are over. i'm scared of deep ocean water

Bash: could've fooled me

Audre: wyd

Bash: i'm out @ a music venue, Brooklyn Steele. u been there?

Audre: I've never been anywhere

Bash: yo the craziest shit happens to me. last weekend, I was in tribeca leaving some

kid's party, and I got in the wrong uber.
there was already somebody in there, this
female rapper from alabama. her accent
went crazy. she freestyled for me on the
spot! Anyway she put me on the list for her
show tonight at brooklyn steele

Audre: what even is your life?
what's her name

Bash: i forgot. hold pls

Bash: .....

Bash: pia colada. video incoming

A few seconds later, Bash attached a dark, shaky video from the vantage point of two or three rows from the stage. It was a tiny club, standing room only. The video was hard to make out, but there was a tiny woman on stage. Pia Colada looked to be in her early twenties. She wore lime green space buns and matching thigh-high stiletto boots. It was hard to tell with the fuzzy sound quality, but she seemed to have no rap skills. She was hot and charismatic, though. And she kept pointing to Bash as she was performing. Every time she did, the group with Bash screamed in delight.

Audre zoomed in to see if she knew anyone Bash was with. And then, clear as day, Clio popped in the frame. It was only a second, but it was clearly her—dancing cutely right next to

Bash. She threw her arms in the air and let out an enthusiastic "Whooo!"

Clio. His "acquaintance." Audre told herself this was fine. Because it *was*. Bash said they weren't boyfriend-girlfriend, and she had no choice but to believe him. Besides, there was nothing between her and Bash, anyway. Audre just had a one-sided crush.

The truth? Audre suspected he would've run back to the beach to rescue and return *Barry's* cell phone. That's just the kind of guy he was.

Bash: did u hear what she said

Audre: i couldn't make it out!

Bash: she put me in her song

"Come for my girls expect a backlash

Ass on squish I'll give you whiplash

See me in VIP with my boy Bash"

Audre: AYYYEE! love this for u

Bash: it'd be more fun if u were here

Audre: ikr. good night, B

Bash: Good night, A

Just before she fell asleep, she looked again at the video Bash sent. When he turned the camera on himself, she barely recognized him. He looked a little untethered, adrift. Like physically he was at the show, but mentally he was far, far away.

1, 2, 3, 4 ... THRIVE!
A Teen's Rules for Flourishing on This Dying Planet

By Audre Mercy-Moore

Rule 6:
This isn't a rule, it's a question. If the person you like is super nice to everyone, how do you know if they like you specifically? I guess the rule, here, is that crushing on a sweet guy isn't any less confusing than crushing on a player.

Chapter 16

"But you were in Argentina for less than two weeks! How did you cause so much trouble in so little time?"

"Look, none of it was my fault. I didn't mean to catch the most devastating cold of my life. Plus, I didn't know the production assistant was gonna look like Victoria Monet."

Audre, no longer grounded, was thrifting in Soho with Reshma. It was a bright day, both girls hiding behind sunglasses and dressed in roomy jeans and Y2K-era tube tops. They looked like cross-ethnic twins. It was a humid, drizzly afternoon in late June, and the only people out there besides them were tourists. Audre couldn't buy anything—Soho vintage spots were too expensive for her—but it was fun to window-shop.

Now they were at the Vintage Twin on Broadway. Reshma was trying on tops while Audre sat on a plush ottoman outside the fitting room, idly shaking her iced latte.

"I told you that you were gonna date someone."

"It wasn't even that deep. I was so contagious, we barely even kissed," she said through the curtain. "It was just an emotional affair."

"What was the age difference again?"

"Almost three years, that's all! Spiritually, I'm older, anyway. It's more that my parents just wanted to get rid of me. Why'd they make me go in the first place? They record overseas precisely so that they don't have to deal with me."

Reshma came out in a fuchsia corset top. It was so cute.

"Too tight?" she asked a sales guy, who appeared out of thin air.

"Just right," Reshma whispered to the wall mirror. Then she turned to Audre. "The problem is, my parents are old-ass Gen X famous people. They're used to publicity teams smoothing out every minor inconvenience. They don't know how to deal with an iconic daughter."

"So many unhealed family dynamics," remarked Audre wisely.

"Speaking of...have you talked to your dad?"

"I'm thinking of calling him. I should give him a chance to apologize, I guess." She sipped her iced coffee. She hated talking about this. It was bad enough thinking about it. "But I've been trying to stay busy, so..."

"Tell. Me. Everything," demanded Reshma, who slipped back into the fitting room. "Last I heard, you were going to meet Bash to do the 'physical activity' challenge. And then your phone went dead. How was it?"

"It was fine," said Audre simply. "The Experience Challenge is doing what it's supposed to be doing. Umm...anyway, please buy that top so I can borrow it."

Reshma came out of the fitting room, still in the corset. Her mouth was open.

"Audre. You're changing the subject."

"I'm not."

"Yeah, you are."

"There's no subject to change," protested Audre. "So, you hungry?"

"Don't play with me. I don't have time for this—you know fitting rooms scare me."

It was true. Reshma suspected that they were portals to an alternate dimension. Especially ones with double mirrors.

Reshma stuck her arm out and pulled Audre behind the curtain. Knocked off-balance, Audre toppled onto the dressing room stool.

"Speak," ordered Reshma, standing over Audre with her hands on her hips.

"Well...Bash isn't exactly who we thought he was. He isn't just some party ho. He's actually sweet and kind."

"Interesting. Say more."

"The rumors about all the different girls? Either I've been red-pilled by this kid, or they're all misunderstandings. Bash is nice to everyone. It's easy to get the wrong idea. Like, he hung out with Barry."

"Not Barry!"

"Swear," whispered Audre. "Now they're tight! Which is basically how Sparrow said she felt after she met Bash once. And I get it! Each time we hang out, I feel like something important happened. Even though it's just a dude being nontoxic and friendly while also being fine. A triple combo rarely seen in Brooklyn."

"It's rarely seen anywhere," muttered Reshma. "So what was your physical activity?"

"Well...he took me surfing. But I didn't actually surf." She couldn't bring herself to explain the Smurf Incident. "Also, I might've freaked out a little bit."

"Oh no, babe. Panic attack?"

"I wanted to die. Like, just thinking about it is just...ugh." Audre shuddered. "But Bash was cool about it. He calmed me down, even. Made me laugh. And then, look."

Audre showed Reshma their text thread from three nights ago, while he was at the Pia Colada show. "See? He's so pure."

Reshma scanned Audre's phone, her eyes slowly widening.

"What?" asked Audre.

"He loves you."

"Stop it."

"He loves you bad."

"No, he doesn't."

"And you love him, too."

She refused to admit her low-level attraction. It wasn't even her brand. Audre was an intellectual. She was supposed to like a diamond-in-the-rough guy that shone only for her, barely noticed by anyone else. Wouldn't it be more special if he was off the radar? Not someone who was name-checked in some rapper's song after hijacking her Uber.

"You know he's not my type."

"But what's your type? Remember the crush you had on that skinny, morbidly pale white boy we met at bowling?"

"Wade. I know, he looked like he was actively decomposing. I was thirteen! It was my Tim Burton era," protested Audre. "Maybe I don't have a type. But I know it's not a guy who barely buttons his button-down."

"You know nothing of the sort," said Reshma in a purposefully posh British accent. "So, are you ready for your next challenge?"

"Ugh, it's the dildo one. I don't want to do it!"

"You have to. It'll be *hilarious*."

"Hilarious to who? And what could I learn by humiliating myself in a sex shop?"

"You can buy dildos at Target. Self-checkout." Reshma tossed her hair and continued. "The Experience Challenge is about doing silly activities so you let go of the perfection addiction and *live*. What could be sillier than dildo-shopping with a guy you low-key love but has baby mama rumors and also possibly a girlfriend?"

"You have a point."

"Do we know Bash's backstory, by the way?"

"He's not the most open person," she said, jiggling her iced latte. "I know he was a track star in Oakland—"

"Time to research!" interrupted Reshma, with glee.

They googled "Bash Henry" on Reshma's phone, but there were no results for a competitive track champion. Which didn't match the story he told Audre. But then she remembered that his dad was California University's track and field coach, and they found him instantly. Milton Wallace. Bash looked exactly like him, just taller, leaner, and a few shades lighter—and without the gray hair.

Detective cap on, Reshma entered "Bash Henry Milton Wallace Oakland Sprinter," and the first entry was a *San Francisco Chronicle* shot of a straightlaced-looking Bash gripping three oversized trophies. His dad posed a few paces in front of him. The caption explained it all:

Sebastian Wallace, USA Today Boys Track & Field Athlete of the Year, 2024, with his proud dad, Milton Wallace of California University. The world-class track and cross-country runner earned three gold medals at the California Class 2A championships as well as the Nike Outdoor Nationals. And he's only a junior! We've got our eye on this rising senior, who's been heavily recruited by top D1 track and field universities like Baylor, University of Arkansas, and Louisiana State. He's not sure where he'll go but hopes to run for the US in the Olympics.

Sebastian Wallace. "Bash" was a nickname for Sebastian. So, that part made sense. But when did he become Bash Henry?

"This kid's an actual enigma," whispered Reshma.

"It says he's a world-class runner," said Audre. "What happened in February that made him quit track, leave home, and start over?"

"At the actual end of his senior year? A brutal time to be the new kid."

"And why'd he move in with his mom, a woman he barely knows?"

"Just ask him to explain."

"I would, but he's super private. It's *frustrating*. But I'm respecting his boundaries. Besides, if I was his girlfriend, I wouldn't want some other girl prying into his life."

"He has a girl, but he's out here with you?"

"Platonically!"

Reshma rolled her eyes at this. "What do we know about this alleged girlfriend?"

"I saw her in the park with him, and they had this intense lovers' fight. And when we hung out, she kept calling. I'm so confused. Apparently, he told her about me, the Experience Challenge, all of it. He says she's an 'acquaintance.' But does this look acquaintance-y to you?"

Audre showed Reshma the video of Clio dancing next to Bash at the show. Reshma watched. Then she did a double take, zooming in on her face.

"Th-that's her?"

"Yep. She's cute, right?"

Reshma's jaw dropped. "Fuck yes, she's cute. Is her name Clio?"

"Yes!"

"Babe. *I just met her.* Go to her IG, see if Bash is on there."

They searched through her Instagram, and deep down, there was a pic of her and Bash, posted two years ago. No location was tagged. The caption simply read: *Till the wheels fall off.*

"What does that mean?" whispered Audre.

"Like ride or die? They're in this relationship until their metaphorical car dies."

Audre gasped. "Where did you meet her?"

"She saved me from a murderous swan."

"Typical."

Stunned, Reshma sat down on the stool next to Audre. A sales guy knocked on the wall outside the curtain.

"You girls okay in there? Can I switch something out for you?"

"No, we're good," called out Audre.

"Just having a petit crisis," said Reshma, putting on her posh accent. "We'll be right out."

"Umm . . . okay, but there are people waiting."

Reshma stuck her head out from behind the curtain. "I'd like to speak to the manager."

"I'm the manager," said the guy tiredly.

"I don't love the way you're treating us. You haven't seen the last of me."

"I've barely seen the first of you," grumbled the guy, turning on his heel.

Reshma tossed her hair and popped back into the fitting room.

"Audre," she whispered, "I need you to be so serious right now. Do you like Bash? If you lie, I'll know."

She took a deep breath. This was her best friend. Why was she so protective over her feelings? It's just that everything this summer felt so fraught and tension-filled. Every move she made seemed high-stakes. She was emotionally raw. And, in just the few weeks she'd known Bash, they'd shared so much, so fast. He didn't even want her to therapize him. He didn't want anything from her. He just wanted her to have a good time and to feel safe.

Everyone else in her life needed something from her. It was too lame to say out loud, but Bash didn't even want payment for his services.

How could she not have feelings for him, even the smallest, tiniest ones, after he traveled over two hours to the beach and back, and smuggled her phone through Barry?

And there was that moment on the beach. Right before everything fell apart. The shimmering tension in the air between them. She wondered if he'd felt what she felt.

Don't even go down that road, she told herself.

"Yes. Yeah, I guess I like him a little bit. But he has a girl-friend. He says he doesn't, but it's not adding up. And boys lie. I really think he and Clio are together."

"What if they weren't, though?"

"But they are."

"But what if they broke up?"

"What do you mean?"

"I could split them up," she said, tapping her fingertips together with glee. "I have ways."

Audre just stared at her for a moment. Too stunned to find the words. "First of all, that's so evil and anti-woman. Why would you deliberately ruin another girl's relationship? If they're happy together, they should be happy together."

"It's not like they're married. Come on, it's not that serious. I've never seen you light up like this over a guy. You deserve this."

"But why do you think the only way Bash could like me back is if you removed an obstacle for me? Why do you think I need your help to get a guy?"

"Because you do need my help. I mean, obviously."

Audre winced. "Excuse me?"

"Look. I orchestrated all of this, didn't I?" Reshma giggled. "Cute boys make you nervous, and then you get overly bossy."

Audre stared at her, mouth slightly agape. Hurt sliced through her like a knife. Reshma's tone was so factual. It was as if Audre's cluelessness was simply a known truth. "You really think I'm that hopeless? That I can't get a guy on my own?"

"I didn't mean it like that," groaned Reshma, rolling her eyes.

"You basically said I suck at pulling guys. You think I'm a loser."

"Audre. You're gorgeous and funny and smart and cool. You know I didn't mean that."

"I know what you meant. You're the star in the friendship. There can only be one."

"Come on, don't get upset."

"I think I should go now," said Audre quickly. "Listen, don't get into Clio and Bash's business. And don't do me any favors."

Audre was so angry—so offended—she could barely get the words out. Brusquely, she hooked her tote on her shoulder and walked out. Reshma didn't try to stop her. Audre was so controlled, she barely ever showed her anger. But when she did, it was serious. So Reshma knew to give her space.

Five minutes earlier, she'd asked herself why she protected her feelings from her best friend. Well, this was why. Opening up to Reshma? It never ended well. And in this case, it could be as explosive as tossing a lit match into a bucket of gasoline.

If Reshma inserted herself into this situation, Audre would die.

Chapter 17

"Do we have a dildo-buying strategy?" asked Audre.

"You tell me," said Bash. "I've never done this before."

"So, how are you helping, exactly?"

"I'm here as an enthusiastic cosigner."

"This challenge is dumb. What am I supposed to learn from buying a dildo?"

"Okay, you gotta stop saying the word *dildo.*"

"Why?"

Why? thought Bash. *Is she really asking me that? How do I even answer?*

Bash and Audre were walking toward the Atlantic Center Target in Downtown Brooklyn. The whole world was outside. Millennial couples, stylish toddlers, high school kids chilling in clusters. As they zigzagged through the crowd, Bash thought about her question.

I need you to stop saying that word, he thought, *because I picture what it's for, and I'm not chill enough to associate YOU ... with ... THAT ... and act normal. It's hard enough pretending that everything about you doesn't throw me off! Your brain, your perfume, your bravery, even your arrogance. Especially your arrogance. And your crazy-beautiful skin and lashes and dimples that all blur together into an explosion of cute every time you smile. You have to stop saying it, because I'm just a guy, and my poker face is trash, and you're fucking up my brain . . . and I momentarily forget that I shouldn't be thinking of you as anything but a friend. And we're becoming really good friends.*

And that it's safer for you if we stay friends only.

Bash obviously couldn't tell her all of that. Turns out he didn't have to say anything at all, because they'd reached the Target entrance. She swept by him in a cloud of soft, citrusy perfume, looking summertime-fly in an oversized tee and a miniskirt made of some stretchy material that made Bash's head hurt. He looked away, fast.

Audre's Audre-ness was driving him crazy. But, again, he had to control his feelings. Audre and Bash were just friends. He'd slid right into the role, like it was the easiest thing in the world. Which was why, at some point, he'd have to tell her that she was way off about Clio. It was only fair. But the truth was too painful. And hanging out with Audre felt too good.

He knew he was running from his problems. But running was what he did best, right?

"If we're gonna do this," she said, "you have to relax. 'Dildo' is just a word. Be mature."

"I think you're overestimating my maturity."

"Bash, come on."

"I'm kidding. I'm kidding." He turned his Raiders cap to the back and neutralized his expression. "I'm ready. Let's go. What's the move?"

"I guess we just wing it. Go with God?"

"Bet."

"And you swear to me that this is cool. You're not crossing some sort of line with Clio?"

"I swear, it's cool. Are we gonna do this every time we link up? Besides, I'm not buying a dildo. You are."

"Right, that's true," she said, and she seemed to deflate a bit. Her expression was etched with slight worry. Or embarrassment? Which one was it?

Bash realized that he wasn't fulfilling his end of the deal. He was supposed to be Audre's cheerleader. "You got this, okay? Look, I know you're not easily scandalized. You listen to people's deepest confessions and don't blink. Let's just ... um ... find the sex toys aisle ..."

"Sexual wellness aisle ..."

"... and get this over with."

Audre nodded, her mouth in a tight line. "Honestly? Dealing with other people's dark truths is easy. Because it isn't about me. I'm gonna say something embarrassing right now."

"I'm listening."

"You're frowning."

"This is my active listening face."

Her mouth dropped, and then she laughed despite herself.

"You're making fun of me now?"

"Yep." He bit back a smile. "Sorry, continue."

"No, it's just that I always try to carry myself with decorum." She lowered her voice to a whisper. "I mean, I'm the class president."

"Yeah, but you're not *the* president."

"And that's not all. I wear this cameo ring, see? It was my mom's, my grandma's, my great-grandma's, and so on. They're power women, okay? The ring makes me feel like I belong to a coven or something. Do I really wanna buy a sex toy in front of my ancestors' ring?"

Bash nibbled his lower lip in thought. Without thinking, he took her right hand in his and turned her ring so the cameo faced inside. She met his eyes. A current passed between them, a warm surge of electricity. He blinked slowly. Something fluttered in Bash's stomach. Gently, he let her hand go.

"Now they'll never know. Right?"

She nodded silently, the corners of her mouth curving into a smile. And then she averted her eyes. "R-right. Thanks. I was being silly anyway." She cleared her throat. "Let's go!"

She rushed off to find The Aisle in Question. Bash hustled to catch up with her.

"Why're you in such a hurry?"

"Hurry? I'm not in a hurry."

"Yo! Slow down." Bash stepped in front of Audre, smoothly intercepting her. They paused for a breath, realizing they were standing way too close to each other in the kitchenware aisle. They both took a step back.

"Your brain can't think properly when you're moving so fast."

Audre raised her eyebrows, interested. "Based on what evidence?"

"Mine," he admitted. "Have you ever been on the go, just doing shit on fast-forward, and then you try to remember something? Someone's name, maybe? Or where you put your phone?

Think about what you do next. You stop in your tracks to think about it. 'Cause while you're moving, your brain shuts off."

Audre pondered this. "That's true. Wow. Sounds like you're speaking from experience. I guess a world-class runner would know something about moving fast."

World-class runner? So specific. Where did she get that from? Bash had never said those words to Audre. She only knew what he'd told her—which was that he ran track at his old high school, and he was good. She didn't know about the nights where agonizing muscle spasms kept him from sleep. The tutors falsifying his tests so he could compete. His permanently dissatisfied father who pushed him to the brink. Audre couldn't have known all that, and yet she was eyeing him like she could see right into his brain.

"When I ran," he said, "I didn't think about anything. Just the basics. Happy, sad, hungry, cold, stress, move, win. No complicated thoughts."

"No complicated thoughts," repeated Audre in a dreamy voice. "Must've been nice."

"The running part was nice. But the pressure that came with it was stressful. It was like a vise tightening around my head."

"I know how that feels. I like student government. I like school, even. But when I step away and think, I just worry that I'm not good enough."

"Same," he said. "That I'll fail everyone who believes in me."

"That I'll end up a loser."

"That I'll waste my talent."

They looked at each other. Game recognizing game.

"When I first moved here, I decided to say yes to everything," explained Bash. "My whole life used to be a 'no.' No McDonald's, no late nights, no drinking, no weed, no sleeping past 4 AM, no mention of the grown-ass adults bribing me to lose or win depending on their bets." He shifted his weight from foot to foot. Why was he revealing so much? "Whatever. The point is, this is why I said yes to you. But, look, we can abort this mission. Come up with a different challenge, even. Who says Reshma's the boss?"

"What's not gonna happen is that. I know she thinks I'll chicken out."

Bash cocked a brow, sensing some edge in her voice at the mention of Reshma. "Let's just get it over with. And then we'll go to Tacombi. Their tacos smack."

"You mean slap."

"Slap? No, no, no. That's what y'all say out here? *Music* slaps, not food."

"Excuse me, the tacos smack." She laughed, her mood lifting. "Hey. Can I please therapize you?"

"Nooooo," he groaned, turning to walk down the kitchenware aisle. She followed him with a cheeky, dimpled grin. *God*, Bash thought, *she's so endearing*. "I told you, I don't believe in therapy. Not everything means something."

"It actually does, though."

"Nah, man. Therapy is manipulative. Is it trauma, or just a generic bad memory? Is it gaslighting, or someone's perspective clashing with yours? Is she a sociopath, or just hungry?"

Audre giggled at this. "You're so wrong I can't even begin to explain how wrong you are. Plus, everyone could use therapy. Don't overestimate your mental fortitude, B."

"I'm just trying to put one foot in front of the other, A."

"You must have some plan. What college are you going to?"

He pretended to check out some generic wall prints. "College isn't for everybody."

Audre's eyes widened to unreal dimensions. "Why bust your ass to excel at a sport and not reap the rewards? At least get a scholarship out of it."

"Nah, my athlete days are over. Besides, does excelling at a sport have to equal college?"

"Why else do we work so hard if not for our future?" she challenged.

"I'd rather be happy in the present."

"But you can afford that. You have generational wealth from your mom. My parents do well, but they worked for everything they have. There's not a lot left over after my tuition."

Bash frowned at this. "My mom has money, yeah. It's not mine, though. I won't take it."

"But that's your choice. You have a safety net. Most of us don't."

Bash and Audre faced each other, their eyes sparking with challenge. They were on opposite ends of the same experience. Excellence was their brand. But where it motivated Audre, it broke Bash down.

"The point is," he started, "I don't think college is necessary to have a good life. All I want is a tattoo chair at a solid studio. Have some steady clients. Live near a beach so I can surf. That's my dream. And it's my life, right?"

"It just feels unorthodox."

"What? Nah, bruh, I don't believe in religious discrimination."

Audre stared at him. "No, I mean 'unorthodox' as in unusual."

"Oh." He paused and then hung his head in shame. "Fuck. Maybe I do need college."

"I'm an obnoxious former spelling bee champ—ignore me."

"I've noticed something," said Bash carefully. "You like pointing out the competitions you've won."

Audre flinched, immediately embarrassed. "I...I guess I want to seem impressive."

"But you're impressive without winning. You're impressive just standing there, trying to figure out why you're in Target buying a sex toy with a guy you didn't know two weeks ago."

Audre smiled bashfully, casting her eyes downward. "Thank you."

"Back to college, though," he said, feeling a little dizzy in her presence. "All I know is that every part of my life was logged on a spreadsheet. And now I have choices. I love it."

She nodded. "Makes sense."

He wanted so badly to tell her about the Fifth Angel Ink call. He hadn't told anyone. He hadn't even said it out loud yet, made it real.

"I kind of have news. So, there's this well-known tattoo shop, Fifth Angel Ink? A few months ago, I sent them my portfolio. And the owner just asked me to come in for an interview. I might be working there by the end of summer. Professionally."

Audre stopped walking, her eyes wide and shining. "Are you serious? Bash, that's incredible! Damn, you're really good, huh?"

"I told you I was!" he said, laughing.

"Where's the shop? Brooklyn? Is it in the city?"

"Nah, it's down in South Carolina. Myrtle Beach. The surfing there is legendary, too. It's kinda like too good to be true, though. I shouldn't get my hopes up."

The vibe changed for a split second. She tilted her head to one side, nodded to herself, and then kept walking down the aisle. Bash hurried after her.

"Bash Henry, you should absolutely get your hopes up," she said, using her businesswoman voice. She sounded more like a guidance counselor than a peer. "You're gonna get this job. Mark my words."

Why does she sound like that? wondered Bash. *Does she . . . not want me to leave?*

"What does your mom think about you moving?" she asked. "South Carolina is far. Really far."

His stomach sank a little at her question. Of course, why would she care if he left?

"My mom'll probably be relieved. We've never spent any time together anyway."

"Really? You must have some standout memories with her."

As they moved through the aisles, Bash gave this some thought. "The last time I saw her, I was twelve. She'd invited me to spend my birthday in Brooklyn. I flew across the country by myself, which was cool. And she took me to Dave and Buster's. I was so excited. The few birthday parties I had were at the track, with my team before or after practice."

Audre glanced at him, her expression filled with empathy. "You never got a break, huh?"

Bash shook his head. "Anyway, Dave and Buster's wasn't as

cool as I'd hoped. I just sat there eating stale nachos while Jennifer went on about how Trump's administration canceled funding for social programs."

"Did you play games at least?"

"Nah, she's a germaphobe. She said I could play if she wiped the controllers down with Clorox wipes. For dignity reasons, I declined."

Before Audre could answer, they were there. In the sexual wellness aisle. Surrounded by shelves stocked with fruit-scented lube, butt plugs, and packs of "adult party cards." Everything was locked up behind a case—which meant they'd have to ask a clerk for help. Mortifying.

Bash clapped his hands together. "What's the move?"

Audre chewed on a cuticle, scanning the shelves. "These are all vibrators. No, we need a dildo. Hmm. Wait, here a few. But which one do I get?"

Bash swallowed hard, stuffing his hands in his jeans pockets. *Please stop saying it, just pick one out and let's get outta here expeditiously,* he thought.

"I read a psychology book once with an interesting theory." Audre turned to face him. "It said that if you're a woman without IRL sexual experience, sex toys could be a problem. Because they might work...too well...and then you'll expect that... feeling...when you're with an actual person. It sets up false expectations."

Bash blinked at her, flushing hot. His T-shirt was sticking to his back. Desperate to look busy, he pretended to study a jar of Sexytime Gummies through the clear case. "Interesting. But who's to say you won't get that feeling with an IRL person?"

"Because women's bodies are complicated. It takes nothing for boys to get... excited," she whispered. "But girls take more work. It's Sexual Health 101."

"Well... why not find out what you like before you're with an actual person?"

"Why?" asked Audre with a wide-open, innocent expression.

Bash raised his brows, scratching the back of his neck. "It's just that... what if the guy doesn't know what he's doing? If you have dildo experience, you could... you know, guide him."

Audre raised her chin, her coppery braids glinting in the superstore lighting. In her face was a knee-weakening mix of competitiveness and vulnerability. Bash's mouth went dry.

"I don't need dildo experience to guide a guy. Why assume that virgins are prudes?" She stuck a fist on her hip. "My brain is slutty. You'd be shocked by what goes on in there."

What?

Bash's heartbeat roared in his ears. Hanging on to sanity by a thread, he pointed to a large wand sealed in plastic. "How about the Indulge Double-Sided Vibrator?"

Audre's eyes widened. "What does it do?"

"Unclear. But one charge gives you an hour of continuous use."

"An hour of continuous use?" She winced. "Ouch."

"And why is it double-sided?"

They tilted their heads together, reading the instructions on the back. With a shocked gasp, Audre backed away from the case like it was on fire.

Just then, a Target sales associate approached. "Can I help you? Oh! Holy shit, it's Audre! And Bash."

The associate was Wilder Katz, a local legend. Two years ago, the five-foot-three math prodigy was the Cheshire Prep valedictorian. Halfway through his first semester at Harvard, he came home for good—a hollowed-out shell of the boisterous guy he used to be. Could've been burnout. Or emotional challenges. But soon he was found wandering the halls at Cheshire—wearing a Harvard hoodie and asking underclassmen if they knew of any jobs.

These days, he worked part-time at Target. The rest of the time, he posted up on Fulton Ave., belting out tunes from the *Shrek* soundtrack while playing an accordion. He was neither a singer nor a musician, but he was beloved.

Bash gave him a pound, and Wilder drew him in for a quick hug.

"You two know each other?" asked Audre. "I have to hear this story."

"We met in Fort Greene right after I moved here," answered Bash amiably.

"I was performing 'All Star,' and he watched my whole set! You were with a Hillcrest girl . . . was it Delilah Lange?"

Bash's eyes darted to Audre's, then back to Wilder's. "I don't really remember."

"Anyway, we bonded on music shit and we got coffee. Bash, you're a real-ass dude."

"I appreciate you, man. We need more artists in the world."

"Yeah, I'm living. I don't miss school, either. I make enough to pay my parents' rent. I eat La Villa pizza whenever I want."

"La Villa smacks," said Audre, glancing at Bash. He gave her a thumbs-up.

"I just got burned out, man. There are no jobs. The economy

is trash. No one's in charge. Gun violence is gonna kill us all anyway. How's the Ivy League gonna save us?"

"This is what I'm saying," exclaimed Bash, gesturing at Audre. "We're doomed as fuck. So do what makes you happy."

"Exactly." Wilder nodded. "Audre, that's why you're looking for sex toys, amiright?"

Audre's face went slack, like she'd stared into the void and barely escaped to tell the tale.

"Don't be embarrassed," said Wilder. "Couples experience mad mutual pleasure with toys. Plus, it's safe sex."

"Wilder, I love you but please stop talking." Her cheeks were on fire. "And we're not a couple."

"Right, and it was just a dare," said Bash, wanting to save Audre from embarrassment. "We're not, like, trying to find mutual pleasure at Target."

"Who dildo-dared you?"

"Reshma Wells," she sighed.

Wilder burst out laughing. "Okay, see, that tracks."

• • •

Bash and Audre were so caught up in their conversation with Wilder that neither one of them noticed the redhead peering over at them from the hair aisle, grasping a Dyson blow-dryer. It was Sparrow.

She was too far away to hear what Audre and Bash were saying, but their body language (and the sex toys) spoke loud enough.

And she was outraged.

1, 2, 3, 4 ... THRIVE!
A Teen's Rules for Flourishing on This Dying Planet

By Audre Mercy-Moore

Rule 7:

Success is what you decide it is, for you and you only—it's tacky to force your idea of happiness onto someone else. So play the accordion like no one's watching.

Chapter 18

Audre felt so fancy. It was the first time all day that her thoughts weren't consumed with her involuntary crush on Bash. She didn't want to like him. She didn't want him to be her last thought before she fell asleep or to get indescribably giddy with every morning text. But she did.

And he wasn't even going to live in Brooklyn by the end of the summer. If everything worked out, he'd be moving seven entire states away. She shouldn't have felt so crushed—after all, they were just friends—but the idea of losing him in a few weeks? It made her nauseous. It made her mood dip.

It made her want to pull away, to protect herself.

Especially when she remembered Wilder saying to Bash, "You were with some girl."

There's always some girl, thought Audre. *Maybe I'm just some girl, too.*

But she abruptly pushed these thoughts out of her head. She was lounging on a plush ivory love seat, sipping a champagne glass filled with sparkling apple cider. Amsale Bridal Boutique knew how to create a glitzy atmosphere. The mahogany floors, the glass side tables, the sparkles accenting the gowns—everything in this boutique glowed. Including Eva.

When she emerged from the dressing lounge, Audre gasped. She looked gorgeous. Holding up her skirt, Eva climbed on top of the little platform in front of a four-way mirror. The strapless lace mermaid gown was the third dress she'd tried on. It was dramatic but elegant—and just right. Audre knew this dress was the winner.

"That's the one!" gasped Audre.

"I know, right?" Eva primped in the mirror. "Sigh. This day is everything I wanted it to be."

It's true. Eva had wanted a gown by a Black designer (Amsale Aberra was Ethiopian American). She wanted both of her daughters to help her pick it out (Baby Alice was zonked out in her stroller, which was parked next to Audre). And she wanted to wear her favorite Jordans with her gown (present).

"You look so pretty, Mom."

"Are both y'all smoking black tar heroin?" drawled Grandma Lizette from FaceTime on Audre's phone. Her disembodied head was as glamorous as ever—CoverGirl red lipstick, shoulder-length bobbed waves, and cheekbones kissed by angels. She was sixty-five, looked forty-nine, and sounded eighty with her raspy, cigarette-inflected, Louisiana bayou drawl. In her accent, the line sounded like "Ahh both y'all smokin' black tahh HAIR-win?"

She'd demanded to be included in the dress-choosing process. And she'd even postponed one of her pageant training sessions so she could be available. According to Eva, Grandma Lizette never rearranged her plans. She was a businesswoman, and business came first. (Which, Eva said, was one of the reasons they rarely saw her.) Harsh, sure, but Audre didn't hold it against her grandmother. Men were rarely questioned about their dedication to their careers at the expense of family time. And Grandma Lizette was a single woman business owner in a cutthroat profession. The fact that she was virtually "here" was a big deal.

Good thing I remembered to turn my ring back around, thought Audre. *Grandma Lizette was serious about her heirloom.*

Eva sighed. "Black tar heroin, Mom? Really?"

"You want the truth, don't you?"

"Fine, Mom. Why do you hate it?" she asked through gritted teeth.

"I think she looks beautiful," said Audre.

"Of course she does, bé," said Grandma Lizette. "She look like me."

Eva rubbed a temple. "Then what's the problem?"

"It don't fit. It's all lumpy around your hips. Y'all don't see it?"

"This is a showroom. This dress isn't my size. It's held together in the back with pins. I'm gonna get it tailored."

"Oh. Well then, what you need me for?" Sounded like: *Whatchoo need me fuh?*

Audre put the phone face down on her thigh and grimaced at Eva. Eva rolled her eyes and squeezed her hands into fists.

"You okay?" mouthed Audre.

"It's fine, I'm used to it," whispered Eva.

Grandma Lizette wasn't finished talking. "Audre! Show me your mama again, bé."

Audre aimed the phone in Eva's direction.

"The good news? Shane loves you regardless. You could show

up naked 'cept for clown shoes and a flowerpot on your head, and he'd be happy as a clam," said Grandma Lizette in an attempt to compliment her daughter.

Just then, Baby Alice stirred. She started to cry but then saw Eva in her big gown and went silent. A huge, gummy smile, plus two teeth, spread across her plump face. And then she debuted a new skill. Clapping.

Eva yelped. Lizette yelped. Audre sipped her sparkling cider.

"Did the baby clap?" asked Grandma Lizette via FaceTime. "Somebody answer me—I feel like I'm in a looney bin, yapping to the walls."

"Yes!" said Eva, hopping off the platform to give Baby Alice a bottle from her diaper bag. "She's so smart, Mom. Audre, you were just like that. You hit every milestone so early."

Audre looked over at Baby Alice, who always looked so angelic in front of an audience. (As demons often did.) It occurred to her that Baby Alice was already getting the "exceptional child" messaging. One day, her little sister would find out how heavy that crown was.

Good luck to you, kid, thought Audre. *May you handle the pressure better than I do.*

"Genevieve—I mean Eva . . . was advanced, too. Y'all get it from me," said Grandma Lizette. "Audre, you still got our ring on, right?"

Genevieve? Who the hell was Genevieve?

Audre held up her hand at the phone screen. "I never take it off, Grandma!"

"I know that's right! One day it'll go to Baby Alice."

"Does it have to?"

"Now, Audre. Can't keep the juju to yourself. Best pass it on, or it stops workin'. Don't you want your sister to get some of the Mercier girl magic?"

Eva, who was examining her train in the mirror, straightened her posture. "Mercy girl."

"Right. Mercy," said Grandma Lizette.

"Mom, have you been drinking?"

"That's between me and the Holy Trinity."

"Which Holy Trinity? Tequila, lime, and ice?"

"The Father, the Son, and the Holy Spirit!" snapped Grandma Lizette.

And then, for a reason she couldn't place, Audre couldn't help but think of the weird note on her mom's Post-it. *Lizette: Where's the line between telling the truth and shaming my mother?*

Grandma Lizette was a mystery. But so was her mom. Who were these women, who had so much love between them but also an undercurrent of something dark? What were they keeping from Audre?

(Or maybe her mom was just being funny or sarcastic on that Post-it, in some cryptic way. Private thoughts didn't have to make sense. Maybe Audre was searching for meaning where there wasn't any.)

"I'm done here," Grandma Lizette was saying through the phone. "Now, y'all go 'head and proceed without me. I gotta get up out this house. The electricity's out and it's hot. Like spendin' an hour in the devil's pocket. Y'all be good."

With that, Grandma Lizette disappeared. Audre glanced at her mom, who was staring at herself in the mirror. She wished she could've read the expression on her mom's face. It was a cloudy mix of sadness, frustration...and something else. Something deep down and closed off, where Audre couldn't reach.

"Don't let Grandma Lizette bother you. You know she's just loud and opinionated."

Eva pasted on a big smile and fake-laughed for her daughter's benefit. "Oh, she doesn't bother me. It's just exhausting, watching her try to mimic human emotions."

"Was she like that when you were growing up?"

Eva met Audre's eyes in the mirror. "Like what?"

"Hard on you."

"Oh, I don't remember. My growing-up years are a blur. We moved around a lot, you know."

Eva was always so vague about her childhood with Grandma Lizette. Their single-mom-plus-daughter life mirrored Audre and Eva's in so many ways. But where Audre and Eva were always close, Eva and Grandma Lizette weren't.

Her mom always told her rapturous stories about Grandma Lizette's proto-girlboss work ethic, but their actual relationship was a question mark. They barely spoke. There had to be more to the story than the time difference, or Eva being busy writing, or Lizette hating to fly. Audre would've killed to learn the secrets between her mom and grandmother. Because she was curious, sure. But also because somewhere in those secrets were clues about who she was, too.

"Why don't you two talk more? Don't you miss her?"

"Of course I miss her," said Eva, gathering her skirt and joining Audre on the sofa. "Your grandma's a great woman. Truly. The strongest lady I know. You're lucky to have such a trailblazer for a grandmother."

Audre noticed that she always referred to her as "your grandmother." Not "my mother."

"But," continued Eva, clearing her throat, "my life's busy. And so's hers. It's hard to find time to talk. That's life, you know?"

"I hope that doesn't happen to us," said Audre. She couldn't imagine adulthood making her drift apart from Eva. Her mom was her touchstone. When she was little, she wanted to jump into Eva's shadow, to feel what it was like to be her. It wasn't lost on Audre that she wanted to write a book at sixteen. Was it to beat her mom's record of publishing her first at nineteen? Was it normal to feel a need to one-up your own mother? Any good therapist would say no.

"It won't happen to us. We're different."

Eva slung her arm across Audre's shoulders. It was a light, breezy move, but her voice sounded strained. She was hiding something. It was so obvious.

"Mom?"

"Daughter?"

"When can I read *Back to Belle Fleur*?"

Instantly, Eva drew back her arm. "You? Reading one of my books? Since when?"

Audre had never read a word her mom wrote. Up until *Back to Belle Fleur*, her mom had only written supernatural erotica. Reading actual sex scenes her mother wrote about a nineteen-year-old witch and a five-thousand-year-old vampire banging throughout fifteen books? Kill her now. Plus, Eva's rabid fandom freaked her out. It was nauseating, experiencing middle-aged white women in witch hats make orgasmic noises about their vampire crush at book signings.

"Yeah, but this one's a memoir about the Mercy girls," said Audre. "It's not just your history, it's mine, too."

"I promise I'll let you read it before it publishes, this fall. First, I just need to explain . . . you know, figure out . . ."

Before her mom could finish the thought, Audre's phone went off in her pocket. Her stomach flip-flopped a bit, hoping it was Reshma. They hadn't spoken since she'd stormed out of the vintage shop. And Reshma owed her an apology.

It wasn't Reshma.

> **Ellison:** r u ever gonna answer me? just making sure u haven't told anyone. i cld potentially get in big trouble. don't want it to f up college admissions. i made a huge mistake & i apologized. hope ur having a great summer

Audre sucked in a gulp of air. With trembling hands, she turned her phone off and slipped it in her jeans pocket.

"What's wrong?" asked her mom.

She was tempted to tell her. Weirdly, after the beach incident, they'd grown closer than they'd been in ages. It was as if their tension had reached its boiling point and was now cooling off. For the first time in forever, Audre's muscles didn't tighten into knots when Eva walked in the room. Maybe she was finally getting used to being in Brooklyn for the summer. Maybe they were finally getting over the almost-two-year relationship slump. Whatever it was? Audre would take it.

But she couldn't bring herself to tell her mom, so radiant in her wedding gown, that her golden child could barely make a move without being seized with panic attacks. And that she was so traumatized from prom night that she hadn't had a full night's sleep since May. So, she pasted on a smile.

"Audre, are you okay?" repeated Eva.

"Totally." Nonchalantly, she sipped from her champagne glass, her hand still trembling. She got up and handed it to Eva. "Is everything okay with you and Grandma Lizette?"

"Totally," she said, sipping apple cider.

They were both lying. And it was obvious.

"Quick question," said Audre, fiddling with her cameo ring. "If you're wearing Jordans, can I wear my Converse?"

1, 2, 3, 4 . . . THRIVE!
A Teen's Rules for Flourishing on This Dying Planet

By Audre Mercy-Moore

Rule 8:

If you grow up around older family members (aunts, uncles, grandparents), ask questions about their past. When you don't know your family history, you can feel like an escaped balloon — no anchor, just floating away to who-knows-where. Alone.

Chapter 19

Four miles south in Brooklyn, Reshma was soaking in her bathtub. Lazily, she was stirring Le Labo Rose 31 bath salts in the water with her white-polished big toe. And she was strategizing. She had to apologize to Audre. She didn't mean to imply that Audre couldn't pull Bash on her own. Or that she *needed* Reshma's help. Reshma *wanted* to help. There was a huge difference.

Could Audre handle herself on her own? Maybe. But the thing was, she wasn't as experienced, and getting her man might take forever. Reshma was wily. She was clever. And she was daring. With her tactics, she could speed up the process a little.

Why couldn't Audre see that? she wondered, pressing her hands over her upset stomach. She'd been nauseous since their fight, but the hot bath was helping a bit. This antique claw-foot tub was her favorite spot in the house. It was the very same tub where Sparrow had lain, dry, during Reshma's last-day-of-school party as she wept about her love of Bash.

So it was a full-circle moment when, just then, Reshma's phone rang from its perch on her bath tray. It was Sparrow.

"I know we're not close friends," she was saying, "but I feel like I can trust you."

Why? wondered Reshma. *You shouldn't.*

"Of course you can trust me, doll," she said. "What is it?"

Reshma heard Sparrow suck in a big, shuddery breath. "I was just at Target."

"There's nothing wrong with Target," said Reshma, withholding a yawn. "Their throw pillows are elite."

"No, it's not that. I was there, and I saw Bash. With... with..."

Abruptly, Reshma sat up straight, splashing steaming water onto the black-and-white checkerboard floor tiles. "With who?"

"Audre."

"Omigod." Silently, Reshma clapped her hands with glee.

"I know! She *knows* I like Bash. She knows we shared a moment. I told her everything in confidence. She pretended to be my therapist and then went after MY GUY."

Reshma couldn't help but smile. They must've been doing the dildo challenge. "Sparrow, I know that must've really hurt. Can I ask you, though? Did it look like they liked each other?"

"Oh, they like each other. Audre was *assaulting* him with her eyes. I know that look—I've described it a million times in my *Naruto* fanfics." And then her voice dropped down low. "They were in the sex toys aisle."

Just as Reshma thought. Her mind was racing. Okay, clearly they really liked each other. But, once again, Reshma knew Audre would never make a real move if Bash was taken. Which sucked. More than anyone, Audre deserved love. Or at least a satisfying hookup.

Reshma was already in planning mode. "Don't worry. I'll get to the bottom of it."

• • •

Reshma was bored. That was the problem. Whenever she was bored—or even sensed boredom brewing on the horizon—Naughty Reshma popped out of the bushes. She became a mischievous imp. Pagan goddess of mess.

When she didn't have enough to do, when life slowed down for her, she got into trouble. Her only other option? Shutting down altogether. It had happened before. Everything went deep, dark purple, and the only place she felt okay was in her bed. In total darkness. With the AC turned down to a frosty sixty-six degrees. In the cold, cold darkness of her bedroom, she'd hide under a pile of blankets. Then she'd pull up every avatar-making app available, creating new illustrated versions of herself. It captivated her, seeing her face through the lens of a million different illustration styles.

And it wasn't vanity. Her folders of animated "Reshmas" made her feel like she existed, somewhere. But she didn't want to fall back into that pattern this summer. The good news was that she had an idea. A brilliant one.

When Audre talked about Bash, it was like a ring light appeared out of nowhere, illuminating her face like she was holy. She glowed! Audre had it bad, and no one deserved to be "in like" with a boy more than she did. It was hopeless, though, if he had a girlfriend. Audre had morals. But Reshma knew what Audre didn't—there wasn't anyone she couldn't seduce.

Her plan? To lure Clio away from Bash. Once she was out of the picture, Audre would be free to date him! Yes, Audre had explicitly told Reshma not to get involved. But Audre had no idea what she was doing. She *did* need Reshma. And what she didn't know couldn't hurt her.

And now, she and Clio were sitting on a bench at the edge of the pond. For an hour, they'd strolled around the perimeter of the lake, sprinkling the embankment with oats, birdseed, and grated carrots—the lunch of choice for the swans of Prospect Park.

"That one's Melba," said Clio, pointing over to the right. Melba was swimming all alone while a group of five or six swans slowly drifted by, looking swanky and standoffish.

"But why doesn't she join them?"

"Because she belongs to an enemy family. They've been fighting each other for generations. But we had to remove them after an infection, so for now, she's...*flying solo.*"

Reshma giggled at her pun but could barely follow what she was saying. The whole idea had been to capture Clio in her web. But as the afternoon wore on, it got harder to remember her mission. Instead, she was sinking into the tingly chemistry simmering between them. Was she imagining it? It was always hard to tell if a girl was queer, bi, bi-curious, or a Flirty Straight. The few times she'd incorrectly clocked a girl's interest were soul-cringing.

Zoning out, she took in Clio's curled dreadlocks. Her soft, slightly spicy perfume. Retro New Balances. A tee emblazoned with Princess Nokia's face. She was bad as hell.

Tee with a queer female rapper on it, mused Reshma. *Encouraging.*

"So, Melba and the Mean Girls have beef? Who knew swan life was so treacherous?"

"Oh, they get active. That big one leading the Mean Girls? Look closely at her."

Reshma leaned forward, squinting. Then she gasped. "Only one eye. A war wound?"

"She fought Melba's mom over a male swan. Jerry belonged to the streets," said Clio, shaking her head. "There's always one."

"Always," chuckled Reshma. "It's usually me."

"That's not surprising," said Clio.

"So, what made you so interested in swans?"

"My passion is aquatic birds. Ducks, herons, seagulls, swans. I loved that book *The Ugly Duckling* when I was little. Did you ever read it?"

"About the abandoned duckling who gets adopted by swans?"

She smiled, nodding. "And when he grew up, he realized he'd been a swan all along."

"Now, that's a fairy tale," said Reshma. "In my elementary school back in London, we had a transfer student from Copenhagen, Denmark. That's where Hans Christian Andersen wrote *The Ugly Duckling*. The swan is their national bird. He had special Danish notebooks with a tiny gold swan stamped on the corner of each cover. So beautiful."

Clio smiled softly. "At such a young age, you saw beauty in little things. Nice. Most people never learn how to do that. Are you an artist?"

"No," she laughed. "No, I don't know what I am. My parents are."

"Who are your parents?"

Groaning, Reshma pulled her waves over her face like a curtain. "The Well Well Wells."

Clio froze in the middle of throwing her seeds to the swans. "The Well Well Wells? The duo with the greatest harmonies of the nineties? The king and queen of the mellow ballad?"

Reshma grimaced. "Coming to a supermarket playlist near you."

"'So Far So Good' is my mom's favorite song. Adbhut!"

Reshma's jaw dropped open. She got full-body chills, and every follicle on her head tried (and failed) to stand up.

"Hold on. Did you just say *abdhut* in a flawless Hindi accent?"

Clio batted her lashes.

"Do you know what it means?" asked Reshma, heart pounding. A few of the swans, eating several feet away, looked up at Clio. Wow, she really was a Disney princess.

"It means wonderful," she said shyly. "It's no big deal, really. I had an Indian nanny."

And then, because she was so transported by this enchanting girl, speaking in one of the tongues of her birth country, under the glow of the midday sun, she spoke before her brain caught up. "Mujhe aapakee aavaaz pasand hai."

Clio gasped in delight. "I'm not fluent! What did you say?"

"Not telling. Look it up later," she said, now embarrassed. She never spoke Hindi in front of anyone. It made her feel vulnerable, skinless. Stripped of all her bravado.

First of all, she didn't speak it well. Her parents weren't the kind of white people who exposed their kid of color to their birth culture. She did not grow up in an "Angelina Jolie doing the Electric Slide at Zahara's Spelman welcome weekend" environment. So, in secret, Reshma tried to figure out the language of her ancestors on her own—through a patchwork combination of

Duolingo, Bollywood movies, and "teach yourself Hindi" books. The results were mixed. But she'd never stop trying. She didn't want to die a fake-ass Indian.

Secondly, no one she knew spoke Hindi, so she never had a reason to use it.

"Okay, then tell me this," said Clio. "What does it feel like to have genius parents?"

"Don't know. Ask Blue Ivy, Sir, and Rumi."

"Got it. So you're not close to the Well Well Wells?"

"I'm close to running away," she joked, grabbing a handful of grains from Clio's hemp bag. "Are your parents cool?"

"My mom is. I don't know my birth dad. But my mom's boyfriend is chill. He likes animals, too. And he drove me to school on really cold days when I couldn't handle the train. He's a stand-up dude, you know? I could do a lot worse."

"What high school did you go to? I can't believe we've never met."

"'Cause you're a Brooklyn girl, and I'm from Jackson Heights, Queens! I graduated from George Washington Carver High last year. Now I'm studying veterinary medicine at Cornell," she said with pride. She glanced at her phone. "Speaking of, I should go. I have some summer school coursework to finish."

"Yeah, no it's cool," said Reshma quickly, realizing that she'd forgotten her objective. That she was there to pull Clio in. To distract her from her boyfriend.

She'd been having so much fun that she'd lost track of time altogether. And it wasn't like she had in Argentina, with Kiki, where she intentionally passed the time with her, like a cat spending a lazy afternoon batting a toy. She'd never gotten lost in Kiki.

With Clio, she'd forgotten to be strategic.

Remember your mission, thought Reshma. *Mastermind this shit.*

"Can I ask you something?" She bit her bottom lip and tried to look bashful, turning on the charm. "And tell me if I'm being too forward."

Clio tossed off a breezy shrug. "Depends on what it is."

"I guess . . . I'm just wondering if you're seeing anyone."

Clio sighed, letting her head fall forward.

"Uh-oh," said Reshma, fixing Clio with her upturned, smoky eyes. Clio returned the glance for a moment. Their eyes locked. And then she tore her eyes away, gazing out at the pond.

"You're wondering if I'm seeing anyone? Or asking?"

"I'm asking."

"I'm seeing someone," she admitted, fiddling with her bag. "But I don't know if we'll last. We were long-distance at first. And now we're not. Which is weird. Plus, he's the artistic type, so he's all over the place. And doesn't want to commit."

Makes sense, thought Reshma, her chaos-agent senses tingling. *Bash had been in California till now. And he's definitely all over the place.*

"A boy?"

Clio nodded, still looking toward the water. The swans had all headed back in, listlessly floating in the heavy humidity, leaving swirly patterns in the water.

"Hmm." Reshma stretched, taking in this information. "Can I ask you something else?"

Clio faced her with an unreadable expression. "Sure."

"Why are you here with me, then?"

Something flashed behind Clio's eyes. And, after a beat, she slowly leaned in closer to Reshma. Her long, Bambi lashes fanned out, casting shadows on her cheeks. Her scent was intoxicating. Their knees were touching. Reshma held her breath, silently praying that Clio would make the first move.

If she kisses me first, it's good, she thought, her mind racing. *If she kisses me first, I didn't start any of this. It was her. It's on her.*

"Ask me again," said Clio, her voice lightly daring.

"If you're serious with him," asked Reshma, "what are we doing here?"

Clio sighed, the soft warmth of her breath blanketing Reshma's mouth. Despite herself, Reshma let out a tiny, barely audible noise of anticipation.

"I'm here to feed the swans," answered Clio. "What are you here for?"

And then she pulled away with a wicked expression, leaving Reshma speechless. Which never, ever happened. She felt like she was suspended on the wrong side of an hourglass.

It wasn't until this very second that Reshma understood this was no longer her game.

Later, long after Reshma helped Clio pack up her blanket and then walked her to her train, Reshma found birdseed in the pockets of her cutoffs. She carefully plucked it out and poured it into a delicate, empty earrings box. For safekeeping.

Not mastermind behavior, at all.

Chapter 20

Late-Night Texts, June 30–July 4, 2025

Bash: u ever start wondering random shit when it gets late

Audre: yeah like what

Bash: like are my cells dividing right now

Audre: lol lol lol

Bash: srsly! we're just lying in our beds. but our organs are experiencing a whole other reality inside our bodies

Audre: it's giving science fiction

Bash: here's another one. why can't we keep weather as a pet?

Audre: LOL LOL LOL

Bash: don't laugh, I have a thirst for knowledge

Audre: so do I, tbh. i researched NYC tattoo certification laws. u need to be 18 to get a license

Bash: that law is ageist and I refuse to recognize it

Audre: ur cool w operating an illegal business? living outside the law?

Bash: laws are arbitrary. it used to be illegal for women to have credit cards. wait why'd you look up tattoo laws

Audre: no reason

Bash: checking up on me, huh

Audre: i was just bored in the house, being nosy

Bash: house. i'll never get used to new yorkers calling their apartments houses. just say apartment. or use a generic term like crib

Audre: do u miss Oakland?

Bash: nah not anymore

Audre: why?

Bash: ...

Bash: ...

Bash: idk, I guess I really like being your funsultant. even though I haven't seen u in days

Audre: my stay-out-past-10 challenge is up next. aren't you taking me to a party?

Bash: but that's over a wk away

Audre: you're counting the days?

Bash: i'm counting the minutes

Audre: ...

Audre: oh

Audre: (same)

Audre: I think being a funsultant is your calling

Bash: maybe I'll design a logo

Audre: yeah, it should be your next tattoo

Bash: if you could get one, what would it be

Audre: i'm scared of needles, remember

Bash: I'd make u feel safe, promise

Audre: but it's illegal

Bash: just trust me

Audre: what if we get arrested

Bash: what if it's worth it

Audre: menace

Bash: good night, A

Audre: good night, B

NEW DAY

Audre: i think I'm sick.

Bash: what kinda sick

Audre: idk, my throat is scratchy and i sneezed twice today. maybe I shouldn't go to the party

Bash: ur going. i have a whole thing planned

Audre: i might be contagious

Bash: contagious doesn't always mean dangerous

Audre: ???

Bash: think about it. yawns are contagious. if somebody yawns in ur vicinity, u do it too

Audre: ok that's true

Bash: and aren't periods contagious? like when a bunch of girls are on a sports team together or live in the same dorm

Audre: WHAT

Bash: no?

Audre: periods aren't contagious! girls' cycles sync up when we're around each other for a long time

Bash: ur so fucking smart

Audre: it's science!

Bash: smiles are contagious too. yours is, at least

Audre: wait what

Bash: when u smile, I wanna smile too. See? contagious, not dangerous

Audre: ...

Audre: . . .

Bash: ur smiling now, I can tell

Audre: 😋

Bash: ur coming on friday. take some tussin & feel better soon

Audre: FINE. *sneeze*

Bash: night, A

Audre: night, B

NEW DAY

Audre: u know, the other night, when u were thinking about your organs?

Bash: i'm always thinking about my organs

Audre: i think about mine, too. i sometimes wish I could have a constant x-ray streaming to see what's going on in there

Bash: i love x-rays

Audre: NO, I LOVE X-RAYS. speaking of, I have something to confess

Bash: i'm ready

Audre: promise to still be my funsultant when I tell you

Bash: i promise on mamas

Audre: i have a tooth in my chin

Bash: ...

Bash: ...

Bash: whut

Audre: it's an adult tooth that never pushed up! it's laying down sideways, deep down in my chin. the baby tooth it was supposed to replace? it never fell out

Bash: UNHINGED I LUV IT. does your chin hurt?

Audre: i can't feel it. and my baby tooth fits in w the rest. no one would ever know. his name is robert

Bash: whose name?

Audre: my chin-tooth. when I was little, dr. gregg told me to name it and make friends with it. so it didn't freak me out

Bash: this is the greatest news I've ever heard. can I see the X-ray?

Audre: maybe one day

Bash: since we're doing this, I have a body secret to tell u too

Audre: i'm scared

Bash: i have 3 nipples

Audre: YOU HAVE 3 WHAT

Bash: the third one's small! it's on my stomach, u can barely see it. harry styles has 4

Audre: did u name yours?

Bash: should I?

Audre: roberta

Bash: YES. robert's sister

Audre: it's weird that we trust each other like this

Bash: idk it's not so weird to me

Audre: night, B

Bash: night, A

NEW DAY

Bash: i did some research on panic attacks

Audre: (embarrassing)

Bash: it's not, tho. therapists get anxiety too

Audre: i know, i know

Bash: ever heard of the 333 method

209

Audre: ofc, i've prescribed it a million times. when u feel panic coming on, u focus on 3 senses. something u can see, hear, and touch

Bash: so why don't you try it?

Audre: cuz then i'd be admitting that I have panic attacks. admitting that I have panic attacks makes me wanna have a panic attack

Bash: nah, man. ur gonna start doing 333. okay?

Audre: okaayyyy

Bash: ur stubborn as hell

Audre: duh i'm a taurus. u know what else tauruses are? curious. which is why i solved the 1980s smurf lunch box mystery

Bash: !!!!!

Audre: a huge cargo box got stuck in the rocks offshore in 1983! and over the years, the lunch boxes get swept out to shore

Bash: THAT'S WHY??!

Audre: i'm obsessed and kinda want one now

Bash: i'll find you one. now I'm even more determined

Audre: night, B

Bash: night, A

Audre: and thx for the 333 tip. ur really sweet

NEW DAY

Bash: childhood confession time

Audre: k, u first

Bash: when I was a kid, I saw this h'ween simpsons episode where a witch cursed everyone to turn into their costumes. so I always picked costumes that I'd be cool with for eternity

Audre: that's adorable. what was your fav?

Bash: captain america. he was an artist before he was a superhero. i always knew I wanted to design things. i could be captain america forever

Audre: perfect. did I ever tell u I used to be an artist? paintings and collages, mostly. i won a statewide competition in seventh grade

Bash: why did u stop

Audre: idk. The older i got, the more i realized i wasn't THAT good. i get impatient when i'm not the best at something

Bash: why not do it 'cause it feels good

Audre: maybe idk

Bash: what costume would u pick if u had to wear it forever

Audre: dr. melfi, the therapist on the sopranos

Bash: never watched it

Audre: i have so much to teach u

Bash: ur turn. childhood confession

Audre: don't judge me. in dept stores sometimes, i used to get lost on purpose. just to hear them call my mom to the front desk

Bash: whoa. that's deep. why?

Audre: idk. if a client told me that story, i'd have it figured out in 2 min. but I can't therapize myself

Bash: maybe u just craved her attention. we all want recognition. i think it's a normal thing, don't u

Audre: i don't know what's normal anymore, tbh

Bash: night, A

Audre: night, B

NEW DAY

Bash: wyd

Audre: lol it's almost midnight. i'm at my house

Bash: house?

Audre: crib

Bash: u hungry? wanna get something to eat? that diner on sixteenth is open 24 hrs

Audre: ...

Audre: which challenge are we doing?

Bash: no challenge. but it's 4th of july! we should do something

Audre: are we allowed to "do something" outside of a challenge

Bash: i just want to see u

Audre: but i'm wearing a bonnet

Bash: so am i

Audre: u r not. um i guess you can come by my window?

Bash: omw

Chapter 21

Bash didn't run to Audre's building. He didn't want to look as thirsty as he felt. Instead, he walked. Fast. Minutes later, he found himself standing beneath her third-floor apartment, texting her to come to the window.

It was 11:30 PM.

As he stood there on the wide, elegant sidewalk, he wondered what she was thinking. If she felt as dizzy as he did. As rearranged. They hadn't spoken in person in days, but it didn't matter. Just texting with her turned him upside down.

Audre Mercy-Moore had done this to him.

All night, Bash had been lying on his bedroom floor, rereading their old texts, listening to Frank Ocean, and feeling antsy. He needed to see her.

So weird, he thought. *The person who makes me feel crazy is also the only one who can calm me down.*

He waited. The seconds stretched into minutes. Everything was quiet. The streetlights were on, but otherwise everything was bathed in darkness. It was a warm night, made bearable by the soft, linden-flower-scented air wafting over from the park. His heart thundered in his chest. He squeezed his eyes shut. What if she changed her mind?

Then he heard her voice—the low, whispery, late-night version—calling down to him.

"Hey."

Bash's eyes flew open, and he looked up. There she was, framed by her living room window. Too pretty to even deal with. Her face had a late-night vulnerability he'd never seen before—and she looked adorably cozy in a roomy Cheshire Prep sweatshirt. They were in contact every night around this time, texting each other the most random, unhinged stuff. But seeing her in real life in the middle of the night? This was different. A mindfuck of epic proportions.

His smile happened before he could even control it.

"Where's your bonnet?" he asked.

"Where's yours?" she asked with a small smile.

Bash bit his bottom lip shyly. They gazed at each other for a moment in silence. Time stretching into something loopy, surreal.

God, did Audre have to be so beautiful? Her braids were swept into a high bun, showcasing the smooth, deep walnut skin of her neck. He wondered how her skin would feel there, under his fingertips. Under his lips.

Bash was losing it. And he needed to pull it together. He wasn't supposed to like Audre for real. He wasn't supposed to like anyone for real. When he moved to Brooklyn, he promised himself he wouldn't. He was still too scarred from what happened. The tragedy.

Overwhelmed, Bash tore his eyes away from hers and peered

down at the sidewalk. "Now that I'm here, I don't really know what to say."

"Why did you want to see me?" she asked softly. "It better be something good. I was halfway asleep in my bedroom."

"And by 'bedroom' you mean 'couch.'"

"Right."

"I didn't feel like texting anymore. And I didn't want to Face-Time. I wanted to, uh . . . see you in person. I guess."

Bash saw her take in a sharp breath. She blinked a few times and then nodded. "I know the feeling."

"Plus, I just wanted to take a walk. It's a nice night."

"Yeah, Brooklyn's kinda nice in the summer. It's no cottage in Malibu, but there's something magical about it."

Bash was standing under a linden tree, a ubiquitous presence on Brooklyn sidewalks and in parks. Yellow blossoms breathed out a sweet, soothing scent. Blended with the streetlights, the reflection from the blossoms cast a warm glow on Audre's face. Hypnotized, Bash was rooted to the spot.

"There is . . ." He stopped, cleared his throat, and deepened his voice. "There is something about the summertime here, yeah."

Audre was right there, but still too far away. It was scrambling his brain. And she shouldn't be having this effect on him. They were just friends. They couldn't be anything more. He'd already ruined one life, back in Oakland. He didn't want to ruin another.

Clio warned me about this, he thought, remembering an angry conversation they'd had before he left California. *She told me I need to face what happened before I tried to move on.*

"But enough about the weather," said Audre, cutting through the tension.

"I know, right? We're talking like we don't know each other."

"Speaking of knowing each other... can I say something?"

"Yeah. I'm listening."

"You flirt with me," she said. "And it has to stop."

Bash's jaw dropped. He didn't know what he expected to hear, but it wasn't that. "You flirt with me!"

"I don't even know how to flirt."

"You might not know you're doing it, but you are."

"It's not the same," she said, her voice raising to a louder whisper. "I think... let's agree to stop flirting. We're just friends, right? I just don't want things to get confusing."

His stomach plummeted. His mouth felt dry. Suddenly, the air felt too hot and uncomfortably still. Her words sliced through him—but the worst part was, they made sense.

For him, things were already confusing. Yes, he had feelings for Audre. He couldn't help that. But he could help what he did about it.

Why couldn't he have met her before his life fell apart?

"No, you're right. Let's keep it professional." He nodded in enthusiastic agreement.

"Also, I'm... I'm not ready to hang out outside of my challenges."

"Oh. Oh? But, why?"

"I'm a logical, analytical person, right? I've been thinking a lot about this," she said slowly. "Right now, we're just friends. But the way we... are with each other? I think that if we hang out too much, I could start feeling things. And I'd end up hurt. Because you talk to a lot of girls. Like you said before, you 'dabble.' And I know Clio means something to you."

"I wish you'd trust me about her. I don't cheat. We're not together."

"But you're not denying that she means something to you."

"No," he said quietly. "I'm not denying it. But it's not what you think. I just can't talk about it."

Audre nodded as if to say *My point exactly.*

"I'm not like you," she said. "I can't date a lot of people. I don't want to dabble."

"What do you want?"

She glanced at him for a few breaths and then looked away. A siren went off, far away. Someone's dog, on a late-night walk, started barking.

"I want to be with one person." She said this line with steely confidence, but her eyes were wide and vulnerable. "And I don't wanna want something I can't have. I have a book to write. And a future to plan. You know how that goes. You're planning to move for your career. Permanently. All the way to Myrtle Beach."

Bash looked up at her, struck silent.

"Aren't you?" she asked.

"There's a chance I could move. I hope it works out. Fifth Angel is my dream. But that has nothing to do with...I mean, you shouldn't..." He stood there, gesturing at her and not making any sense. Overwhelmed, he stopped talking.

Bash felt a million miles away from her. Confused, hurt, in almost physical pain. Seeing her so tortured and knowing that his vagueness was the cause? It was killing him. "Can you come down? I feel like some fucked-up version of Romeo out here."

She chewed on her bottom lip, her dimples popping. Was she

thinking it over? Whatever she was doing, it was taking too long. And he was a man of action.

"I'm coming up," he blurted out.

"No, you can't! My parents are asleep. No."

"Can you sneak outside?"

"No, Bash. This is a firm boundary."

"I respect your boundaries, but please just come down. I know I've been confusing. It's my fault. Let me explain."

"No, Bash! There's nothing to explain. I'm embarrassed enough as it is. I'm gonna go to bed now, okay?"

"Audre..."

"I'm fine, Romeo. Go home. We'll talk later."

She smiled tightly, then shot him a quick wave and closed the window. He peered down at his phone in his hand. It was 11:50 PM. He leaned against the tree, hands thrust in his pockets. Lost in thought.

When he finally turned to head home, he glanced back at his phone.

It was 11:57 PM. Seven minutes had passed.

Chilled to the bone, he walked back to his building in a near trance. He couldn't forget what he already knew—that it only took seven minutes for everything to change.

Chapter 22

And just like that, Audre stopped returning Bash's texts. She was mortified. Basically, she told Bash she liked him. And she did it from her window, like in a cheesy fairy tale. And he didn't have a response. She went out on a limb and he left her there. Why'd she have to be so melodramatic? They weren't dating. Why'd she jump forward a million steps and break up with him? Why had she been so honest?

The problem was, she felt safe saying anything to him. As a therapist, she was used to people spilling their guts to her. But Audre never reciprocated—and because of that, no one ever actually got to know her. This was her armor, the safest way to move through the world. If no one knew your weird stuff, they couldn't hold it against you. Audre loved controlling how she was perceived. But with Bash, she couldn't control anything. Ever since the beach panic attack, it was like he had a key to her psyche. All her boundaries dissolved and blew away, like pollen on a breeze.

She tried to ignore his "let's talk" texts. But then, late at night, he'd started sending his random, stream-of-consciousness thoughts...

> **Bash:** when ur watching a movie set in long-ago times, do u ever think about how everyone smelled

> **Bash:** should i try to grow a mustache

> **Bash:** did u know ur never more than 3 feet from a spider

> **Bash:** what if u ran into urself in an alternate dimension? what would u say to alternate-dimension audre? i think i'd wanna make out with myself. see what it's like

That last one was too deranged to ignore. So she folded. She missed him! And slowly, they built back up to the place they were before. Calling, FaceTime, talking on the actual phone about nothing and everything. But now they followed Audre's new rules—no flirting, and no seeing each other outside of the challenges.

Audre had to say, she was pleased with herself. Out of sight almost meant out of mind. It was easier not to fixate on Bash when they weren't talking on the phone, FaceTiming, or being in each other's presence. She was good, generally. The problems started late at night. Super late, when the house was quiet and dark, and everyone was asleep but her insomniac ass, and she'd reread old texts they'd sent each other . . . and swiftly tumble down the rabbit hole. Did she google his old track videos, spiraling over slow-mo footage of his strong, long legs as he left his competition in the dust? Uhh, yes. Did she listen to the same CBSSports.com post-meet interview several times, feeling soothed by the slow, deep cadence of his voice? Yes. But did her late-night thirstiness exist if no one knew about it? Nope!

On the best friend side of things, Reshma and Audre finally made up—Reshma enthusiastically and Audre hesitantly.

"I was wrong to imply that you need my help to get a guy," she told Audre over the phone in her expressive, Londonese-American accent. "You know I just be saying shit."

"You really hurt my feelings."

"I'm so sorry, babe. I never meant to. I'll never meddle again. Forgive me?"

"Say you're an emotional terrorist."

"I'm an emotional terrorist."

"You're forgiven," said Audre, and she meant it.

"Good, now we can discuss what really matters. That party with Bash on Friday."

"I was thinking about the red cami top and jeans?"

"Purrrr," she said approvingly. "WAIT. Challenge number three is staying out past 10 PM, and challenge number four is hooking up with a boy you have chemistry with. Do both at the party. You can't waste that 'fit. Every guy in town'll be there."

"Are you going?"

"Please. You know I only attend high school parties when they're at my house."

Audre had to admit that completing two challenges at once sounded like a good idea. The faster she could get through her list, the sooner she could start writing her book—and the sooner she could move on from Bash.

And maybe making out with someone would help her move on, too.

·   ·   ·

Friday night came faster than expected. Audre told her mom she was going to "a random get-together and don't worry the parents will be there," which wasn't a total lie. Eva, preoccupied with wedding planning, simply insisted that she honor her 11 PM curfew. Ever since their post-beach fight, Audre knew she better be on her best behavior. So, she happily agreed. After 9 PM, she started yawning anyway. Good thing she only had to stay out past 10 PM.

The plan was to meet at the party. But when Bash texted her the address of a local bakery, she was confused. He assured her that he knew what he was doing. So, trusting this maniac, she showed up exactly five minutes after their meeting time of 9 PM. He was standing in front of the bakery, looking stylish in an orange PEACE IS POWER sweatshirt, cuffed cargos, and a mini crossbody bag.

It had been forever since she'd seen him (i.e., a week). She'd forgotten that simply looking at him was...a lot. The slightly sunburned, bronzed skin. The dreamy, abstract ink snaking up and around his arm. His impossible height. The tension between the hard metal of his rings and the soft, long taper of his fingers. God.

"Hi, friend!" she said, sneaking up behind him. Startled, he jumped a little, and then turned to face her. In a flash, his face went from stranger-danger to goofy-smiley.

"Whoa." His eyes widened, scanning quickly from her face to her feet and back up again. She was wearing the red cami outfit, and she'd swept her hair half-up, with a few loose braids in front. "Wow. Okay. Hi."

"Hi," she said, repeating herself in a breathless voice she barely recognized. For a moment they just stood there, drinking each other in, not talking but switching between nervous fidgeting and blatant staring.

"Wow," he repeated. "You look—"

"Thanks, so do you," said Audre quickly, before Bash forgot the no-flirting rule (and she did, too). She nibbled on her bottom lip, trying desperately to control the helpless smile that was plastered all over her face. "Since when do you have a brow piercing?"

He shrugged shyly. "I don't wear it all the time. Is it weird?"

"No, it's giving Myspace era. Cute."

He grinned and peered down at his feet.

Audre had to change the subject 'cause the sparks between them were already flying and it was going to be a long night otherwise. "Now, tell me why we're at Chevalier's Bakery and Café for a party? Cafés don't stay open late."

"Right, but after hours in the summer, Chevalier's opens the backyard. And it turns into a party. Full bar."

"But we can't go to a bar," whispered Audre, looking from left to right. "I'm sixteen and you're seventeen. And I don't have a fake ID. Reshma does, and maybe if you're nearsighted and racially blind we sort of look similar..."

"Chevalier's doesn't card," said Bash. "It's an open secret."

Audre's eyes widened.

"Just trust me."

"Okay, I'll trust you. But first, I should tell you that Reshma and I sort of raised the stakes. We decided that I'm gonna do the next two challenges tonight. Staying out late and successfully making out. I'm killing two birds with one party."

Audre refused to allow this to be awkward. The best way to deal with it was to be direct.

"Really." He said it fast and flat, like it was punched out of him. "The kissing challenge—I forgot about that. So, you're saying I'm a wingman tonight?"

"Yes."

Crossing his arms, he thought this over for a second. And then his brow tightened. "I don't think you need me for this one."

"Bash, you *promised*. We shook on it, like gentlemen."

Visibly flustered, he grabbed an elastic out of his pocket and scraped the top of his hair into a bun. "I, as a man, cannot help you, as a woman, hook up with some fool."

"Why are you assuming I'd kiss a fool?" She paused. "Actually, Reshma told me I have no taste. Let's just say my taste is developing."

"I don't know, bruh. When I agreed to this, I didn't think this far ahead."

Stop me, then, she thought, ignoring all common sense. *Tell me you don't want me to kiss anyone else.*

"Why does it bother you?" she asked pointedly.

"I just think it's morally dubious, A."

"How's it morally dubious, B?"

" 'Cause we're taking advantage of some poor kid who doesn't know he's just a pawn in your game."

"I have a lot of things, but 'game' is not one of them. Which is why I need you." She paused. "Are you going to break your promise?"

Bash rolled his eyes dramatically. And then exhaled even more dramatically.

"Fine," he said.

"Fine?"

"Yeah, I'm down. I don't break promises."

She lifted her pinky, he hooked his pinky in hers, and the night began.

. . .

Bash was right. Inside, it was Brooklyn high school central, with a generous sprinkling of Manhattan kids, too. Chevalier's front room was generic and homey, with French café tables and baguettes painted in watercolors on the ivory walls. But in the back, beyond French double doors, was an outdoor courtyard packed with people. Everyone was smashed together—drinking, dancing, and spilling into the café. Behind the register, three girls in halter tops and intense eyeliner were filming a TikTok. Two people Audre knew from Cheshire's gender-neutral soccer team were groping each other under a café table. A clique of uber-rich boys was taking selfies while unironically throwing up gang signs.

The only light came from a flashing disco ball hanging over the courtyard. No AC. No one in charge.

Audre and Bash stood on the outskirts of the action, peering into the crowd.

"You look like a deer in headlights," Bash hollered over the music. "What's up?"

"You've lived here for five minutes, and you knew about this party? I grew up here and had no idea. What does it say about me that I was never invited? Am I that uncool?"

"No! Folks probably put you on a different level. Like you're above these antics."

Fiddling with her cameo ring, she looked down at her skimpy cami. She felt a sickening surge of insecurity, like she was trying too hard to be sexy. "Well, do I *look* uncool?"

"You're the prettiest girl in here. And it's no contest."

Bash paused, looking stunned. And embarrassed?

"What?" Audre thought she'd misheard him over the noise.

He shook his head, as if ridding his brain of all intrusive thoughts. "Nothing. I meant that whoever you decide to hook up with is a lucky man."

Audre smiled hesitantly. Then she hopped up and down a little, shaking out her arms. "Okay. How do I do this?"

"First, find somebody you wanna make out with."

She quickly scanned the crowd.

C. J. Jacobs? she wondered. *Kinda fine, but could I ever have chemistry with a guy obsessed with competitive subway surfing? Dangerous, and not in a hot way. Hmm ... Maxwell Reynolds? Ugh, he'd become such a player ever since he returned from rehab five inches taller. Definite no. There's gotta be someone here who's cute. Cute and not Bash.*

Just then, she landed on Manny Sanchez. He wasn't conventionally good-looking, but he was confident and smart as hell—plus, they'd had chemistry one year at a debate championship. He was bobbing his head to the throwback DJ Khaled banger pounding through the speakers.

"Him. Manny. The guy by the double doors."

"Really? *That* guy?"

Audre narrowed her eyes at Bash. "You're supposed to be helping, not judging."

"You're right, my bad. Yeah! He's the one," agreed Bash with forced enthusiasm. "You know him?"

"I do, but what do I say? Why am I so nervous? I don't think I can do this."

Bash turned to Audre and gripped her shoulders. "Look at me."

She did.

"You ran for class president at the most academically rigorous school in Brooklyn. You're a therapist. You're great with people. Just talk."

"But how?" wailed Audre. "I'm great at running for office. Or counseling somebody. Any activity when I'm in charge. But I'm not in charge here. Plus, everyone's two hours into drinking, and I never drink. I feel so stiff."

"You never drink?"

"Well, I had some sips of champagne at my California cousin's wedding."

Bash nodded slowly, giving this careful consideration. "Bet. Here's what we're gonna do. I'll grab you a beer. You won't get drunk off one beer. Just hold the cup and sip so you have something to do."

"Perfect. Beer. I'll sip a beer."

"And can I give you some party advice? You're gonna be tempted, but resist the urge to lecture or correct people."

"I don't understand. Example, please."

"I mean...hmm...like if somebody's talking about celebrity gossip or whatever. Like the Kardashians. Don't be like, the Kardashians are oppressors and cultural rapists!"

"But they are," she deadpanned.

"Of course they are, but people are entertained by them. It's a party, let people be problematic and toxic. I know you'll want to psychoanalyze. I know you feel safest counseling clients in bathrooms. But this challenge is about breaking you out of that."

How did Bash know she felt safest counseling people in bathrooms? It was true, but she'd never actually said that out loud, to anyone. Is this what it felt like to be seen? To be understood without words? A warm, potent feeling surged through her. She quickly squeezed her eyes shut and opened them again, trying to chase away this sensation.

For her sanity, it had to go away.

"Right," she said, her voice unsteady. "If I get stuck, I'll just tell everyone you have a third nipple."

"Okay, chin-tooth," he said with sparkling eyes. "Come on, let's get you into trouble."

Chapter 23

Audre and Bash made their way to the deejay booth. The deejay, a guy wearing a striped bikini and body glitter, was overseeing the Spotify playlist *and* the drinks cooler. Bash bought a Fireball shot for himself, but there was no more beer. Audre decided that the red punch looked doable.

"What's it spiked with?" Bash, looking worried, asked the deejay.

While wiggling to his beats, the deejay yelled, "Everything."

So, Bash bought a cup of punch and a bottled water—and watered it down for Audre.

"Just take sips," he hollered over the music. "Little sips."

"Little sips." She nodded.

"If you feel like you're getting too drunk, tap your teeth. If they're numb, stop drinking."

She saluted him—a super-goofy move that made Bash erupt in laughter. When he recovered, he saluted her back. Everything was chill! But by the time they approached Manny Sanchez's friend group, Audre was holding her cup so tightly, her fingers were shaking.

He whisper-yelled in her ear, "Just have fun! Go-with-the-flow energy."

She nodded and then said to the group, "Hey, y'all! WHAT'S UP, WHORES?"

Maybe a little less energy, he thought.

The group turned around. Seeing Audre, they greeted her with tipsy hugs and "girl, how are you?" and "let's take a pic" and "omigod you're here this summer?" and "let's get fucccked up" and "wait, you're really drinking?" and "you know Bash?"

By the time everyone had finished the initial niceties, Audre had almost finished her punch. Bash had made it less potent, but as he watched her, he realized the punch had zoomed right to her head. Almost immediately, her face went all warm, gooey, and smiley.

Her expression was simply the most adorable thing he'd ever seen.

Soon, Audre was talking to everyone in the group—except Manny. Was she intimidated? Bash didn't get it. He was just a short king in a polo shirt and khakis. What was so scary?

Bash stepped in, giving Manny a pound. "I didn't catch your name?"

"Whassup, dawg, I'm Manny."

"Good to meet you, Manny. You know Audre, right?"

"Yeah, we go way back, right, Audre?" Manny winked. "That debate championship."

Audre smirked goofily. "Back in 2021, yep. I killed you," she said a bit too forcefully. She tried to dull the edge with a little laugh, but it came out as a witchy cackle.

"I wouldn't say you killed me. If memory serves, I let you win, 'cause you were cute."

"Manny Sanchez, I murdered you. It was a bloodbath." She pretended to point a gun in his direction. "Manny down!"

Manny fake-laughed, then turned to talk to the girl next to him. Audre was bombing.

"You're being too competitive," Bash told her, blocking his mouth with his cup in case Manny was a lip reader. "This guy needs to be the alpha. I can tell by his little . . . outfit."

"Fuck that. *I'm* the alpha."

"I know, I know," he said, grinning because she was adorable. "You want some advice? It's misogynistic, but it'll work on him."

"Tell me," she said, leaning in closer to him.

"Compliment him. Ask him to explain something. Be positive, upbeat. Laugh at his jokes, not at *him*. You think he's cute, right?"

"He's in the vithinity . . . vicinity of cute," she slurred. "I guess I lisp when I'm drunk?"

"Listen, you just made it to ten PM. So, you're one challenge down. All you need to do now is . . . uh, kiss this dude, and we're done. Let's focus."

"I need another punch," she said, looking around for the deejay. Bash, with a worried expression, saw her sway a bit.

"Did you eat? You seem hella tipsy."

She tapped her two front teeth. "I'm not hella tipthy."

"Nah, I'm cutting you off."

"You can't cut me off."

"Maybe this was a bad idea. I'm supposed to be looking out for you. Yeah, let's go."

"It's not up to you! What are you gonna do, pick me up and carry me out of here?"

His gaze met hers for a few charged moments. She looked up at him, all radiant eyes and impossible dimples. She was *too much*. As if pulled by an invisible string, he leaned down close to her ear. And then, he lightly grazed her earlobe with his lips and replied, "Don't tempt me."

A shuddering tremble rolled through her. Her mouth parted and she sucked in a gasp, her cheeks flushing a deep, ruby red. The air crackled with tension.

"Hey! Y'all dating?" asked a tipsy, college-age brunette neither of them knew.

"We're just friends," they responded quickly, jolted out of that blazing moment.

"Love that for me. I can talk to you, then?" The brunette licked her lips, cozying up to Bash. "I've got some eddies... you want?"

"Who's Eddie?" asked Audre.

"Eddies are edibles." Cackling, the girl hooked her arm in Bash's. "OMG she's so cute."

Bash didn't want this girl hanging on him. But he knew that if his face showed what he was thinking, then everyone would know he was crazy about Audre. For her challenge to work, Manny had to believe there was nothing between them. So, the girl stayed.

But there was no way to communicate his strategy to Audre. She saw that chick all over Bash and, in her intoxicated state, was not amused.

"I'm ready for my challenge," announced Audre. She finished off her cup, crushed it in her hand, and slammed it into Bash's chest. A little too hard.

"Cool. I'll just chill here with, uh..." Deeply uncomfortable, Bash shot the girl a smile that was closer to a grimace. "Sorry, what's your name again?"

"Fiona. As in Apple."

"Great to meet you, Apple," said Audre, who almost got it right. She tossed her braids, turned her ring inward, and then scooted over to her target.

"So, what brought you out tonight?" Audre asked Manny. Her smile revealed lipstick on her teeth. Subtly, Bash caught her eye and ran his tongue over his teeth. Audre mouthed *stop being weird*. He shook his head, fast, and mouthed *lipstick*. With a yelp, she quickly scrubbed her teeth with a finger.

"Hmm, why am I here? I'm just vibing." Manny winked at her. "Soulmate searching."

"The concept of soulmates," started Audre, "was invented by the patriarchy to tie a woman to a man so she could cook and clean for him while bearing his seven children."

Bash shot her a frown over Fiona's head.

"Um... I like your tan," she said to Manny with a feathery giggle.

"Yeah? Just got back from the Hamptons. Eboni Green's having a party at her beach house next weekend. You pulling up?"

"I might," she said in a sultry voice. "How are you getting there?"

Just then, Bash's phone lit up in his palm. Clio's pic flashed on-screen—and, of course, Audre saw. His stomach sank, knowing how bad it looked. Clio, his not-girlfriend, was calling him on a Friday night.

A fiery expression thundered across Audre's face. Abruptly, she grabbed Manny's punch. "You're not gonna finish this, are you?"

Before he could answer, she downed half of it in twenty seconds.

"Noooo," groaned Bash, running his hand over his face.

"You're wild, Audre!" exclaimed Manny. "I didn't know."

"I am wild as hell, boi!" she exclaimed.

"Audre," started Bash, "what are you *doing?*"

"Why do you care?" grumbled Fiona.

"Good queth-tion," slurred Audre.

"Let's get outta here," Manny told Audre. "Ever been to Brooklyn Steele? Not to brag, but I'm kind of known there. My cousin bartends on weeknights. Anyway, he said some no-name rapper, Pia Colada, is performing?"

"Oh, Bash saw her last week," said Audre, glaring at him.

"She any good?" asked Manny, who was disinterested in talking to Bash.

"She had some skills," said Bash, who was even less interested in talking to Manny.

"She wasn't all that," said Audre.

"You weren't there," said Bash.

"I was there!" exclaimed Fiona, who wasn't but hated losing Bash's attention.

"Well, I saw that video." Audre hooked her arm in Manny's. "He's impressed 'cause she rhymed Bash with whiplash."

Bash smirked. "Can you do better?"

"Can I do better? Can I do better?"

Manny looked fascinated. "Wait, can you do better?"

"Y'all aren't ready," exclaimed Audre, buzzing with liquid confidence. "Manny, do you beatbox? I need a beat. No fuck that, I'll freestyle a cappella."

"Omigod, A, please rethink this," hissed Bash under his breath.

"I got bars, B! I'm only telling y'all this 'cause I'm drunk, but every night before I go to sleep I think of rhymes that would kill Pia Colada's in a battle."

Bash's mouth fell open. "You do what?"

"Every night," she repeated, too tipsy to feel shame. Then she took a deep breath—and started spitting.

Off the top of her head.

Poorly.

Four-point-oh but I got a fatty
J/K about the ass but I'm still a baddie
I'm talking to this kid, yo his name is Manny
I get thleepy . . . I mean, SLEEPY after nine but I gotta rally
Let's keep it a bean, tho, I came with Bash
Hot like fire yo he gives me, um . . . what else rhymes with Bash . . . oh,
     I got it, HEAT RASH
Can't stay all night, bitch, I gotta dash
Apple's a broke bitch but I got that cash

"BROKE?" exclaimed Fiona, offended.

By the time Audre reached the end, a group had formed

around her, cheering and clapping, cell phones recording every moment. And suddenly, she felt a lot less drunk. Rapping in the middle of a party when you're not, in fact, a rapper? Definitely sobering.

Frantically, Audre reached for Bash's arm. "Get me out of here, immediately!"

"Say less," he answered.

Without saying goodbye, Bash grabbed her hand and led her through the maze of the dance floor, back to the entrance. Until Audre abruptly stopped walking, jerking Bash backward. She was frozen to the spot.

Bash looked down at her. But her eyes were focused on something off to the right. He followed her sight line to a guy standing in a small group. He was a stocky dude wearing short twists and a letterman's jacket. In ninety-degree weather?

Audre squeezed Bash's hand, hard, digging her fingers into his palm. He saw what condition she was in and, without asking questions, said, "Three-three-three. Remember? Focus on something you can see, hear, and touch."

"Right." She squeezed her eyes shut. "I see darkness. I hear a light-skinned Bieber song. I feel you holding my hand."

She exhaled shakily, then she opened her eyes and peered up at him. Bash nodded and squeezed her hand. Then her gaze landed on that guy again, and she started trembling.

"Audre, what's going on?" asked Bash, starting to panic himself.

She just shook her head, eyes welling up.

"Talk to me. What's wrong?"

"It's E-Ellison," she rasped, her voice almost too flimsy for him to hear. "He...he was my prom date. He recorded me having a panic attack. And he laughed at me, and..."

She wasn't finished. But Bash was gone. He'd approached Ellison, knocking into his shoulder. To him, time seemed to slow down and speed up at the same time. The music faded, the humid surge of the crowd disappeared, and all that was left was him, Ellison, and Audre.

"Watch where you're going, man," said Ellison. "Do I know you?"

"What's your name?" asked Bash calmly.

"Ellison."

"Who was your prom date?"

"Audre Mercy-Moore..."

"Did you laugh at her?"

Ellison's jaw went slack. "You saw the video? How? We deleted..."

He never finished. Bash, in a white-hot rage, reared back and punched him in the jaw—putting all one-hundred-and-ninety pounds of lean, powerful muscle behind it. Ellison went flying into a group of girls, innocently shaking their asses, and then they all toppled to the floor. Bash was on him in seconds, trapping him in a headlock as Ellison blindly punched at nothing. Then the party devolved into mayhem. Bash and Ellison were rolling around on the ground, tripping people up. Folks were screaming, chairs were flying, and people were recording it all on their phones. Unfortunately for Ellison, Bash was a whole head taller than him and quick on his feet. Unfortunately for Bash, Ellison was a quarterback and a wrestler, and knew how to slide out of headlocks.

So, he flipped Bash over and clocked him in the nose.

"Stop recording!" a curvy blond girl screamed at her three blond friends. "Recording two African American guys fighting is a wild microaggression!"

"It's a *macro*aggression!" yelled her boyfriend. "PHONES DOWN."

Quickly, everyone in the vicinity stopped recording and deleted.

That's when Audre jumped in, stunning Ellison with a quick, hard kick to his shin. As he roared, she helped Bash to his feet. Suddenly hit with an overwhelming sense of purpose, she grabbed his hand and dragged him outside. Then they took off running into the night.

Chapter 24

Powered by pure adrenaline, Audre and Bash ran several blocks and then turned a corner, stopping at a bodega. And now they were sharing a bottled water and pacing. He was bruised and furious. She was shaky and shocked.

"Bash, what the hell?" Audre's breath came in short gasps. "Why'd you punch him?"

"I couldn't let him get away with hurting you like that," he said, pacing, his fists opening and closing. His right eye was puffy and turning purple, and he had a bloody cut along his cheek.

"But I didn't ask you to do that!"

He stopped pacing, standing in front of her and practically vibrating with anger. "You think I wanted to jump that guy? I fucking hate fighting, man. I'm a pacifist! I walked out of *Creed 2*! I did it because he hurt you."

"Oh, of course you did." Audre was now raging herself. She stormed over to him so that they were face-to-face—only a few feet apart.

"What's that mean?"

"It means you *think* you did it for me. But the truth? Men always use women as an excuse to perform toxic masculinity, and if I'm being honest, I—"

"Audre!"

Her eyes widened. Bash took one step closer to her, his expression mellowing from fury to wide-open, vulnerable hurt. And something else. Something Audre couldn't place. Not then. Because in that moment, she was physically too close to Bash to think clearly. The air went vivid, so electric it crackled. There was a steady buzz under her feet, like she was standing on a subway platform. She was lost in the overwhelming intensity of his expression, his physicality, his words.

Lost.

"Doesn't he know that was a private thing?" rasped Bash, overcome with emotion. "He saw something that you don't show anyone. It was a privilege that he ever got to be that close to you. To see you like that. Why didn't he make you feel better? Try to help, or comfort you, whatever. Why wasn't he good to you? You deserve that. And now you'll always remember your prom like that. I wish I could correct all your bad memories, Audre. Erase them and give you better ones. If I see him again, I fucking promise you, if I see him . . ."

Bash's face was pulsing different colors under the neon lights of the bodega. Something that was frozen in her melted into a puddle. Audre was standing there in front of him, but she didn't feel whole. She felt shattered into a million pieces.

Later, they wouldn't be able to remember who reached for who first. But they collided into each other, locking into an all-consuming embrace. It wasn't careful, polite, or unsure. It was *certain*. The entire length of their bodies were pressed against each other's. And still, it didn't feel close enough.

Audre clung to him, inhaling his sunny, beachy scent. Intoxicated, Bash buried his face in the warmth of Audre's neck. A low, vulnerable sound escaped his throat. Arms wrapped around her, he bent down, drew her in even closer, and then stood up to his full height—lifting her feet off the ground.

Had her feet touched the ground since she met him?

They stayed that way forever. Hearts thundering against each other, drowning in sensation. Finally, slowly, Bash lowered Audre to the ground. They were still in each other's space, though. Audre was close enough to count his eyelashes. To feel his breath on her skin. Bash Henry was overwhelming.

"You fought for me. You fought. For me?"

"And I'd do it again," he whispered, ghosting his lips against hers.

The chemistry was so strong, she gasped and pulled away, pressing her knuckles to her mouth. Then he dipped back down, drawing her into a *real* kiss this time. Hot, passionate, searching. She didn't know how to kiss like this—but it was okay because, oh, Bash knew what he was doing. His soft, sensual lips ignited her, lighting fires throughout her body. Tenderly, he nibbled on her bottom lip. She whimpered a little. He smiled a little. And things got serious. He gathered her braids in one hand, tilting her head back, and kissed her deeply, hungrily, sucking her tongue into his mouth.

That's when she *melted*.

Tingles fluttered throughout her body, scrambling her brain.

He kissed her till she was liquid in his arms, till her head was spinning, and if she wasn't already tipsy, Bash's mouth would've taken her there.

Her curfew was the last thing on her mind. Turns out? It was the least of her problems.

1, 2, 3, 4 … THRIVE!
A Teen's Rules for Flourishing on This Dying Planet

By Audre Mercy-Moore

Rule 9:
Unless your last name is Thee Stallion, there's never a reason to rap in public.

Chapter 25

Audre and Bash kissed forever. Could've been min-utes, but it felt like hours. And when they finally stopped, the vibe was still there. It was almost one week past July Fourth, but Brooklyn Bridge fireworks flared far in the distance, brightening the inky sky. They walked around the neighborhood in a hazy daze—but touching each other the whole time. Holding hands. Hooking arms. Hug-walking, which was complicated given Audre's buzz.

They didn't mention the kiss, though. It was like they had an unspoken agreement not to go there, because there was too much to unpack. Was Audre's whole "strictly business" thing out the window? What did it mean? Where did they go from here? Who's responsible? Neither one was prepared to answer these questions. No, tonight, they just wanted to be lost in the feeling—no matter how unrealistic the feeling was.

They barely spoke at all, to be honest. Too many words would've ruined it.

One hard truth, though, was that Audre needed to sober up

before getting home. So, Bash stepped in. At a corner store, he bought her a one-liter bottle of water and a soft pretzel. He sat with her on a bench until she felt normal. It wasn't until she successfully walked in a straight line down the sidewalk that they decided to head back. But first, Bash checked his phone.

"Umm . . . Audre? When did you say your curfew was?"

"Eleven." She exhaled contentedly, her head leaning against Bash's shoulder. Then reality hit and she bolted upright. "Oh no. Oh God. I haven't checked my phone at all."

"It's 10:48. You're only fifteen blocks up." Bash stood up and reached out to her. "Here, hop on my back."

Audre cocked her head, disbelieving. "You're joking. Who are you, Edward Cullen? You're gonna fly me through the blue-tinted evergreens of Washington State?"

"Basically. But I'm gonna run. We can make it."

"With me on your back?"

"There's a whole Finnish track and field sport where men run while holding women up on their shoulders. Google it later. Come on, we don't have time to debate this."

Did she have any other options? Not really. So, Bash bent down, and in one fell swoop easily hoisted Audre up on his back. And then he took off. Ten minutes later, he was dropping her off at her front door—exactly two minutes early.

• • •

Unfortunately, Audre's apartment door flew open before Bash had a chance to run down the stairs. (He was fast, but not that fast.)

Audre's stepdad, Shane, was at the door. He looked like he'd just run out of a burning building—incorrectly buttoned flannel shirt, baby-food-stained joggers, and a wild expression.

If Audre wasn't totally sober before, she was now.

"Who the hell is this?" Shane asked her without so much as a glance at the tall kid frozen next to his stepdaughter.

Audre and Bash looked at each other, eyes huge and mouths sealed shut.

Shane took a step forward. "I said, who the hell is this?"

Audre, who had never heard this even-keeled, unruffled, chill-as-hell man raise his voice, nearly jumped out of her skin. Shane wasn't a disciplinarian. He was like her fun uncle. She could count on one hand the times they'd gotten annoyed with each other. And it was usually about something dumb, like who ate the last Girl Scout Samoa cookie.

Shane never yelled at Audre.

"It's B-Bash," she stammered. "This . . . this is Bash. My friend. My new friend."

Shane looked at Bash, who was two inches taller than he was. Audre couldn't imagine what was going through his head. She'd never brought a guy home. The last time a boy was even in her house was four years ago, before Shane was in the picture.

Eva had been out at a book event, and Audre snuck half her seventh-grade class over to do one-on-one therapy sessions. Her babysitter snitched, though. So, Eva came home early, made Audre return the two hundred dollars (cash!) she'd made that afternoon, and then double freaked out 'cause one (1!!) of the clients was a boy. It would never make sense to Audre why her mom—a card-carrying, super-progressive Black feminist/girl power/shero advocate—was so threatened by the presence of unchaperoned boys within six feet of her daughter. Nothing about Eva was conservative, except for this one hangup. Whatever the reason, Audre had gotten in so much trouble that one time in seventh grade that she never invited a boy over again.

And, judging by the way Shane was shooting daggers at Bash, Eva had gotten to him, too. She knew how bad it looked. Bash had a black eye forming and a jagged cut on his lower cheek. Plus, his arms were all banged up from tousling on the cement courtyard floor.

The sleeve of his shirt is torn, noticed Audre, cringing. *He looks like trouble.*

And with her tear-smudged mascara and blotchy skin from crying, she probably didn't look much better.

"Hi, I'm Bash. Um...Sebastian. Good to meet you," he said politely, sticking out one extremely tattooed arm to shake his hand. Shane glared at him until he dropped it. And then he turned back to Audre.

"Where were you? I was texting you all night. Your mom had an episode. I wanted to take her to the ER, but she was in too much pain to just sit in a waiting room all night. I convinced the paramedics to give her some IV pain meds at home, on the couch. She's resting now. It's been a nightmare."

Audre shut her eyes, going limp against the doorframe. "Oh no. Oh no, Shane. And I wasn't there to watch Baby Alice."

"That's why I was calling you. Since when don't you pick up your phone?"

"Wait, where is Alice?"

"One of your mom's friends picked her up. We've gotta get a fucking babysitter—there just hasn't been any time." He ran his hand over his face. Audre saw he had dark circles beneath his eyes.

"I'm...I'm really sorry. I am," she said emphatically, her eyes pleading. "Look, I was out and accidentally forgot to check my phone. So much was going on..."

"So much," cosigned Bash. Seeing the murderous look on Shane's face, though, he shut up.

"But I made curfew!"

"Question. Since when are you so unreachable? First the beach, now this. Since when do you ignore your phone?"

"And who's this kid who looks like he was knocked out in the first round?" asked Eva.

Her voice was weak and small but clear enough to travel from the couch to the doorway. Audre stuck her head into the apartment and saw her mom propped up on the couch (i.e., her bed) wearing boxers and an old Cheshire Prep tee. She had an icepack tied to her head and a series of Band-Aids along the inside of her arms.

"Eva, lie back down," said Shane lovingly but firmly. "Just rest, okay? I've got this."

"I'm fine," she said. "You guys, get in here, out of the doorway."

Shane shut the door, joining Eva on the couch. Sheepishly, Audre and Bash skulked into the apartment, awkwardly taking their places in front of Baby Alice's playpen. Of course, there was nowhere to sit, thanks to the never-ending renovations.

Eva peered up at them with one eye open. "Who's the fighter?"

"Me?" asked Bash. "I'm Bash, ma'am. Sebastian."

Shane and Eva glanced at each other.

"What were you doing with my daughter?"

251

"Excuse me?" said Audre. "He wasn't doing anything. What are you assuming?"

"Are you kidding?" Eva's voice was a trembly rasp. "You're practically hyperventilating. He's bleeding. Who knows what you guys were up to!"

"But why would you assume the worst? Yes, Bash got in a fight tonight. But he was fighting for me. To defend me."

Shane groaned, dropping his face in his hand.

Eva sighed with her entire body. "Defend you from what, exactly?"

Audre's heart was thundering. Sweat beaded on her forehead, and her head pounded. The only people who knew about Ellison and prom night were Reshma and Bash.

She took a deep breath and dove in.

"He was defending me from my traumatic prom date. Ellison." Audre blurted this out, shocking herself at her directness. As she heard herself say the words, she decided she couldn't go further. The panic attack, the video? Nope. There was no way she could reveal that to her mom and Shane.

All the color seemed to drain from Eva's cheeks. Shane's jaw clenched, his hands curling into fists.

"Traumatic prom date?" whispered Eva. "That little shit, what did he do?"

"It's not what you're thinking. It's . . . something else."

"I'll kill him," muttered Shane.

"No, *I'll* kill him," said Eva. "Audre, why didn't you tell me about this?"

"Well, I would've, if you were interested in anything other

than your baby and the wedding and your book. You barely even asked me about prom. All you cared about was if parents would be at the after-party. What are you so scared of?"

"This!" yelled Eva, aiming her index finger at Bash, then Audre, then back at Bash. She was painkiller-woozy—but not too zonked to yell at Audre. "This is what I'm scared of. You, becoming unreachable. You, keeping whatever horrible prom thing happened from me. You, getting in over your head with some boy. Exhibit A... Bash, who thinks defending your honor means allowing himself to get absolutely rocked in the jaw by some lowlife."

"With all due respect, ma'am, I won," said Bash quietly. "He was a lowlife, though."

Shane shook his head, the corners of his mouth pulled down. "Not now, son."

Bash put up his hands in surrender and shut up.

"I'm trying to protect you," said Eva.

"From what, though?"

"The fact that you don't know what horrors can befall a teen girl if she's not careful."

"Horrors?" Audre shook her head, furious. She didn't deserve being treated like a criminal in her own home. "Come on. I'm a perfect kid. You should feel lucky. Okay, fine, I missed your calls tonight, but what about all the times I didn't? What about all the times I was here, worrying about you? Watching you for any signs that you were struggling? Pretending I was ready to end our movie date or brunch date or playground visit or *American Horror Story* marathon 'cause I could see in the way your shoulders crept

253

up toward your ears that you were dying. Can you imagine what that's like as a kid? To always be on alert? Before Shane, there was me, taking care of you."

"You think I don't know this, you ungrateful little..." Eva caught herself, and started again. "I know you were on alert. It haunts me, every day of the world, that my illness affects you so deeply. But I'm your mother. Everything you feel about me, I feel about you times ten. When I can't reach you, the bottom falls out. When it happens twice, I think you're dead."

"But why do you jump to me being dead, Mom? Why are you scared?"

"She just is," answered Shane quietly. "Listen to your mother."

"Audre, you're a great kid. You're my favorite person. You're my idol. Please don't rebel till you go to college. My heart can't take it."

"But I don't want to be your idol. That's an impossible standard. Yes, you're perfect. And Grandma Lizette's perfect. And our maternal bloodline is so girlbossy, you wrote a book about them. But I just want to be normal."

With finality, Shane dropped his palms on his thighs and stood up. "Look, we've all been through it tonight. Eva, Audre—let's sleep on it and revisit tomorrow. I'll see you out, Bash."

Audre followed them as Shane walked Bash to the door.

"Where do you live, son? Should I get you an Uber?" asked Shane.

"No thanks, I'll walk. I'm on Prospect Park West."

"Oh word?" And then Audre watched her stepdad become Mentorship Shane, which, after Chef Shane, was the most vivid Shane. "I think I see what happened here."

"You do?"

"Yeah. You live on the Park, niggas around the city think you're bougie, so you're out here fighting to prove you're tough. Listen, dog, you have nothing to prove. You understand? Black manhood is so much more nuanced than what these white kids think."

"Umm...that's not..."

"One time, when I was your age, I had a job at a gas station. It was freezing, ice everywhere. A customer, this preppy white guy, was like, 'Watch out for the black ice!' I thought he said, 'Watch out for the Black guys.' I'm looking around like, 'I'm the only Black guy here.' So then I felt called to beat his ass. For what, though? It was pointless. I spent a night in jail, and to this day a confused white man is walking the earth wondering why a gas station attendant tackled him in '05." He paused. "Keep it a buck, that part I don't care as much about."

"Shane, please," sighed Audre.

"I'll get you an Uber," he whispered to Bash. "It's late. You want some ice for that eye? An Advil?"

"Really, I don't even feel it. And I'm sorry about..." Bash gestured toward his bruised, cut face. "This...really isn't what it looks like."

"Never is, is it?"

"It's just, I really like Audre. Someone disrespected her and I can't allow that."

Even in the middle of family chaos, Audre went all warm and tingly all over. Shyly, she looked down at her toes, her heartbeat roaring in her ears.

Bash stood up for me like an actual knight in shining armor, she thought. *I didn't know this was something I needed or wanted.*

Meanwhile, Shane had slapped Bash on the back. "Good man. Between us, I'm glad you looked out for Audre. But be safe, understand? Things can go from a tousle to jail faster than you can blink. Especially for us."

"I know. My brain just shut off. Like a light going out. Pffft."

"That happens sometimes, when you have strong...pla-tonic...feelings for someone."

Audre's cheeks went hot. She and Bash shared a split-second glance before looking away.

"You seem like a really present stepdad, sir. You're cool. My dad never talked to me like this. He just yelled."

At this, Shane's ears perked up. "I'm sorry to hear that. If you ever need to talk, you know where I stay. No pressure, but I lead a teen mentorship group on Saturdays at Park Slope Methodist Church. If you ever find yourself needing a present stepdad."

Bash nodded shyly. "I might take you up on that one day."

Audre watched this interaction go down, feeling heart-warmed. In a different context, it seemed like Bash and Shane could be friends. Too bad her mom only saw him as a threat.

Bash gave Shane a pound. Then he awkwardly waved goodbye to Audre. She smiled, wearily, and wiggled her fingers at him.

"Have a nice evening, you guys," said Bash, heading for the stairwell.

"Same to you, kid."

●   ●   ●

Ten minutes later, Audre and Eva were still going at it. Shane sat next to his wife, arms crossed and frowning at the floor.

And Audre was in a fiery rage. (Underneath her rage, though, was relief that Eva hadn't noticed she'd been drinking.)

"You were awful to him, Mom. For no reason. You don't understand me. All you care about is appearances. And I know what you're thinking. 'Mercy girls don't run around with guys who get in fights.' But he didn't do anything!"

"You have no idea what I'm thinking, Audre." She was talking as if she were in a daze or a trance. "And it's my job to steer you in the healthiest direction. I don't care if you're mad about it."

With that, Eva grabbed her icepack and blanket and stormed into the bedroom.

Shane clasped his hands together, elbows on his knees.

"What?" asked Audre.

"I don't know, man." He shrugged. "I kinda like the kid."

Chapter 26

Much later, Audre was lying on the couch, too depressed to change out of her clothes. She was frozen, staring at her mom's gallery wall—the framed portraits Audre had painted of the two of them, from the time Audre was two up until age twelve. Her eyes unfocused, welled up with tears, and then focused again. It had almost become a kind of meditative exercise. The longer she stared, the more she disconnected from the trash fire of her life. The longer she zeroed in on those relics—artifacts from a younger, simpler time—the easier it was to pretend that she hadn't gotten herself into a world of (unfair, undeserved) trouble. How did she end up here?

Audre rewound it all in her mind. A mere month ago, she had hoped she was entering her best summer ever. But then her dad decided she was no longer welcome in his home. And Reshma insisted that she "live a little." And then she met Bash and he scrambled the synapses in her brain.

But what was her part in all of that? What was so unsatisfying about her world that drove her to unravel everything she'd been building her whole life? To torch her relationship with her mother? To be the reason the sweetest guy in the world got in a public fight in front of a hundred wasted, heat-fried people? If someone panicked and called the cops, the repercussions could've been cataclysmic for Bash.

Mercy girls don't run around with boys who get into fights. How dare Eva say that to her. As if Bash was just "a boy who got into fights." She didn't know him. She hadn't even asked what happened. It's like Eva took one look at them standing in the doorway—admittedly looking guilty of something—and decided she knew the story. Bash was only guilty of trying to defend her. You'd think an overprotective mom would love that.

Audre was an evolved person. Like Bash, she didn't believe in physically laying hands on anyone. And she wasn't a fan of violence masquerading as "chivalrous" or "gentlemanly" behavior. But she had to admit—it lit a fire in her to see Bash knock Ellison out! Ellison fucking deserved it. For months, her traumatic prom secret had been gnawing at her insides, her self-esteem ripped to shreds. She'd been terrified that the video had leaked somehow. But tonight? For the first time, she felt like her anxiety balloon had popped, and the pressure was slowly seeping out.

And Bash did it for her. She couldn't pretend that it didn't make her melt. No one had ever fought for her before. She didn't even know she was the kind of girl who could inspire a guy to take such action. And definitely not a guy like Bash, a sweetie-pie cinnamon roll who had philosophical conversations with lanternflies.

And then there was that kiss. That endless, dizzying, so-good-you-forget-your-name kiss. Yes, it completed her fourth challenge, but it was so much more than that. Bash Henry's mouth, arms, hands, everything—he'd practically changed the molecular structure of her entire body.

But now that she was home and sobering up, insistent little questions began to emerge. What if it hadn't been special to him? What if he kissed every girl like that? Including Clio? Besides, Audre knew that he was kind to everyone he came across. For God's sake, he'd even charmed Barry the Silent Neighbor and Wilder the Valedictorian *Shrek* Singer.

But what if she was really, really falling for Bash? What then?

She could feel her chest start to rise and fall, fast. Then it got tight. Her breath was coming in short gasps, and her heart thundered against her rib cage. Her palms started to tingle. And then the tears came, and she felt like all her atoms were flying away from each other, in opposite directions. She was having a panic attack, right there on the couch. She tried to keep quiet, to avoid waking up her family. She didn't want them to know she had this affliction, that she wasn't their perfect daughter. That she barely made it through her award ceremony speech. That she was falling apart.

Remember the 333 method, she told herself. *Focus on what you can see, hear, and touch. I see a rocking chair blocking the hallway, waiting there until the nursery renovation is done. I hear a fire engine siren through the cracked window. And I can touch my cameo ring, which witnessed me get absolutely wasted tonight. Great. This is having the opposite effect.*

She lay there, trying to ride out the violent attack. When it didn't work, she climbed out onto the fire escape, dangling her feet over Barry's garden, her head tilted back against the scratchy brick of the building. Tears streamed down her cheeks as she shook uncontrollably and wrapped her arms around herself.

The night air washed over her, carrying the powdery-sweet scent of honeysuckle and freesia from Barry's garden. She breathed in and released, breathed in and released, until she finally started calming down. Her hands stilled. Her breathing slowed. And then her phone rang.

Bash.

"Hi!"

"Hi. I'm so sorry..."

"No, I'm sorry..."

"No, it's me, it's my fault..."

"It's mine. If I hadn't told you about Ellison, you wouldn't have gotten into that fight, and I wouldn't have ignored my phone, again, and tonight wouldn't have happened."

"No," he said with quiet composure. "No. It was me. I have a habit of messing things up. I feel terrible that your mom got so mad at you. I know how close you two are, and how much she means to you. I should've been taking better care of you."

"Taking care of me? But I don't need to be taken care of, Bash. The whole point of the Challenge Experiment was to stumble and fuck up and make mistakes. And to learn from it all. My mom is mad at me, yeah. But when I write an amazing book and get into Stanford, she'll be proud again. She will."

"Do you have to be getting an A-plus in life for her to love you?"

"I don't know. I've never not gotten an A-plus in life," she said honestly. "Until now."

"Until me."

No. She couldn't have Bash thinking that tonight's blowup was his fault. This was about her and her mom, and years of a codependent relationship that functioned beautifully when Audre was at her mom's service but imploded when she went her own way. It wasn't about Bash. And more importantly, she didn't want this to chase him away. Especially not before they could figure out what they were. Why the emotions were so high, why it felt like the air between them was shimmering, moving, sparking every time they were together.

"Listen . . ."

"No, you listen."

Audre stopped talking because she'd never heard Bash take such a firm, stern tone.

"I think you were right before," he said. "We shouldn't hang out anymore."

The bottom fell out. Audre's mouth went dry, she sat up too fast, the world was spinning. She dropped her forehead to her knees, folding herself in half.

"What do you mean?" she whispered into the phone.

"I like you too much to start ruining your life," he said, unconsciously dropping his voice to a whisper, too. "I've done this before."

"What do you mean?"

He said nothing—she could barely hear him breathing.

"When did you do this before? With who?"

"It doesn't matter. But I can't do it again," said Bash, who sounded more like he was talking to himself than to Audre.

"Is this about Clio?"

"No."

"Why is she always calling you?"

Silence.

"I'm sick of this. Why are you such a mystery? Why won't you just tell me who she is? Why won't you tell me whose life you ruined? And what really happened with your dad? Who are you? I know your name isn't Bash Henry. It's Sebastian Wallace, and you're one of the top five high school sprinters in the country. So, what are you doing here? Not running, and not even planning to go to college? What happened to you?"

"How did you find that out?"

"Google is free, genius."

"Did...did you find out anything else?" He sounded panicked.

"No. Do you hear yourself? What don't you want me to find out?"

"Nothing. It's just...better for you if we don't talk for a little while." His voice was choked, strangled. It was as if someone had written a script and they were forcing him to read his lines. He didn't sound convincing. He sounded lightweight, flimsy, and fragile, like a strong wind would've blown him miles away.

"Don't do this." She'd always told her clients not to beg for someone's affections. If he wanted you, he'd show you. If it was real, you wouldn't need to convince someone. But maybe she wasn't as wise as she thought she was.

Fuck it, she thought.

"Please," she whispered. "I've never had a friend like you."

Audre wished she had the guts to go further, to say *Please tell me you like me as much as I like you; please tell me that Clio and all the other girls don't matter; please tell me I haven't imagined something between us; please please please don't move all the way to Myrtle Beach.* But she wasn't that brave. Or crazy.

Good thing she didn't go there, because Bash's silence was deafening. After minutes that stretched on forever, he finally spoke. And his voice was unrecognizable.

"I don't want to be friends," said Bash.

Audre shut her eyes. The air went out of her, like she'd just absorbed a vicious punch to the stomach.

"Why." She said it like a statement, not a question.

"You don't understand what I'm saying. I can't just be friends with you. I can't kiss you without wanting to do it all the time. I can't talk to you without wanting you forever. And if I hurt you, I'd never forgive myself. That's why I need to go."

The connection went dead.

Chapter 27

"The city looks so cinematic from here," said Clio. "Like a postcard."

It certainly did. On a whim, Reshma had invited Clio to the rooftop bar at the William Vale Hotel in Williamsburg, home of the longest outdoor pool in the city and insane views of the Lower Manhattan skyline. Reshma and Clio weren't supposed to be there without parental guardians. But Reshma's parents had a lifetime day pass (such an oxymoron, "lifetime day") and the bouncers had a soft spot for Reshma. At the beginning of every summer, Reshma slipped them a few bottles of wine lifted from her parents' wine cellar, and in exchange they turned a blind eye to her underage presence.

The rooftop pool seemed like the perfect place to hang out with Clio. She was an outdoorsy girl. Outdoorsy people didn't waste beautiful days being indoors. So, a museum, coffee shop, or shopping date felt off-brand. And it was a beautiful day. Bright, sunny, warm-but-not-sweltering, and shimmering with possibility. And up on the glitzy rooftop—crowded with twentysomething hotties—Reshma and Clio were living the life. They were lying under a cozy, striped cabana, sipping fruity drinks and gleaming from Reshma's Supergoop! sunscreen.

"Isn't it like being in a resort in Ibiza?" asked Reshma, adjusting the hip tie on her lipstick-red string bikini.

"I wouldn't know," admitted Clio. "I've never been to Ibiza. Or anywhere in Europe."

"You're basically in Europe now." She lowered her sunglasses and looked around. "These people aren't American. They're rich international kids playing with Mummy and Daddy's money."

"How can you tell?"

Because, she thought, *I'm one of them.*

She motioned for Clio to come closer and whispered, "Stilettos at the pool. Heavy on the upper-lip filler and WAG boob jobs. I see two gays with fox eye lifts like Bella Hadid. Also, we're surrounded by a *violent* amount of Louis Vuitton. None of these people work for a living."

"You're so good at that," said Clio in awe. "What's a WAG?"

"Wife and Girlfriend. It's what Brits call women who date or marry pro athletes."

"I'm learning so much. I feel like I should teach you something now. Want to learn about the healing powers of honey?"

Reshma burst into a wide smile. She wiggled her toes to the deejay's Bad Bunny mix, feeling goofy-happy. Something about Clio made her want to slow down and listen to her every word. Hell yes, she wanted to hear her explain the healing powers of honey!

But then Clio said, "It's funny, I didn't hear your accent until you said 'mummy.'"

"It comes and goes. It usually pops out when I'm tired, or buzzed, or..."

"Or what?"

"Really comfortable with someone." Reshma heard herself say this and couldn't believe how corny she sounded. But this had been one of the best days she'd had in this entire, miserable year. She may have started out with an ulterior motive—to lure Clio away from Bash—but now, it was so much more than that. She'd forgotten Bash Henry existed. They'd gotten ice cream, and dim sum, and now they were enjoying lazy-day banter in the sun. What could be better?

Reshma felt like all roads had led her to this moment. Which she was sharing with this exquisite girl. Who did not, in fact, look like she belonged at the Vale pool.

Clio wasn't wearing a full face of makeup. Nor was she dressed in a flashy way. In fact, she was simply wearing a short T-shirt dress over a one-piece swimsuit. But with her freckled cheekbones, sunflower earrings, and lavender-scented locs tumbling loosely to her shoulders... she was breathtaking. It was like she'd been airlifted here from some island paradise.

And Reshma was nervous. Clio was unlike anyone she'd ever had a crush on. She was so... herself. Reshma wasn't herself. Reshma had no idea who she was. Maybe she had more in common with the plastic weirdos partying around them than with Clio.

"So," started Clio, "you feel comfortable with me?"

"I do. I've never invited anyone here." She paused. "Do you feel comfortable with me?"

"Take off your sunglasses and look at me."

Reshma did, cupping her palm over her eyes to block out the sun. (Unfortunately, the glare from her mirrored acrylic nails nearly blinded a nearby pool boy.)

"Believe me, I wouldn't be here if I didn't," said Clio.

Reshma grimaced a little. "I know, this is kind of a scene. Should we go?"

"No, I love visiting your world. We fed swans for me, and now we get bougie for you." She slid on Reshma's sunglasses and leisurely tucked her hands behind her head.

Reshma giggled. "My sunnies look good on you."

"Here's the thing. I know Bella Hadid's famous, but I couldn't tell you what for. And all of this"—she gestured around the pool— "isn't really my world. But it's fun to pretend sometimes."

"This place makes me feel better when I'm depressed. I feel like I'm on top of the city. Everything that's stressful is under me. I feel above it all."

"You know what instantly brightens my mood? Replacing a boring word with a fancy one. Like 'autumnal.' Anybody can say "It's September, fall is here.' But 'It's September and the vibes are autumnal' has flair."

"I love this! My birthday's in October. Autumnal is my birthright. *Autumnal.*"

"Feels good, right? What is it in Hindi?"

"Not sure. I think *sharatkaal ka.*"

"Even prettier."

They smiled at each other for what felt like fifteen minutes.

"Hey, is your name short for Cleopatra?"

"Nope, just Clio. I don't know why Mom named me that. Maybe it was my dad's idea. But I wouldn't know. He's not in my life."

"Oh, I didn't mean to pry," said Reshma.

"No, no, it's not a big deal. I never knew him."

"You can't miss what you've never known, right?"

Clio gazed out at the skyline, going quiet for a moment. And then she shook her head, fast, as if shaking it off. "How are you so wise at only sixteen? You sound like you've lived a million lives."

"I kinda have. I mostly raised myself. My parents are always on tour, or recording, or something. I used to travel around with them, but when I turned thirteen, I started staying home, and they hired people to come check on me. Sometimes I feel British, sometimes I feel Indian, but mostly I feel American. I dream in broken Hindi sometimes, but I think and speak in English. I have godparents on four different continents." She sighed. "I feel like a patchwork of a bunch of different shit that doesn't match. Like a horse with a human head."

"A centaur," said Clio, and then her phone buzzed with an incoming text. With an exasperated noise, she clicked off her phone. Groaning, she tucked her hands behind her head. "Do you ever feel like you've outgrown someone?"

Reshma's breath hitched. Was she about to open up about her boyfriend?

"Why, what's going on?"

"Just drama with . . . the guy," she said haltingly. "Is it cool if I bring him up?"

"No, sure. Of course! I know you're not single."

Clio's mouth tightened a little. "Even though we were long-distance forever, I felt so connected to him. He's artistic, kinda weird, sweet. Tall, which is important when you're a five-ten girl like me. Just a good guy, you know?"

"Mm-hmm. So, what's the problem?" she asked, trying not to seem overcurious.

"The problem is, what I thought was cool at sixteen is annoying now. He thinks he's so edgy 'cause he's slightly femme and has an eyebrow piercing. It's giving 'I'm-the-only-Black-guy-in-an-emo-band.' His energy's just exhausting, you feel me?"

It was all Reshma could do not to guffaw. Clio had described Bash to a tee.

"I absolutely know that genre of guy," she said. "It's like, dude, you're not a unicorn. Welcome to Brooklyn."

Clio chuckled a little and then went all pensive. "Can I ask you something? When did you know you liked girls?"

It's no coincidence, thought Reshma, her heart racing, *that she's asking me this right after complaining about Bash. She's mine, she's mine, she's mine.*

"I never didn't know," she responded, trying to steady her breathing. "But I remember my big sexual awakening. I had a massive crush on the lady elves in *Lord of the Rings*. They rode on these beautiful horses, and ate delicious salads, and lived in forests with waterfalls. They were so at one with the earth." She didn't even realize how Clio figured into this description. "But I didn't want to be one. I wanted to marry one."

"A foresty, animal-loving elf lady was your sexual awakening."

"Your turn. When did you know?"

"I was in love with Clawdeen Wolf from Monster High." She giggled. "A sexy brown werewolf with fire makeup and trendy clothes who was dangerous but had a soft, sweet side."

They looked at each other and couldn't help but melt into nervous laughter.

"Am I Clawdeen?"

"Am I an elf?"

Reshma looked at her. "You have a boyfriend."

She didn't want to say Bash's name. She didn't even want to acknowledge that he existed in their world. It would taint the moment.

"For now I do. But I guess I'm queer-curious."

"I'm really a lesbian," said Reshma. "I'm not searching or curious. I'm certain."

"And you don't want to waste your time with a girl who's just trying it on. I know it's annoying." She paused. "But here's the thing. I've had other opportunities to date girls. Hello, I'm a junior park ranger. Name a gayer job."

Reshma smiled and nodded.

"I'm not here because of an experiment thing. I'm here because of a you thing."

They lay there, flat on their backs, sun beaming down on them, party raging all around them, but it felt quiet. Slowly, Clio inched her left hand toward Reshma, closing the gap between them. Reshma met her in the middle. Gently, their pinky fingers brushed against each other's. A wave of tingly warmth rushed through Reshma. And Clio? Clio gasped. She must've felt something, too.

They turned their heads toward each other, staring in wonder.

"Let's get outta here," said Reshma.

Chapter 28

"Audre Audre Bo-Baudre!"

"Hi, Dad."

"You sound weird."

"I wonder why."

"Are you ever going to forgive me? I told you, honey, I didn't choose my unborn son over you. I really didn't."

"You literally did, though."

"We just didn't have room in the cottage this summer. I was thinking of you. I didn't want you to be uncomfortable."

"You didn't even give it a chance, Dad!"

"This decision was about logistics only. If I had a bigger house, you could've come."

"But I would've stayed in a sleeping bag on the floor. I would've slept in the bathtub."

"I promise you, Audre. I'll make it up to you once your brother's born."

Her brother. Dreading this addition to her already sprawling, complicated family, Audre slid from her sitting position on the couch down to the floor. And there, she stayed. Sprawled flat on her back on the living room rug, surrounded by soft baby books and stuffies—and still in her pajamas at noon. Thankfully, she had the house to herself. She didn't know where the rest of the Mercy-Moore-Halls were, but she hoped they stayed there a while.

In the meantime, her dad was talking at her. He hadn't reached out to her in two weeks. What was the point of him calling her now? Unless it was to admit he'd ruined her life, and/or to change his mind about Dadifornia, though that probably wasn't the case (after all, it was almost August).

Honestly, she wasn't that interested in what her dad had to say.

"Your brother's due date is approaching," said Troy, overflowing with glee.

"Great."

"Audre, I know it was a shock. But what's done is done! You can't un-ring a bell."

You can't un-ring a bell. Her dad wasn't a philosophical kind of guy, but she had to admit that was a smart line. Audre made a mental note to remember it.

"We keep a list of baby names on a dry-erase board in the kitchen," he was saying. "Athena always thinks of great ones while she's teaching her prenatal yoga class. Exciting stuff, isn't it?"

"Thrilling."

"Well," he started, "don't you want to hear them?"

Audre exhaled noisily. "Hear what, Dad?"

"The names. We're leaning toward Canyon, Wisdom, or Truth."

Audre stared up at the ceiling, resisting the urge to say something bitchy.

"So, what do you think?"

"I think those are perfect names."

"Seriously?"

"Yeah, if you're raising a toxic barista."

"Haha. I know you're making fun. But I bet you didn't know that Athena's very active on CoffeeTok."

"Then everybody wins," muttered Audre. "Dad, Mom said something weird to me yesterday. She said there's a lot I don't know about her. What did she mean?"

"Well, I couldn't possibly know. Maybe you should ask her?"

"We're not in the best place," she said, slowly spinning her cameo ring around her finger. She wondered if her ancestors had ever fought their moms to the death. Surely not. Too busy being iconic. "Actually, we've been fighting a lot."

"You two? Lorelai and Rory Gilmore?"

"Dad, you know I don't like it when you call us that. I love *Gilmore Girls*, but we're not them. It's a very narrow, white feminist version of single motherhood."

"Yes, you've pointed this out to me. Several times," he said gently. "I just meant that you and your mom can talk about anything. I'm surprised."

"Well, this summer's been full of 'em," she said. "Mom gets so mad at me when I get the smallest taste of freedom. And I just want to know why. What makes her be so... unfair to me."

"Maybe she's stressed about editing her new book. Isn't *Back to Belle Fleur* about her life, her mom's life, and her grandma's life? Memoirs must be hard to write. Like one long therapy session."

Audre stopped fiddling with her ring. Abruptly, she sat upright.

One long therapy session. The book! Of course.

She was so stupid. The answers were probably right in front of her, in her mom's manuscript. Why hadn't she thought of this before? She needed to read the book. Her mom said she'd "explain everything" to her before it published, but Audre couldn't wait. (And what did that even mean?) The Post-its, Grandma Lizette's bizarre name slipups at the bridal boutique . . . she craved answers.

". . . anyway, I need to go," her dad was saying. "Athena wants me to make her Cream of Wheat with barbecue potato chips sprinkled on top. Pregnant women eat the silliest things, don't they? What a wild ride!"

Long after they hung up, Audre stared at her phone. Lost in thought.

Audre had a hard-and-fast rule, that she never read any of the fifteen books in her mom's Cursed series. Erotica books about a horny witch and a vampire with a nonstop erection. So. Extremely. Embarrassing. Not the sex, but the fact that it was her mom talking about sex. Eva, to Audre, was specifically and exclusively her mother. She wasn't supposed to know about stuff like that.

But Eva's new book wasn't fiction. It wasn't sexy, and it wasn't made-up. It was all true. And it was about the women in Audre's family—including Eva herself—and her mom had been traveling to Louisiana, researching the book for years. Her mom's new book was probably three hundred pages of tea.

If there was something to know about Eva, it'd be in there.

Audre lay on the floor for two more minutes, tops. And then, like she had been shot out of a cannon, she hopped up and scurried into Eva and Shane's bedroom.

She had to work fast, before they got home.

Barely breathing, she sprinted over to her mom's desk. Eva's laptop was sitting atop a pile of novels. She didn't even have to look for it; it wasn't hidden. Eva had no reason to think that Audre would go snooping because she never had before. But there was a first time for everything.

Moving quickly, she opened it, typed in the password (ironically, GilmoreGirls2), and searched the desktop for the file. Audre pulled up the Word doc and quickly scrolled through to the prologue.

> This is a story of my family. Me, my mother, my grandmother, and my great-grandmother. Four women, born into challenging circumstances, who did whatever they needed to do to survive.
>
> For so long, I didn't know where, or who, I came from—beyond my mother, Lizette, who regaled me with family lore that sounded more like fantastical fables. Was she a reliable source? Not sure, but she was the only source I had. We lived all over the country, but never close to Belle Fleur, Louisiana, the birthplace of Lizette and my ancestors. It's a Creole town as old as America (by definition, Creole describes Black people who are a mix of enslaved Africans, French colonists, and Indigenous peoples). By the time I was old enough to travel there myself, my grandmother and great-grandmother had passed. I never met them.

Nor had I ever met my father, grandfather, or great-grandfather because they're missing from this story. Which is a story itself. There were no sons and no fathers in my maternal bloodline. So, we just kept passing down our maiden name, Mercier. It was as if men weren't even necessary. Were we too strong to have a man around? Or was it something else, something darker? Could be. After all, wherever we were, scandal and tragedy seemed to follow.

As a child, my mother told me that Mercier girls were cursed.

If there is a curse, it ended with my daughter. She's different—a truly self-possessed teenager, a tower of strength. At her age, I was a self-destructive addict, racked with pain both physical and emotional. A runaway. A loner. A lost girl haunted by darkness.

My daughter broke the curse. Or maybe I broke it, back when I was nineteen and moved to New York to begin my adult life.

Back in the dark ages. When I changed my name from Genevieve Mercier to Eva Mercy.

1, 2, 3, 4 … THRIVE!
A Teen's Rules for Flourishing on This Dying Planet

By Audre Mercy-Moore

Rule 10:
You can't un-ring a bell. And you can't un-know the truth. So don't chase it down if you're not ready to face it.

Chapter 29

Audre didn't know where she was going until she ended up at the F train. Two transfers later, she found herself at Rockaway Beach. Her internal compass had led her to the same pier that she visited with Bash. It felt like five years had passed since that day. Nothing about her life looked the same.

Audre sat on the sand, crisscross applesauce, staring out into the ocean. The waves weren't quite high enough to ride, so the surfers were hanging out on the sand, picnicking, sun-worshipping. Shutting her eyes, she felt the warm, coconut-sunscreen-scented air whoosh over her skin, ruffling her braids. She had so many questions.

Why had she tried so hard to be perfect her entire life? For what?

Why had her mom lied to her about their family? Her past?

Why was her mom such a hypocrite? *Eva* was the bad teen, not her.

Did she ever even know her mom? Her mom, whose name was, in fact, Genevieve Mercier. Not Eva Mercy.

Audre felt tricked. She felt duped into a false sense of security, of familial pride. It felt like nothing had ever been real in her life. If she'd believed she was one thing and found out she was another, was there any security anywhere? Eva was so hard on her. She'd set unrealistic expectations for Audre, and the pressure had caught up to her. It was the reason for her panic attacks. Her constant anxiety. Her perfection addiction, with the bar rising higher and higher—to heights no normal teen could reach. What was the point of any of it?

Audre wondered who she might've been if she hadn't been such a perfection addict. Who knows? Maybe she wouldn't have busted her ass to win class president every year since 2019. Maybe she wouldn't have taken to her bed for days after placing second at her fifth-grade science fair. Maybe her PSAT tutor wouldn't have quit (in tears!) due to Audre's intensity.

Maybe she wouldn't be the kind of girl who freaks out about taking chances.

She stared out into the water, remembering how Bash dove down deep to chase the Smurf lunch box. It seemed like a silly thing, hunting a 1980s-era relic at the bottom of the ocean. But Bash thought it was cool, so he took a chance and went for it. Weirdly, Audre was jealous—she wished she could be that carefree.

But it hurt too much to think of Bash. It shattered her in almost a physical way, causing her to double over, hugging her knees to her chest. Hot tears spiked behind her eyes. God, to be so close to something real...and then having it blow up in your face? It cut deep.

Her emotions were exploding in her brain like paintball

pellets. She was furious at her dad. She felt betrayed by her mom (and Shane, to be honest!). She was annoyed by Baby Alice. And she was still offended by Reshma assuming she couldn't handle Bash on her own. And she was miserable without Bash.

The way she felt about him wasn't a crush. It wasn't just physical attraction, either. They weren't just friends. When Bash kissed her and held her in his arms, she could feel his heart beating between them, like it was outside of his body. When he palmed her cheek, his hands were shaking. She hadn't imagined it or exaggerated it in her head. Bash was just as overwhelmed as she'd been.

Bash dropped her because he was afraid of hurting her. (Whatever that meant.) But there were two of them in this situation, and it wasn't fair that he got to make the decisions. It wasn't fair for him to decide what would hurt her—before she had a chance to see for herself.

And hadn't Eva done the same thing? She'd created a string of pretty lies to teach Audre before she had a chance to hear the truth about her mom—and judge for herself. Audre's whole life, she'd elevated her mom to idol status. She was her prototype for womanhood, for Black feminist excellence. But she had her all wrong! Eva had a . . . dark past. And they weren't alike, at all. Eva was the opposite of who Audre was. It was outrageous.

But at the bottom of her outrage was something else. Something weirder, something harder to define.

She was in awe of her mom.

Eva said she'd been a runaway. A delinquent. Not a day went by that Audre didn't wish to be someone who didn't care—about expectations, other people's opinions, or being the best. She was always fascinated by kids who skipped class, didn't turn in their homework, and never worried about their future. What she wouldn't have given to live a day in their shoes.

Chin resting on her knees, she stared out into the Atlantic, wondering if that Smurf lunch box was still there. And if it was gone, had another one washed up? She yearned to jump in and find it. After all, Audre was a strong swimmer. She'd been swimming in Malibu for as long as she could remember. Why not just jump in?

But she couldn't bring herself to do it. With her luck, something would go wrong. Maybe she'd get captured by a member of that water tribe species from *Avatar* and dragged down to her death. It wasn't worth the risk. Besides, if she were successful, who would she tell? She'd been rejected by the one person who would've celebrated with her.

But that was the old Audre, wasn't it? Doing great things so other people would be proud of her. What if she did it just to impress herself?

She raised her chin up from her knees. As the roar of the sea filled her ears, she stood up, dusted off the sand from her skin, and stared out at the preternaturally still water. With the faintest hint of a satisfied smile, she ran for the water.

Chapter 30

"So, first week of August, then?" asked Mack Rhodes, Myrtle Beach's tattoo artiste extraordinaire. "My assistant emailed you your travel confirmation, right?"

"Yep, yesterday." Bash nodded, though Mack obviously couldn't see him through the phone. "Is there anything I should bring?"

"Nah, we have everything at the shop. Just bring yourself and an open mind. You'll be working on dummies, so think of this as the chance to take risks with your designs. Wherever your bar is today? Raise it. Your week at Fifth Angel will be the most important audition you'll ever have. Treat it as such."

"Bet. Will do."

"Looking forward, kid. See you in a couple weeks."

Just bring yourself and an open mind. Hadn't Bash basically said the same thing to Audre before they started her Experience Challenge? He had, and she did. And now everything was ruined. He'd fallen for her and then freaked out. And now, whatever they almost were, was done.

And the job opportunity he'd been dreaming of? He was starting to feel conflicted about it. He'd been so dead set on moving far away, starting his adult life somewhere new. But that was before he met Audre.

God, he missed her. And he was miserable. It was as if the color had been drained from the world, leaving everything a dull, faded thrift store print. A sad reminder of former vibrancy. Which was more depressing than no color at all.

Lost in thought, Bash placed his phone by his side and continued exercising. He was lying flat on his back on the kitchen floor, a stability ball between his ankles. Slowly, he rotated his legs to the right, and then to the left. This was his favorite recovery exercise from his competition days—it calmed his muscles down, helping him relax after running at breakneck speed. During meets, he ran like he was surging out of his body, shedding his mortal skin and transforming into a superhuman speed demon. But afterward, he loved sinking back into his skin. Becoming Bash again.

He wasn't competing anymore, but the exercise usually lifted his mood when he felt down. Today, it wasn't working.

Bash more than missed Audre. Was there a level after missing someone? He'd actually googled this, to see if there was a word for it. He'd landed on "anticipatory nostalgia"—or feeling sad about missing memories you haven't made yet.

Audre would've known that term. Audre knew everything.

And he'd pushed her away. Because this wasn't the plan. Bash wasn't supposed to fall for someone in Brooklyn. Brooklyn was supposed to be temporary. He was simply supposed to finish high school and save enough cash from Just Because and tattooing so he could move away and start his adult life.

Bash wasn't supposed to put down roots. To find a best friend who was also infuriatingly pretty. A girl who was his first thought in the morning and his last before drifting off to sleep. A girl who ignited his brain and his heart. He'd only known her for a little over a month, but Audre Mercy-Moore had become essential to his life. It was terrifying.

What was he going to do without her? The thought made him nauseous. Because Bash didn't know what he was going to do with her, either.

After everything he'd been through in Oakland—all the damage he'd caused to innocent people—being in a relationship was irresponsible. But Bash hadn't explained this to Audre. He'd basically broken up with her without telling her why. Confessing about his past. How could he do that to her?

He'd hurt her. And it was gnawing at him, relentlessly. He had to tell her. About Oakland, his dad, Clio, everything. He owed it to her.

In the middle of his stream-of-consciousness spiral, Bash heard the front door open. Surprised, his ankles tightened around the ball, which shot it straight up in the air. The ball landed on his bruised face with a dull *thwack*. He was so out of shape, his reflexes weren't shit. With an annoyed moan, he clutched his purplish eye and stood up just in time for his mom to breeze into the kitchen.

"Oh! Bash, hi! Hi!"

As always, Jennifer sounded shocked to see him. Like she had come home to find a Teenage Mutant Ninja Turtle binging *The Mandalorian* on her couch.

"How are you?" she trilled.

"Good," he answered, dropping his hand from his bruised eye. And then his jaw dropped, too.

She set her structured black handbag down on the marbled kitchen counter and offered him an exaggerated smile. In her hand was a battered, Smurf-shaped lunch box. Decades of salt-water erosion had faded the Smurf's facial features to almost nothing.

Jennifer handed it to him. He took it and just stood there, frozen solid, gawking at the lunch box like it had just burst into song. After a long pause, he found his voice.

"Wh-where was this?" he stammered.

"Propped outside the front door," she said with a confused shrug. "It's for you, apparently. There's a note taped to the back. Incredibly odd, no? It looks a million years old."

Bash flipped the lunch box over and read the note.

Challenge #5, completed. I faced a fear: diving deep into the ocean. These sell for hundreds, so consider this payment for a job well done.

—Audre

Slowly, he shut his eyes. He felt dizzy. Nauseous. As if moving in dreamlike slow motion, he carefully placed the lunch box on the counter.

"Are you alright? Coming down with something?" asked Jennifer.

"No. No, I was just doing some stretches before you came home. I guess I went too hard."

She let out a surprised yelp. "In my kitchen?"

"Uh...yeah. Sorry?" Bash dug his nails into his palm, itching to get out of this conversation, to call Audre, to sprint to her house, to teleport to her couch, to do anything to get to her.

"No, no it's fine! You can work out wherever. What's mine is yours."

Jesus. Talking to Jennifer was excruciating at the best of times. And awkward on both ends. But at this moment, it was particularly torturous.

"Is that a black eye?" The second she got the words out, her phone dinged. She pulled it out and began scrolling through her messages.

Good, thought Bash. *She's distracted—maybe I can get out of this, fast.*

"Yeah, it doesn't hurt, though."

"Mmm," she said, nodding. "What happened?"

"I got hit by a bus."

"Bummer," she said, not glancing up from her phone. Thumbs flying over the keypad.

"And then a motorcycle rolled over my face."

"The worst," she said, dropping her phone on the counter and turning her attention back on Bash. "So, I'm home a bit early from the center. I thought maybe we could hang out."

Bash was genuinely confused by this. "Together?"

She scowled a little. And then she huffed out a short, hard

laugh without opening her mouth. "You're so funny. I'm glad that
we can share light moments together." She tapped on the counter,
visibly searching for something to say. "You wanna smoke some
pot?"

"Nah, I'm good."

"Hmm. Oh! Wanna go to Dave and Buster's? It'd be a hoot.
Like old times."

Old times. Plural? Their Dave and Buster's trip had happened
once, six years ago—and it was one of the *only* memories they had
together. "Sorry, I have to work later."

"Pshaw. You don't need to work. The past year has been hard
enough. I told you, whatever money you need, I can give it to
you."

He shook his head. "Thank you, but no."

"We have generational wealth. If the kids at the shelter had it,
they might not be in the position they're in now. You shouldn't
feel guilty about your privilege."

"It's just not my money. Taking it doesn't feel right."

"That's how generational wealth works, Sebastian. What if it's
a loan? You'll pay me back one day when you strike it rich as . . .
a . . . what do you want to be again?"

Bash was always polite to his mom. He was just wired that
way, to be respectful and kind, no matter what. (Yes, he punched
out Ellison, but that was a public service.) Did he love her? No, he
didn't. In fact, when he forced himself to think about their non-
relationship, he felt resentment, confusion, and, at worst, a sad
numbness. But that didn't justify dick behavior.

However.

This was easily the tenth time she'd asked him about his career aspirations. He was sick of answering this question. It was infuriating. It was bad enough that she gave him away, never tried to contact him, and basically forgot she had a son. But now he lived with her—and she was still ignoring him? It was too much to take.

"Tattoo artist," he snapped. "My answer's always the same. Maybe I could ink the words across my forehead. Double meaning, so it really sticks."

Jennifer flinched with surprise and then folded her arms across her chest. "Why're you being mean to me?"

"This isn't me being mean. It's me being truthful. You just can't handle it."

"But I'm trying to connect with you. I'm offering you money, pot, anything you want. Am I that bad?"

"Literally no one wants to get high with their mother."

"Well, what do you want? I'm trying to be a thoughtful, present mom. It's a lot to learn in four months. You've grown up already. You've finished cooking. What role am I supposed to have in your life?"

Bash just looked at her. Where would he even start? He'd been holding back for so long. What he wanted to say would send their nonexistent relationship straight to hell. And practically, he needed a place to live until he could afford to move.

But then he thought about Audre, who had somehow gotten up the courage—both physical and emotional—to dive into the ocean and rescue that lunch box, even though the last time she was there, she'd had a panic attack. Despite it surely bringing back memories of the two of them. She was braver than anyone he'd ever known. He should be able to finally express what he'd been burying his entire life.

"What role are you supposed to have in my life? You really wanna know?"

"Yes, I do. This is great, we're finally communicating...."

"Nothing. You're nothing in my life," he said with finality. "Let's not pretend I'm here for any other reason than my dad disowned me. We don't have anything to talk about because you're a stranger. And that's on you."

"Sebastian!"

"Oh, you're offended? *I don't have a mom.* Do you understand that?" On the last word, he slapped the back of his hand against his palm. Incandescent rage flared inside him. "I never even had one to miss. Do you know what that's like, as a kid? I never knew what to say when friends would ask where my mom was. Across the country, happily living her life without me in it? In second grade, I told everyone you were dead, and my guidance counselor signed me up for grief camp. Milton had to tell her I made it up. Which felt worse than the lie."

"I told you what happened. Your dad took you away...."

"And you didn't stop him."

"No, I didn't. The truth is, I guess I wasn't ready to be a mom. Sometimes you don't know how you feel about something until you're in it." She exhaled a long, shaky sigh. "God forbid a woman choose herself."

Speechless, Bash just stood there for a long moment, his heart crashing against his rib cage. "Back then, you decided you didn't want to be a mother. Fair enough, I guess. But you don't get it both ways now. We have no relationship. That's just the way it is."

"But I'm trying to make up for it now."

"How? You're never here! I bet you didn't even know I throw parties like twice a week."

"You . . . you've been disrespecting my home?"

"Regularly. I don't even like parties. And I hate throwing them. But my life's . . . nothing, it's been *blank* since I moved here, so I do it to fill in the blanks, and everything's fucked anyway, because I think I might've hurt a girl I really, really like . . . way more than like . . . and I . . . honestly, I really couldn't give a fuck about the lost kids of color you're using to relieve your guilt about the real-life one you abandoned."

She blinked, too stunned for words. "A girl?"

"Her name's Audre. And she thinks there's a strong chance you have narcissistic personality disorder."

Offended, Jennifer huffed and threw up her arms. Her right one connected with the Smurf lunch box, sending it flying. It landed on the floor with a crash, cracking the delicate, decades-old plastic. He scrambled to pick it up, and it fell apart in his hands.

The world stopped.

Bash just stared down at it. All the breath left his body. His heart thundered; his face contorted. In one fell swoop, Jennifer killed something that meant so much to him. Yes, it was a ridiculous '80s relic. But it meant everything to him—because Audre had rescued it. He didn't know how she got up the nerve to dive in that water, but she did. And in her gesture lived all the memories they'd shared this summer. The only summer that'd ever mattered to him.

But now the ruined lunch box was a dark reminder. That even the most sacred moments, memories, and connections could be shattered in seconds.

Without saying a word to Jennifer, or even looking her way, he grabbed his phone from the counter. He called Audre. It rang once, twice, three times.

And then . . .

"Yes?" Audre's voice sounded shaky, raspy, like she'd been screaming or crying or singing at the top of her lungs for hours. None of which sounded like things she'd do. His stomach flip-flopped and he could barely breathe.

"Where are you?" he asked finally.

"Don't know. Walking. Near Carroll and Fifth."

"Don't move," he said, already halfway out the door, ignoring his mom's barrage of questions. "I'm coming to you. Don't move."

1, 2, 3, 4 ... THRIVE!
A Teen's Rules for Flourishing on This Dying Planet

By Audre Mercy-Moore

Rule 11:
Who knew a 1980s relic would give me such confidence? Sometimes, reaching into the past helps you heal in the present. (Maybe that's what my mom is trying to do with her book. But who knows.)

Chapter 31

Fifteen minutes later, Bash found Audre sitting on a bench outside a restaurant. It looked like he'd gotten dressed in the dark. In his rush to get to her, Bash hadn't bothered changing out of his sports headband and mismatched workout clothes. He dropped everything and *sprinted*.

"I found you," he gasped, bending over with his hands on his knees.

"Were you in the middle of a workout?" she asked, her voice flat and numb. Her energy was cold. Distant. Unlike her.

"Yeah, and I ran here." He stood back up, wiping sweat from his forehead with the back of his hand.

She squinted up at him, using her palm to shield her eyes from the sun. Then she shrugged a little, fussing with the hem of her cutoff jean shorts. "I had second thoughts about seeing you. I was just about to go home. And never speak to you again."

"After what I said the other night, I don't blame you," he admitted. "But I was wrong. I was so stupid, Audre. I'm sorry I hurt you. I was just scared of...feeling too much." He took a breath. "So, yeah, I ran. The way I used to run—sprinting so fast it was like I could warp time." He stopped, regulating his breathing a bit. "I used to wonder why I was born with this talent. Like, what for? Maybe this is why."

She looked up at him. "What do you mean?"

Bash peered down at his feet for a moment, trying to collect his thoughts. "Maybe every run before this one was practice. So that I could be fast enough to catch you before you went home."

Audre chewed on her lip. She said nothing.

"You didn't sound good on the phone," he said.

" 'Cause I'm not good. Sit down—you're making me nervous."

He did, but he was careful to leave a respectful amount of space between them. "You, um, really dove into the ocean and found that Smurf lunch box? Why?"

"My last challenge was about fear. I was scared to dive down that deep, but I did it. So, my experiment is over," she said. "I guess I wanted to prove that I didn't need you to finish it. That I'm strong enough to do it myself."

"You're the strongest person I know," said Bash.

"I don't know about that." Audre looked him in the eye for the first time that day. And maybe because it felt like everything was upside down and there were no more rules—she told him everything. How she read her mom's book. How it exposed the truth of Eva and the Mercier women. How her origins, everything she thought she knew about herself, were a lie.

And Bash hung on her every word. As Audre spoke, their hands moved closer and closer to each other's, until she naturally slid her palm into his.

"My mom's always been so hard on me," sighed Audre. "How

dare she? Remember the way she treated you when we came back after the party?"

"To be fair, my face was busted and I'd been out with her daughter," said Bash.

"But it was like she found out we were a demented, flesh-eating couple just back from a cross-country killing spree."

Frowning, Bash asked, "Isn't that the plot of that Chalamet cannibal movie?"

"The thing is, nothing I do could ever be scarier than who she is."

"Maybe that's why she was hard on you. To keep you from making the same mistakes."

"Stop defending her!" Audre whipped her head around to face him, her braids flying. "She lied to me. And we used to be best friends. I feel so betrayed."

Bash nodded, squeezing her hand. "Do you think you sensed she was hiding something? Maybe that's why you're so interested in psychology? You want to fix everyone, because your family was a puzzle you couldn't solve."

"Well, you know what, Bash? I'm a puzzle that I can't solve. I'm complicated, too. I have secrets and hidden layers and worries and wildness! And I bury everything down to please some 'Mercy girl' ideal that doesn't even exist. It's not even our real last name!" She dropped her head back against the bench, gazing up at the dusky, early evening sky. "Nothing matters."

"Nothing," agreed Bash, who stopped trying to hide that he felt as hopeless as she.

"Everything's a lie."

"Everything."

Audre slipped her hand out of his. "Especially you. You've been lying all summer."

"I know."

"And don't try to deny it," she said, too lost in her rant to hear him. "Whether it's an act of omission or making up shit, a lie's a lie."

"I know," he repeated, his brow furrowed with frustration and guilt. "It kills me. There's so much I haven't told you. But I wanna come clean now."

"You can't tell me we're more than friends and then . . . just . . . disappear. Who does that?"

"I'm a piece of shit, Audre. And it's *torturing* me that I hurt you. But listen, I—"

"If you're not who I think you are, Bash, I swear to fucking God—"

"I'm not who you think I am."

She let out a small, defeated sound. "Who are you, then?"

"Can we go somewhere quiet?"

"No," said Audre firmly. "Tell me now. Here."

Bash stared down at his hands for several breaths. "I don't know how."

"Be honest," she said. "Emotionally honest. Anything else is cheating."

Anything else is cheating.

Audre's words hit him deep down, where his darkest fears lived. Where the past tortured him, day after day. And truly, he was sick of being haunted by the memories. Maybe he just needed someone to give him permission to let go of it. So then, right there on a random bench in front of a random restaurant, he finally let go.

"I'd always done everything my dad asked of me. Ever since I was little. It's like, show me a child actor, or musical prodigy, or whatever, and I'll show you an obsessed parent. And my dad was over-the-top with it. He needed me to be special. Because he wasn't. In the nineties, he was a sprinter, too, and he had talent— but not enough to make the Olympic Team in '92. They cut him in the last round. You ask me, I think it fucked him up for life. He got extremely religious. Which is cool, but the church he picked? Harsh. Way too harsh. You get punished for *breathing*. Women and kids should be seen, not heard. LGBTQ+ people are abominations. Men run the show, and they rule with fear. It's the worst part. That place taught my dad that there's only one way to be a man."

"Sounds like a cult, not a church," mused Audre.

"It was," he answered, his brow pinched together. "Anyway, I don't think he sees women and girls as real people with feelings. When he met my mom, he had three blond ex-wives and three daughters he didn't take care of. Mom was the fourth blond wife. She gave him a son—me—and then he divorced her, too. Apparently, I was the Chosen One. His little Olympic hopeful. He even named me after the Christian patron saint of athletes, Saint Sebastian. Bash is my nickname." He glanced at Audre briefly. He felt so open and vulnerable that he might burst into tears if he held her gaze for too long. "He had me doing drills, *hard* ones, by the time I was in kindergarten. Hurdles and shit, things kids shouldn't do. I won almost every meet. But he was never satisfied.

"To him, 'losing' was anything less than first place. If I lost? No food for twenty-four hours. Or I had to sleep on the bathroom floor. Or he'd make me walk across the city to school instead of taking the bus.

"He only hit me once. I was fourteen, and I'd had so many running injuries, my doctor told me I had the body of a forty-year-old athlete. I was fucking *heated*. Like, why am I ruining myself for him? What for? It was never enough. So, I felt all rebellious one day and got my brow pierced." Bash shook his head, remembering. "I knew he'd hate it. But I didn't think he'd punch me in the jaw."

Audre flinched in shock, her hand covering her mouth. Her eyes widened, but she kept quiet and let him talk.

"I just don't think he liked me, you know? I didn't line up with his definition of Black masculinity. He hated my obsession with the beach. He hated that I sketched all over my school notebooks, and that I wasn't a fighter. He hated that I cried at Adele songs or when he yelled at me for too long. Surfing was for white boys. And art was for pussies.

"A couple years ago, a church elder got caught leaving a gay bar. He lost his job, his wife, and his kids had to take an oath in front of the congregation, swearing to God that they'd never speak to him again. This is who my dad was.

"Meanwhile, I'm in the background, right? Keeping my head down, running and crushing it. That was my whole life. I mean, I dated a little, too. I had a few girlfriends. But all genders have had crushes on me, and honestly? Vice versa. To me, attraction isn't about gender. Who I vibe with is just . . . who I vibe with. It's who I've always been."

Bash looked at Audre. Slowly, she nodded.

"I like who you are," she said quietly.

"I know this doesn't seem like some big revelation in Brooklyn. Everyone's queer here—no one gives a fuck. But you don't know what my dad's like." He inhaled, his shoulders rising and falling. "I used to compete against this guy, Jaden, on a rival high school team. We always had a secret flirtation going. Remember I told you about my Oakland friend with panic attacks?"

"It was Jaden."

Bash nodded, his eyes gone cloudy. "Anyway, one time we traveled to an away meet, down in Ventura? Somebody snuck Hennessey into the hotel, and all the teams got wasted. I was chilling in his room, right? And when his roommate passed out, he told me he was in love with me. And had been for years. Then he kissed me. I'd never kissed a boy, but he had. His roommate was right there, sleeping. Which made it feel...exciting. Anyway, his coach walked in on us. His coach told my coach, who called my dad. I didn't know it yet, though.

"I found out that Saturday. I was doing drills at school. No one was there. Just my dad watching from the stands. After I ran one loop, he was waiting for me at the starting block. And I *knew* something was up. He never came down in the middle of a set. He'd sit there in the stands the whole time, watching and waiting in silence until after practice, when he'd tell me everything I'd done wrong.

"Out of nowhere, he grabbed my throat and said, 'You ruined everything. You're not my son. You're soft. You are your mom's mistake.' He kept going on like that. I don't remember much—I guess I've blocked it out.

"The next morning, he'd boxed up my trophies. He called my high school, the colleges recruiting me, the press, everyone, and said I was quitting track and field due to a quote, unquote private family matter. Said I was dead to him. Kicked me out. Gave me a court order approving my last name change—it went from Wallace to Henry, my mom's name. He said he wanted to change my identity so no one could trace me back to him." Bash took a small breath, shaken by the retelling. "The day I moved in with my mom, I still had bruises on my neck."

"Monstrous. He turned his back on his own son? How could he do that to you?"

"Well, there's more," he said, chewing the inside of his mouth. "When I got to Jennifer's, she casually asked me if my dad's chemo treatments were working. I'm like, *chemo*? The fuck? She thought I knew about his diagnosis. That he's dying of prostate cancer."

Audre looked stunned. Instantly, her eyes went huge and watery. "I'm so sorry about your dad. Even though you have complicated feelings about him, I know this hurts. How...long does he have?"

"The doctors say he probably won't make it till Christmas." Now that the story was off his chest, he leaned back against the bench, allowing his shoulders to relax.

"And what happened to Jaden? The boy you hooked up with?"

He shut his eyes for a beat or two, pressing his fingertips against his brow bone. Finally, he opened his eyes. They were reddened. "I spoke to Jaden one more time, right before I left town. He wouldn't let me in his house. He just stood in the doorway, and I was on the porch. I'll never forget what he said to me. 'What do I do now? I can't grow a new heart.' I've never seen anyone look so defeated. He looked like he'd been crying for days." Bash paused for a beat, and then let out a long, shaky sigh. When he finally continued the story, his voice sounded smaller. "The scandal embarrassed his mom. I heard she sent him to some boarding school in Washington State. I've tried to call, to text, but he blocked me."

"None of this was your fault," she whispered. "You realize that, don't you?"

Bash drew his mouth to one side and shrugged. For a long while, he sat in silence, thinking this over. When he finally spoke, his voice was quiet and thin. "It's why I didn't want to fall for you. I don't wanna hurt anyone else. That one kiss ruined lives. I feel radioactive."

"You didn't do anything wrong, Bash. The parents in the story are the villains. Not you."

"If you say so." He went silent for a few more beats. "When I moved here, I decided not to take anything seriously. I wanted to forget. When I met you, I realized I wanted something else."

"What's that?

"You." He sighed. "I wanted you."

The air felt full—like the heavy stillness right before the sky opens up, sending down a crashing, thunderous storm. They sat there, hopelessly tangled in each other's gaze. Looking at her, Bash knew that he was ready to take it all on. His sadness, her sadness, their wild attraction, this tender connection. In a way that was both certain and unexplainable, he wanted it all.

"You want me," repeated Audre.

"I do," he said, his eyes helplessly traveling to her mouth. "Badly."

She let out a faint, barely audible gasp.

"What do you want?" asked Bash, eyeing her with aching vulnerability.

Unsurprisingly, Audre knew exactly what she wanted.

"I want a tattoo."

And then, the sky really did open up, releasing an apocalyptic rainstorm.

Chapter 32

Of all the places she would have imagined being on a random summer Wednesday—sinking into the leather comfort of Bash's tattoo chair wasn't one of them.

Audre's eyes fluttered closed. It was as if she were living a lucid dream. She thought back to the last day of the school year. Before her life got turned upside down. That version of Audre would never have imagined that, on a (seemingly) random day in July, she'd be here, with her arm lying open and vulnerable on the armrest. The smell of leather and a foresty-scented candle wafted through the small back room. Books with titles like *The Language of Tattoos*, *Japanese Tattoos*, *Painted People*, and *Micro Tattoos* were piled on top of an old, rickety stool. Audre loved being around so much art. Once again, she was reminded of her painting and collaging days . . . and missed the freedom it brought her.

Nondescript, slow hip-hop quietly poured through a portable speaker—and it sounded hypnotic, almost like white noise. She felt like she'd melted into the softest, warmest embrace. It was almost too good.

Then she opened her eyes, and it got better.

There was Bash, the lanky leanness of him perched on a rolling stool, hiked up so that it was just a bit higher than her chair. His hands were folded in his lap as he peered down at her shyly. His expression took her breath away. For once, he didn't seem cool. He didn't seem laid-back or breezy. The corner of his mouth twitched, so he started biting his lip. His eyes burned darker and brighter than she'd ever seen them.

"You sure you want to do this?"

"Positive."

"Are you cold? I can turn down the AC."

She was only wearing a halter top and little denim shorts, but in her excitement, buzzy warmth flooded her skin.

"I'm fine. Swear."

Bash and Audre were talking low, almost whispering. It was just the two of them, alone, in their own private world. There was no real reason to speak in low voices. But the moment felt too big, too important, to tarnish with their everyday, ordinary speaking voices.

"But you told me you'd never get a tattoo. Why now?"

"I feel like I'm spinning out. And I need something to ground me."

Bash cocked his head, taking her in. "And you're sure you want me to do it?"

"Yes. Right now, you're the only thing that feels real to me." She said it almost guiltily, like a confession.

"I know the feeling," he said, scratching his fingers along his jawline. "Audre, I'm sorry I didn't tell you the truth."

"Don't be. I understand," she said shortly.

And she did. But she didn't want to talk about either one of their fucked-up families. Right now, she was too raw. She didn't want to fall apart. She wanted to escape.

"I don't want to think about anything," she whispered.

"Then don't. No one knows where we are right now. It's just you and me." Carefully, he picked up his tattoo gun from the rolling cart and attached an ink cartridge. Damn. Watching his strong hands work over the machinery was...sexy. He gripped it with such confidence. Like he knew what he was doing.

Her heart started racing.

"You nervous?" he asked, the corner of his mouth curving upward.

She nodded, shaking out her legs, trying to relax.

"When I was little," she said, "I used to do this thing called chocolate meditation. You sit a Hershey's Kiss in your mouth and slowly let it dissolve, naturally. No chewing. It teaches you mindfulness. You know, how to be in the present."

"Hmm. I don't have chocolate. I think I have an old candy cane?" He rolled over to a drawer, pulled it out, and handed it to Audre. She broke off a piece and popped it in her mouth. He did the same.

"Let it *disssolllve*," she instructed.

He tried for four seconds and then folded, chomping down on the candy. "Can't do it. I failed. Not chewing is hella challenging."

"It's hard, right? That's the point." Audre wiggled her arms and fingers, all restless energy and nerves. "Maybe I should take a shot?"

"No, drinking before you get inked is a bad idea. It makes you bleed more," he said. "I promise you're in good hands, A."

"If you say so, B." And then she allowed her eyes to flutter closed.

"I've been doing this forever. Did I ever tell you I started on grapefruits?"

"Grapefruits?" Her eyes flew open. "Well, in that case."

"Fruit tattooing is valid practice! Ask any professional."

"I know you're a professional." She grinned. "I'm just kidding. I wish I had half of your art skills. That Myrtle Beach tattoo shop will be lucky to have you."

"*If* I get the job."

"You will." Audre hoped she sounded supportive. It'd be too selfish for him to know how she really felt—which was that she missed him already.

"We'll see," he said. And then a smile slowly and sneakily crept across Bash's face. (It was clear he was trying to fight it. He lost.)

"What? What's funny?"

"No, it's nothing."

He bit his bottom lip, trying to erase his grin. But it broke through anyway. Self-consciously, he clapped his hand over his mouth and whispered, "Fuck!"

"Bash! What are you laughing at?"

"It's just that . . . I mean . . ." He stopped, shook his head, and started again. "I've fantasized about this moment a disturbing amount of times."

Audre's jaw dropped, and then she started giggling, too. "No, you haven't."

"I have," he said, and his bashful tone was adorable. "Look, I'm not trying to be creepy. This is my art. I love creating designs for people that they'll wear forever. It's a rush. And I've been wanting to share it with you."

"And show off."

"A little, yeah. But it's not just that. It's more than that." Bash was quiet for so long, Audre wondered if he was ever going to finish his thought. "Do I enjoy seeing you lying there on my chair? Yes. Do I enjoy that you trust me enough to permanently mark you?" His eyes met hers. "Also yes."

"Oh."

Her mouth went dry. Tingles ran through her body. She swallowed, then licked her lips. He blinked, his gaze traveling from her eyes to her mouth. He stopped there. Something flickered in his gaze. This electric, magnetic thing crackling between them was almost too intense to bear.

Her heart was slamming against her ribs, her brain spinning. Outside, the rain pounded against the window. Something in the air changed then.

"You're shaking," he said.

"No, I'm not, B."

"Yeah, you are, A."

"I'm not!"

"Audre." Bash reached out and held her hand, giving her a gentle squeeze. She gasped a little, feeling his hand on hers. "It's okay. I've got you. Trust me."

She nodded. "I'm ready."

Bash nodded back and reached over to the little tray-stand of his supplies. He slid on rubber gloves, with a loud slap. Which somehow made her more nervous than ever. This was really going to happen.

Gently, he reached out and held her wrist down against the armrest. He touched her as if she were something fragile. (And right now, she was.) She gazed down at his gloved hand on her skin, and it hit her. He was about to imprint something special on her inner wrist, an idea she'd whispered to him just minutes before in this intimate, quiet place—and she felt safe under his care. She felt precious under his touch.

"We can stop if you're really scared."

She looked at him, searching his face for a sign that she should stop. There wasn't one. Audre trusted Bash.

"I'm not scared anymore."

"Good. Don't look at the gun. Look at me."

Almost solemnly, Bash turned on the tattoo gun. A slight, humming buzz filled up the silence, in concert with the steady thrum of the rain outside. Following his directions, she focused on his face as he bent over her wrist—concentration furrowing his brow and pulling his mouth to one side. He looked both intense and angelic. How could one person hold so much beauty in their face?

When the needle touched her skin, she gasped a little in surprise, but it didn't *hurt* hurt. It was just a slight, stinging burn as he dragged the needle in soft, short strokes along her wrist. Staring at him helped. A lot. It was damn near euphoric, actually. The soft huffs of his breath on the skin of her inner arm lulled her into a floaty haze.

And then Bash stopped. He was so close, bowed over her arm.

"Is this okay?"

She nodded, breathless. Somehow, she felt both powerful and weak.

"I'm just getting more ink. Don't move."

He stopped then, gently wiping away excess ink on her wrist with a little pad. And then more. She sucked in her breath when the needle sharply touched her skin again. There was a sting, but truly? There was something satisfying in the feeling. The idea that even though it hurt, she was badass enough to push through it. She felt powerful. It was all so meditative, the buzzing of the needle, the scent of the candle, their almost worshipful silence. Turns out? Getting a tattoo was a rush.

It was a rush because Bash was doing it for her.

Every sensation felt heightened. This was exactly what Audre needed. To forget everything. To float away on feeling. To live only for the next breath. Nothing could get to her here. Nothing could get to her when she was with Bash. She didn't notice that he'd stopped until he turned the gun off. Her eyes fluttered open from half-mast.

She peered at her wrist. It was exactly what she'd asked for.

333.

It was so personal, this mark he'd made on her. So intimate. No matter what happened to them, or between them—Audre would remember it forever.

He layered on ointment and then he bandaged up her wrist. With a trembly sigh, she looked up at Bash. His eyes were glassy, and it looked like he'd been holding his breath.

"You good?" His voice was low and deeper than usual.

Her answer, *yes*, came out as a whisper-croak that took them both by surprise. Bash stared at her, just openly gawked, and Audre stared back, matching his boldness. And then the tub of ointment slipped out of his hand, landing with a *thud* on the floor.

Audre caught her bottom lip under her teeth and released it. He stared at her mouth, unblinking. The rain pounded at the window. Then, as if in a trance, Bash ran the back of his fingers along her cheek, stopping at her chin. Then he slowly swept the pad of his thumb across her bottom lip. Tingles surged through her. Her lips parted just a bit, and she touched his thumb with the tip of her tongue.

Audre never knew that hearing a guy groan could be so... hot. *She* made him make that sound. It felt powerful.

Next thing she knew, he'd closed the space between them—propping his elbows on either side of her and angling his face over hers until their lips were almost touching. After a few trembling breaths, she spoke.

"Am I crazy, or was that... you, tattooing me... the hottest thing that's ever happened."

"Why do you think I've been fantasizing about it?" His voice was a low rumble.

"Bash..."

"Yeah..."

"What did you... fantasize about?"

His mouth curved into a sly smile. "You want me to describe it."

She nodded, heart pounding.

"No."

"No?"

"I'll show you instead."

He lowered his strong body on top of hers, gently placing her tattooed arm up by her head (Audre melted, realizing that he was concerned about protecting her at a time like this). She almost said this out loud. But then she couldn't form words at all because he slid his palm up under her shirt, lightly dragging his fingertips along her belly. His touch was *scorching*. Audre arched into him, plunging her hand in his hair. And then he planted an open-mouthed kiss on her throat. A rush of pleasure skated through her. Bash kept teasing her with light, searching touches under her shirt, and his breath was coming fast, and Audre had started to tremble—and soon, it wasn't going to be enough. God, how did things get so intense, so fast?

With a hungry moan, she hooked her legs around him, desperate to get closer. And he dragged his hot, luscious mouth to her ear.

"Did you really freestyle, 'hot like fire yo he gives me heat rash'?"

Audre's eyes flew open. "PROMISE ME WE'LL NEVER SPEAK OF THAT AGA—"

Bash quieted her with a blazing kiss. The night before, their kisses had been soft and searching. But this one was dirtier, wetter, wilder. He kissed her like he'd never get to do it again—like he wanted her to remember it forever.

He grinded against her, making her gasp into his mouth. Slowly, he trailed his hand further up her shirt, sliding over the cup of her bra. *Bash*, she whimpered. With one hand, he unhooked her bra, and then...

...Audre's phone went off in her pocket. Three rings, and

one buzz. Finally, Audre pulled away. Which, along with her AP Biology final, was the hardest thing she'd ever had to do.

Eva had called three times, and then texted. Audre read the message—and wished she could collapse in on herself, like a dying star.

Did you read my manuscript?

Chapter 33

Outside, the late afternoon rain had finally stopped.
The sun was shining, but a mossy-green, damp scent hung in
the air. Gone was the dreamlike, make-believe quality of Bash's
little studio. The cars sloshing by, shoppers remerging after taking cover in cafés, the wet sheen of the street—the world looked
glaringly real.

And Audre and Bash were in real turmoil.

The second her mom's text came through, the spell was
broken. With a yelp, Audre disentangled herself from Bash,
grabbed her tote, and ran out. He was right on her heels, though.
And now, the two were standing under the JUST BECAUSE
neon sign, caught in a heated back-and-forth neither wanted to
have.

"I have to go." For the first time, she really felt her tattoo.
Now, it did kinda hurt. It burned like crazy.

"I know you do—go make everything right with your mom.
But can I just get five minutes? I didn't get a chance to explain
how to clean the tattoo, bandage it up..."

Audre was frantically trying to order an Uber. "Can you text it to me?"

"Are we going to talk about what happened in there?" asked Bash, his eyes pleading. "Look at me."

With an overwhelmed exhale, she glanced his way. He looked so tender, so fucking hot, with his kiss-puffy lips and impassioned eyes. He looked like *hers*. She felt like if she stared at him for too long, she'd projectile-launch herself at him, clinging onto his body like one of those oversized Tasmanian giant crabs. And then she'd never do what she needed to do, which was get the hell home to get answers from Eva.

"We were vulnerable in there," she said softly. "We finally let down our guard and just kind of..."

"...did what we've been wanting to do all summer."

She nodded, biting her bottom lip. His mouth curved into a satisfied smile. And then he kissed her again—a tender, lingering peck. When he pulled away, she breathily whispered, "Did I really just briefly consider losing my virginity on a tattoo chair behind a gift shop that sells ass-shaped stress balls?"

He took a step back and burst out laughing. "You briefly considered what?"

"You heard me!" she giggled, and then gently touched her tingling lips with her fingertips. "What took us so long to get here?"

Bash ran his hand through his wild hair, shifting his weight from one foot to the other. He lightly shrugged at her, his eyes ablaze. God, he was irresistible. "What was I supposed to say to you? That not being near you feels pointless, like wasted time? That every kiss I don't give you burns a fucking hole in me?"

Audre's mouth dropped open in shock. She was hit with a rush of feeling so strong, she couldn't find the words to respond.

"Bash, you really felt—"

"I'm not done," he said. "Those were rhetorical questions. Here's a real one. Will you be my girlfriend, A?"

Audre blinked several times. Died a thousand deaths. Felt her heart in her throat. And then, in a croaky voice, she responded, "Yes, B."

Because the universe has a sense of humor, they hadn't even begun to kiss yet when they were intercepted by a (very) recognizable female voice.

"Bash!"

They both spun around.

"Clio?" exclaimed Bash.

"Reshma?" exclaimed Audre. "What are you doing together?"

The two girls strolled up to them, clutching iced coffees. Clio looked confused. Reshma looked guilty.

"Hey, Audre," trilled Reshma, her voice weirdly chipper.

"So, you're Audre," said Clio with a bright smile.

"Hold on, how do you know Audre?" asked Reshma.

"I don't," she answered. "Bash told me about her. How do you know her?"

"She's my best friend!"

"I'm confused," announced Bash, delivering the understatement of the year.

"Reshma," hissed Audre. "What are you doing with Clio?"

"Uh...uh...nothing," she muttered.

"Uh...uh...nothing?!" mimicked Audre, furious.

"We're dating," said Clio triumphantly. "I broke up with my boyfriend today."

"Your boyfriend?" Reshma pointed to Bash. "Just say his name. He's right there."

Audre narrowed her eyes at Bash in a blind fury. "So it's true?"

"Eww. Bash isn't my boyfriend." Clio laughed. "He's my brother. My half brother."

Audre flinched with her entire body. Her jaw dropped. The world stopped turning. And then she exclaimed to no one in particular, *"Fucking excuse me?"*

Reshma frowned in confusion (her least favorite emotion). "Clio, you said your boyfriend's tall and kinda femme, with 'only Black guy in the band' energy. Plus, y'all were long-distance till recently, right? That's Bash. He just moved here!"

"My boyfriend *is* the only Black guy in a band. Jake-Anthony King. He plays guitar in a 2000s R&B tribute band called Flip It and Reverse It. We were long-distance because the band was on the road for ages. They're finally back in New York."

Audre's brain was spinning. "Wait. *Flip It and Reverse It?* Tell me you're joking."

"Why?" asked Clio, Reshma, and Bash.

"They're playing at my mom's wedding!"

"Oh, that's what's up," said Clio. "I'm glad they're getting steady work. Brooklyn's a tough market."

Audre was too flabbergasted to think straight. It felt like she'd hallucinated Bash and Clio's entire relationship. What the hell? She just stood there for a moment, slowly letting the news sink in. "Bash, Clio's really your sister?"

"Yeah," sighed Bash.

"Your sister. *Your actual genetic sister?*" Her brain was a fog of disbelief. "Is...this an...incest thing?"

"NO!" wailed Clio.

"Audre, listen. I told you my dad was married three times before my mom, right?" explained Bash. "And he had daughters before me? My sisters all live in different states, so we didn't grow up together. Clio's the one closest in age to me."

"Eighteen months apart," said Clio.

"Anyway, in middle school, we found each other on IG and got hella close, even though we lived on opposite coasts. All her calls and texts? It's 'cause she's been trying to convince me to smooth things out with our dad before it's too late."

"Before he passes," added Clio.

"Anyway. Our dad never gave her, or any of our sisters, the time of day. But Clio's heart's so pure, you know? She's been reaching out to all of them, begging them to make peace. And everyone has but me."

Reshma's eyes darted from Clio to Bash and back again, like she was at a tennis match. All the rapid-fire plot twists had stunned her to silence.

Thunderstruck, Audre sputtered, "But...how...why didn't you tell me? I would've understood!"

"Because I'm a coward. I hate that I didn't tell you, and that you were confused. But if I explained Clio, I'd have to explain everything. And I'm fucking ashamed." Bash stopped, glancing up at the sky for a moment, his expression tortured. "Look, my dad's a dick—he's mean to his wives, ignores his daughters, and he fucked up my life. He's dying, and I'm *relieved*. There's no way to explain that to a girl you want to like you."

"But I already liked you. You couldn't tell?"

"I wasn't sure if you liked me or if I was just your Experiment Guy. I'm always that guy. Everyone wants to 'try me on.' Use me to test out their kinks or whatever. No one takes me seriously. I just . . . wasn't sure."

"But Audre doesn't have any kinks," protested Reshma.

Audre glared at her best friend. And then she stepped closer to Bash and grabbed his hand. She was stunned at this revelation. Bash seemed golden. People wanted to know him, and he was the object of a zillion crushes. He was hot and mysterious and new. It never occurred to Audre that Bash might be insecure. Or that he'd question how she felt about him. Hadn't she been so obvious?

To Audre, her feelings for Bash were an obvious truth. As true as summer following spring, or the fact that she always took the lead in group projects.

"I understand," she said.

In response, Bash's face melted into almost giddy relief. With an exhale, he pulled her closer by her hand and kissed her forehead.

"Aww," sighed Clio. "I've been rooting for you two. You know, behind the scenes."

"Hold on," Bash blurted out. "Speaking of 'behind the scenes,' since when are you a lesbian? If the cancer doesn't kill Dad, this will. One queer kid wasn't enough?"

"Oh, now you care whether Dad lives or dies? You won't even call him," said Clio. "Also, I'm not a lesbian. I'm bisexy."

319

"Since when."

"Since Reshma."

"She doesn't need to explain shit to you, Bash," snapped Reshma, stepping in front of Clio. "And watch your tone. I can get *real* urban *real* fast."

Ignoring Urban Reshma (because she was ridiculous), Bash turned his attention to Clio. "Did you or did you not tell me that you wanted to cheat on your boyfriend this summer to make him jealous? 'Cause you're pressed about the groupies on his tour? That's what this is, isn't it?"

Clio's jaw dropped.

Reshma yelped.

"This is so Wattpad," said Audre. "So messy. Everybody's lying."

"Yeah, tell me more about your cat." Bash smirked.

Audre gasped. "You knew that was a lie, B?"

He gazed at her, eyes twinkling. "You're good at everything but lying, A."

Audre bit her lip, her cheeks flushing hot.

Reshma ignored this, because she was *furious*. She took a powerful step toward Clio. "You only talked to me to hurt your boyfriend? How could you use me like that?"

"Oh please," scoffed Audre. "When are you gonna tell Clio you've been lying, too?"

"There's more? Yo, I can't," groaned Bash, shutting his eyes and rubbing his brow bone.

Reshma winced, rapidly shaking her head.

"Tell her, or I will," threatened Audre.

"Fine!" Caught, Reshma threw up her hands. "Clio, at first

I was dating you 'cause I thought you were blocking Audre and Bash. My plan was to seduce you away from him."

"After you promised you wouldn't," wailed Audre. "How could you? Why do you always put yourself at the center of everything? Are you really that attention-seeking?"

"Is this true?" Clio's eyes were wide and hurt. With a guilty sigh, Reshma nodded. And then Clio winced sharply, like she'd grazed an open flame. Slowly, she backed away from Reshma.

"Wait, wait, wait," pleaded Reshma, holding her arm. "It was true. I was trying to help my best friend. It's stupid, I know. But none of it matters, because I fell for you. For real. I've never felt like this before."

Clio snatched her arm away in disgust. And then she stormed off.

Reshma turned to Audre. "Not her being salty! She was using me, too."

"We're not talking," snapped Audre.

Eyes downcast, Reshma turned and walked off. She knew when to cut her losses.

Then it was just Audre and Bash, staring at each other in utter incredulousness. Without saying a word, he swept her into a warm, strong embrace. She nuzzled her face into his chest, his chin resting atop her head. This was the only safe place in the world.

For ages, they stood there, locked in their airtight, healing hug, oblivious to the sidewalk traffic passing them on either side. After some time, she disentangled herself from him.

And then Audre went home to face her mother. Whoever she was.

Chapter 34

"I'm in here."

Eva's voice reverberated from the kitchen. The house felt weirdly still. All the lights were on in the house, even the bathroom. Shane was out with his mentorship group. Baby Alice was with the new sitter (about fucking time). It was just Eva and Audre, alone.

Quickly, Audre grabbed an oversized sweatshirt from a laundry basket and threw it on, pulling the sleeve over her tattoo. Eva would freak out if she saw it—and Audre didn't have an explanation yet.

Holding her breath, Audre entered the kitchen. Her mom was sitting at the kitchen table, waiting for her—and Audre could sense her tension.

The first thing Audre noticed was the box of Honey Nut Cheerios placed in front of her mom. Uh-oh. The Cheerios were a clear sign that Eva was trying to prevent a nervous breakdown. In times of stress, Eva ate dry cereal by the fistful. No milk, no bowl.

The second thing Audre noticed was that her mom looked

weirdly formal. At least for her. Usually a jeans-and-sneakers lady, Eva was wearing a linen maxidress. Had she dressed up for this conversation? Her hands were clasped together on the table so tightly, the skin on her knuckles looked stretched. Audre wondered what she was thinking. Was she angry with Audre? Disappointed? Or, possibly relieved?

Audre sat in the chair across from her. She folded her hands on the table, unconsciously mirroring her mom. They looked like two Mafia bosses having a sit-down.

"I used to be able to trust you," said Eva.

Audre flinched. "I trusted *you*. And you lied to me about your life. About your name. About Grandma Lizette. It was like finding out Santa Claus is Satan."

"Audre. You read my manuscript without asking me."

"I only read the prologue."

"Doesn't matter. It's not okay, and it's never been okay."

"One might argue you left the laptop out on purpose so I could find the file. A classic case of projected self-sabotage."

"What you won't do is therapize me."

Audre threw up her hands. "Why does everyone keep saying that?"

Eva breathed out slowly. "I've been dreading this moment since the day I found out I was pregnant with you."

"Nice that you felt dread when you found out you were pregnant."

"Don't twist my words. I was elated to be pregnant with you," she corrected. "You're my greatest gift."

Audre let out a huff of frustration. "I push myself so hard, Mom. To please you. I've always felt like if I stopped being perfect for one second, the world would end. You put me on a pedestal! Your greatest gift. Your golden child. Your perfect daughter. So-called 'golden' children become anxious adults with inferiority complexes. Haven't you ever read *Never Enough: When Achievement Culture Becomes Toxic* by Jennifer Wallace?"

"No, but I need to. I clearly have a lot to learn," she admitted. "I never meant to put unrealistic expectations on you. You were always so driven, so ambitious. I thought you liked the pressure." She placed her chin in her hand, her fingertips tapping her cheek.

"Why did you lie to me?"

"I wouldn't say I lied. I simply perpetuated a useful fiction."

Audre shot her an exasperated look.

"I was terrified that if you knew the truth," said Eva, "you'd absorb it and repeat history."

"But what *is* our history? 'Cause right now I feel like aliens dropped me from the sky."

"That's not too far from the truth." Eva angled the Cheerios box in Audre's direction, and Audre shook her head. She was so unsettled, she might never eat again. "I've rehearsed this moment for years. And now that it's here, words escape me."

"Okay, writer," said Audre under her breath.

Eva breezed past this snark. She had a story to tell. "Most families have a sprawling family tree, with several branches. Ours isn't like that. We don't have branches, just a trunk.

"Your great-great-grandmother had one daughter, who had one daughter, who had one daughter, and so on. No siblings; no dads that stayed. Just women and our generational trauma. The trauma ended with me. But when I was around your age, it almost won."

Pausing, she reached down to the chair seat next to her and pulled out an old shoebox. "This is my *Back to Belle Fleur* box. Things I've collected while researching."

The box was filled with all sorts of old-timey miscellanea. Newspaper clippings and invitations to long-ago parties. Faded ribbons, satin gloves, and a few loose pearl buttons. Three black-and-white photos caught Audre's eye. Each one had a name and date scrawled on the back.

The first pic was Audre's great-great-grandmother, Delphine, 1922. She was posed with an ancient Ford, her bee-stung lips and flapper hat signifying wealth.

The second photo was Audre's great-grandmother, Clothilde, 1945. A bright-eyed beauty lounging in the grass wearing a WWII-era rolled hairdo.

The third photo was Grandma Lizette, 1977. It was a pageant shot, torn out of a newspaper. She was wearing a tiara, a winner's cape, and fluffy disco hair.

All three were wearing Audre's cameo ring. It wrapped her in warm, cozy pride.

"Wow, how did Grandma Lizette get her hair so big?"

"She'd tease her hair at the crown, stick a folded-up maxi pad in the center, and then pin her hair all around it."

The warm, cozy pride ended there. "Gross."

"You asked." Eva returned to her story. "Honey, you come from a line of very powerful but very . . . tricky women. Complicated, challenging women. Delphine was tortured by pain in her head, back when no one knew what it was. Belle Fleur is a Catholic town. So, the local priest decided she was possessed—and gave her a public exorcism when she was thirteen. Years later, she shot her husband for singing too loud in the fields. Relatable, to be honest. But not good."

"An exorcism? You can't be serious. There weren't any doctors in town?"

"You weren't raised with Jesus, Audre. People get fanatical when they believe their religion is fact," she said, arching a brow. "Clothilde escaped from a turbulent home and fled to New Orleans—where she passed as a fancy white socialite, fooling everyone in town. But she exposed the truth in the suicide note she wrote in lipstick on her bathroom wall. And my mom, your grandma Lizette? She's not who you think she is."

Audre was hanging on her mom's every word. A sick, misunderstood teenager getting the "witch" label. A Black woman tricking high society into thinking she's white. Broken families, race shame, haunted, murderous women. They sounded like characters in a movie, not real life.

"By the time I started school, she'd aged out of pageants. That's when she started escorting. Wealthy men would... well, they'd hire her to be their date." Eva paused to gather her thoughts. "In exchange, they'd gift us an apartment, pay the bills. And when one arrangement was over, we'd hit the road, looking for the next guy. At first, the men were nice enough. But as she got older, they got meaner and cheaper." Eva chewed a nail. "And they got handsy."

Audre gasped, running her hand over her eyes. *Handsy.* What a chilling word. She had so many questions for Eva—and the girl she used to be—but she knew not to interrupt a person who was exposing a hidden truth.

Also, she was furious with Grandma Lizette. She'd held her up as a shero. A feminist icon. When she was little, she'd named her American Girl doll after her. She used to think Grandma Lizette controlled the seasons. From the way Eva talked about her, she seemed all-powerful.

"Lizette used to tell me that Mercier girls were cursed," continued Eva. "And I had no reason to believe she was wrong. Lizette was a mess, and so was I. When I was your age, I had a death wish. I was in constant pain. No friends, miserable home life. That's when I met Shane."

Audre frowned, confused. "And I always thought that you and Shane were wholesome high school sweethearts. Second-chance romance goals."

"We weren't wholesome, honey. We did drugs together, we self-harmed together, and we broke the law. When you came home the other night with Bash? And his face was bruised and cut? I saw me and Shane, and I was scared. It's what I always try to protect you from."

Audre thought back to all the times Eva had been unreasonably strict. She wasn't allowed to go to slumber parties till she'd taken two years of Muay Thai boxing. Eva always assumed the worst was going to happen. Still, Audre thought, it would've been so much easier to just share what she experienced so she understood.

"The best thing we did was escape each other, though. We both got clean. He became a famous writer. I got into college and wrote the first Cursed book. I met your dad, and we had you. I bought this apartment in a fancy neighborhood, sent you to a fancy school. All I cared about was giving you a normal life. A life with problems, sure—but normal problems. Not ones that would land you in a mental institution."

Audre gasped, and then felt bad for her reaction. "You were institutionalized?"

Eva nodded. "In twelfth grade, Shane and I ran away together. We broke into an empty house and lived there for a week. And I overdosed. Afterward, the police ordered me to check into a facility."

"What in the bad-girl *hell*, Mom?"

"I taught you that 'Mercy girls do what can't be done' instead of 'Mercy girls are cursed' on purpose. To make us sound like superheroes instead of victims." Eva reached for Audre's hand, straightening her cameo ring. "I wanted the past to give you strength instead of weighing you down."

Audre tried to take it all in. "I come from a long line of melancholy outlaws. Bad girls. This is my ancestral truth! I've wasted so much time trying to be so good."

"Life isn't that black-and-white, though. There's bad and good in all of us. It wasn't till I wrote my book that I learned to embrace all of it. It's freeing. You're chained to the stuff you can't get over," she told her. "Delphine, Clothilde, and Lizette did the best they could with no resources or support. I accept them, and I accept myself. You can't live a full life until you do."

It made sense. Audre understood why she'd hidden her true self: Genevieve Mercier. Life was complicated and families weren't perfect—and Eva was doing the best she could.

"But if you're all about accepting your past, why couldn't you tell me?"

"I was scared. Putting it off for as long as I could. Because telling you the truth would mean undoing all the half-truths I'd told you over the years." Again, Eva reached out for Audre's hands across the table. "Can you forgive me someday?"

Audre had a million thoughts running through her mind. She hated being lied to. But she loved her mom and wanted her back. So, with a resigned smile, she nodded. "I forgive you."

"Thank you," whispered Eva.

"You are a warrior, Mom. It's like a flaming baton was passed down from mother to daughter, mother to daughter, and when it got to you, you blew it out. That's your gift to me, and Baby Alice, and everyone who comes after us."

"Beautifully put." Eva's eyes filled up with tears. "I was going to tell you before the book came out. You weren't supposed to discover it on your own. You must've felt so betrayed."

"And confused, and angry," admitted Audre. "But at least it got us talking. I haven't felt close to you since Baby Alice was born. Sounds bratty, but it's like you dropped me for her."

"Are you crazy? I loved you first!" Eva dabbed her eyes with a napkin. "We went from a family of two to four overnight. I'm learning as I go."

"Aren't we all," sighed Audre, sounding world-weary. "Mom? There's something I've been keeping from you."

This was the perfect time to tell Eva about the panic attacks. But was she ready to come clean about the prom video, Ellison's laughter, her public meltdown? To say the words out loud—and reveal that she didn't have it all together? That she was messy sometimes? And felt small, which was the opposite of the personality she projected to the world?

Hell yes. Her mom's honesty had given her courage.

And so, she spilled all. By the time they were done talking, they were curled up in Eva's bed with *Hereditary* on in the background. It felt like old times. The two of them, cozy, watching their comfort horror movies and chitchatting about life.

"I'm furious you didn't tell me about the panic attacks. What were you thinking?"

"I'm not supposed to have problems. Plus, you're so busy with Baby Alice."

"You're my child, too. We'll work on this together. I'm calling Dr. Cleveland on Monday morning." She paused, stroking Audre's hair. "And Bash?"

Audre froze. "What about him?"

"You really like him, huh?"

"I like him too much," she admitted after a lengthy pause.

Eva let out a mighty exhale. "Look. I'm not gonna ease up about boys overnight. It's all triggering for me. But it's my stuff, and I need to work through it."

"You should double your antidepressant dosage."

Eva rolled her eyes. "I'm happy you have a fun crush. Life's too short to waste it worrying about bad things that might happen. Look at me, growing!"

"Since you're growing," said Audre slyly, "can I ask your opinion on my self-help book? I know you're against me writing it."

"I just didn't want you to focus on writing *professionally*. It's too much pressure at your age." She sat up a little. "But I'm working on my overprotective streak. Ask me anything."

Audre sat up. "Okay, here's my issue. My notes feel personal to what's happening in my life instead of general advice for everyone.

Will Stanford admissions be like, who'd take emotional health tips from this basket case?"

"Well, why not write to yourself? A self-help book written by you—for you. Like a 'What I Learned This Summer' essay, but with a therapy slant."

Audre sucked in a huge breath. She had the title.

"Hey." Eva's voice sounded odd. "What happened to your wrist?"

Audre looked down. Somehow, her sleeve had bunched up and her bandaged wrist was exposed. Her mind blanked momentarily. Frantically, she searched for an excuse. A quick, easy lie. Anything. But she and Eva had just shared an afternoon of deep truths and revelations. Her mom was growing! It would be a slap in the face to their relationship if she lied now.

So, Audre went there.

"It's a tattoo. A tiny one. Bash did it. He's a tattoo artist! An unlicensed, underage one... but he's got a huge future ahead of him."

She shot her mom a brilliant smile. In return, Eva stared at her, unblinking, for what felt like five hours. Audre had misread the situation completely.

And there it is, thought Audre. *The danger in having a "cool mom." For one, crucial moment, you could get comfortable. You could get tricked into thinking you were friends. You could forget that she was also a capital-M mother who didn't fuck around. The kind who'd sell your Shopkins collection on eBay after you, in a moment of show-offy sassiness at your ninth birthday party, told her to shut up in front of Ms. St. Croix's entire class.*

"You've lost your damned mind, I see."

"But I thought you were working on your overprotective streak!"

"Up to a point," she said through gritted teeth. "But when it comes to my sixteen-year-old class-president-honors-student child sneaking around getting illegal tattoos from a minor? Absolutely fucking not, ma'am. What's he gonna convince you to do next? Freebase?"

"What's freebase? Mom! It's just a tattoo."

"This isn't about the actual tattoo. It's about your decision making. Your impulsivity. The lying. You haven't been yourself since you met him."

She flinched with dread. "But you don't understand . . ."

"Believe me, I do. You and Bash are over, Audre. I mean it. You're breaking up. I won't let him unravel all I've worked so hard to instill in you."

Eva climbed out of her bed and stormed out of her own room—and Audre was left emotionally whiplashed. From Eva's tone alone, Audre knew she wouldn't budge on this.

This reality felt like a fist around her heart, squeezing it into nothingness.

There didn't seem to be enough air in the room. Her stomach plummeted as if she were in free fall, the whole world whizzing by.

You and Bash are over.

How could she break up with Bash? He was already in her veins. He illuminated her entire world. Even when she hadn't known where she stood with him, when their situation had been confusing and frustrating—every moment they spent together was electric. In a *movie* way. In a "this only happens to other people" way. And their tattoo experience? The way he'd handled her, so carefully and conscientiously. His touch, his brain, his kiss—his *heart*—had ignited a flame in her that she couldn't bear extinguishing. She needed him.

She couldn't imagine un-liking him. Un-caring about him, un-adoring him.

But she also couldn't imagine winning a war with her mother—over a boy, or anything else. Turns out, Audre wasn't an outlaw like the Merciers before her. She was a by-the-book, predictable "yes-girl" who craved approval.

So, Audre did what she was told.

Chapter 35

Was it possible to desperately miss someone you'd just seen eighteen hours before? A few months ago, Bash would've said no. But today, it was an enthusiastic yes.

He couldn't remember feeling this happy ever in his life. Was this what it was like? Being so ignited by another human being that all you wanted to do was ... do whatever *they* wanted to do? Be where they are? That's what Audre did to him. In her presence, he felt both peaceful and euphoric—simultaneously. The world's most magical girl looked at him like *he* was magic. And for once, Bash didn't feel lost. He knew he had value. A purpose.

Hanging with Audre all summer taught him that the old cliché was true. Home wasn't a location. It was a feeling. Bash's home was wherever she was.

Physically, of course, he was still crashing at his mom's. In fact, he was currently splayed out on her couch, carefully Gorilla-Gluing his busted Smurf lunch box. But for the first time, he wasn't tortured by it, or itching to escape. It didn't matter where he was, because Audre was his girlfriend. His mom? Far from his mind. (Plus, she was in DC annoying the hell out of at-risk youth, so he was alone.)

In an hour, he was meeting Audre at Nitehawk Cinema. At the thought of seeing her, his face melted into a giddy grin. A warm, tingly thrill surged through him. He hadn't seen her since last night's couples' confrontation. Such an unhinged scene. When he texted Audre afterward to check in, she couldn't talk. She and her mom were having A Stern Conversation.

I hope she's okay, he thought, gluing an arm back on the ancient plastic Smurf. *I hate knowing that any of it's my fault. Also, I hate that I didn't remind her to apply Neosporin before bed.*

He'd tell her at the theater. They hadn't picked a movie to see yet, but it didn't matter. All Bash wanted was to sit with Audre, in the dark, in her orbit.

Plus, he had life-altering news.

Just then, his phone buzzed. It was Clio. Who'd been leading a secret life for all summer. Yes, he'd kept secrets, too—but he had reasons!

"Who's this?" he asked into the phone.

"You tell me. Am I your sister or your quote, unquote acquaintance?"

"Are you Reshma's girlfriend, or Fake-Anthony's girlfriend?"

"You know his name's *Jake*-Anthony."

"When he stops speaking in a fake Caribbean accent, I'll call him Jake-Anthony," he scoffed. "You're half-Jamaican—this doesn't bother you?"

"He used to sing in a reggae band! The accent stuck!"

"Why didn't you tell me you broke up and started dating Audre's best friend?"

"Don't be a hypocrite. You and I *both* had secret relationships this summer."

"Nah, man, I told you about Audre."

"You told me you were helping a friend with a challenge. Not that you two were Rapunzel and Flynn Rider."

"Rapunzel and Flynn *who?*"

"I saw you guys last night, outside Just Because. When we walked up to you, it was like you two were in your own universe. There was a...a...love energy around you two. It was giving 'get a room.'"

His stomach flip-flopped. Was their connection that obvious? "But I didn't lie, okay? At the beginning of the summer, she was just a friend. Everything changed so fast."

"Too fast to tell her I was your half sister? Or that we have two older half sisters? I mean, we don't know them super well, but still. It should've come up."

Bash squeezed his eyes shut. "I know. I know, I should've. But then, I'd have had to explain our fucked-up family."

"Fucked-up or not, family's family."

"If family's so important to you, why didn't you tell me you were cheating on Fake-Anthony?"

"*Jake*-Anthony!" she exclaimed. "It's 'cause I was ashamed to be cheating. Reshma was supposed to be...an experiment that went awry. I wanted to take back the power from Jake-Anthony. Also, I wanted to see if what I've always felt about girls was true."

"And?"

"And it's true. I like the ladies." She sighed. "Or maybe I just like Reshma. Doesn't matter either way, because she was using me. Fuck. I'm so confused."

Bash tilted his head to one side, carefully scraping extra glue off the Smurf's face. "You were both using each other. Just start over. Wipe the slate clean, you know?"

"Maybe." Clio's voice sounded floaty and faraway. "You know what? You sound good. Strong. Healthy."

"I do?" He smiled at this. "I'm currently rehabbing a broken undersea Smurf, so I don't know how healthy that is."

"I'm not even gonna ask."

"But you're right. I am feeling healthy. I made two healthy decisions. You know the tattoo place in Myrtle Beach? They asked me to come down for a weeklong interview after my birthday. And I turned it down."

"Tell me you didn't. Why would you do that? That place was all you talked about for months!"

"I know, I know. But I changed my mind. There's tattoo businesses all over New York. And New Jersey and Long Island, even. I've already contacted six shops. I have two interviews next week. Myrtle Beach is too far."

"Too far? Oh. *Ohhh.* You don't wanna be too far from Audre."

At the mention of her name, the corners of his mouth curved upward. "Not really."

"Did she ask you to stay?"

"I meannn...like...no. But we haven't talked about the future or anything. I don't know, it just didn't feel right to go. Especially when there's opportunity here."

"That's kinda romantic, Bash. Impulsive. But romantic."

"Whatever," he said, bashful. "Call Reshma."

"What's the second healthy decision?"

Bash pulled up to a sitting position on the couch, his feet on the floor. Suddenly nervous, he set the Smurf on the coffee table. His hands felt unsteady, and he didn't want to disturb the delicate, glued pieces. "I decided to talk to Dad. Well, not talk. Write him an email."

Clio's gasp was so sharp and loud, it was like she was sitting next to him.

"You were right. It's not about letting him off the hook. It's about closure before he . . . he's . . ."

"Before he's gone," said Clio.

"Right." Bash swallowed uncomfortably. No one he'd ever known had died. What would it be like for Milton to just disappear?

He already has, thought Bash. *He disowned you. Don't forget that.*

"I just wanna move on," he continued. "I have good things in my life now. But I can't fully feel them because he's just weighing me down. It's like he's the devil on my shoulder, reminding me that I ruined his life. And mine." He paused, waiting for Clio's response. "You there?"

"Yeah! Sorry, I was nodding," she said breathlessly. "I'm so proud of you."

"Don't be yet. I haven't written it. I don't know where to start."

And then Clio began listing off ideas for opening sentences. Clearly, she'd been thinking about this a lot. Nothing she said rang true, though. Her issues with Milton were different than his. She never knew him, but Bash knew him too well.

As his sister talked, he zoned out a bit. Just staring at his patched-up Smurf and racking his brain for how to say goodbye to his dying father. His first champion, his fiercest enemy. A man whose demons, whatever they were, had zero to do with Bash. But he'd made his son pay for them nevertheless.

Bash looked at the Smurf lunch box. The Smurf lunch box looked back at him. No one would've known he'd glued its sad, cracked body back together again. It looked like nothing ever happened.

Like nothing ever happened.

His spine went rigid. That was it. He knew exactly what to say. Hastily, he ushered Clio off the phone. And he began typing into his notes app. No thinking, no second-guessing—just spilling his immediate thoughts onto the screen.

But first, he set the timer on his phone.

Dear Dad,

I was never going to speak to you again. But Clio convinced me to, and I think she's right. It's probably not healthy to swallow my feelings forever. I don't want them to turn sour inside me and make me mean. Maybe that's what happened to you. Maybe something happened in your past that killed your kindness. I don't know, because you never talked to me, person to person. I'll never know now. And that's okay.

I met a girl, and I like her so much it scares me sometimes. She's the smartest person I've ever met. Yesterday, she told me that anything less than emotional honesty is cheating. I don't want to cheat myself. So, here's the truth.

You were a dictator, not a dad. You pushed me till my body broke. You never asked me how I felt. And all I wanted was to please you...on the track, in interviews, at college scouting trips. I tried to be perfect so you'd love me. I failed. But I kept trying to make things perfect.

And now, I think I'm addicted to it. I deliberately throw parties at Jennifer's house just so I can clean up afterward. The other day, somebody chipped one of Jennifer's vases, and I went to the hardware store and learned how to make it new again. I just spent the whole day refurbishing a broken Smurf! There's no high like fixing what's broken. And I think it's a metaphor, right? I do it because I couldn't patch up what broke between us.

And I won't try now. It'd probably take more time than you've got.

The only thing I regret about the "scandal" is that Jaden got hurt. I know he'll have a good life, though. I'll have one, too. You wasted yours despising what you don't understand. Couldn't be me.

I need peace. So, I forgive you, Dad. I hope that, wherever you're going, you'll find peace, too.

Your son,
Sebastian

He checked the timer. Five minutes and three seconds. He'd beaten the time it had taken for Milton to disown him. He'd beaten it. From that moment on, Bash stopped obsessively timing things. The "seven minutes" spell had been broken.

Before he could read over what he wrote—or change his mind—Bash emailed the letter to his dad. And he closed that chapter of his life. It was a door he'd never open again.

Waves of relief washed over him with such force, he felt faint. He flopped back onto the couch and lay there, too wrung-out to do anything but stare at the ceiling. After some unknown amount of time, he snapped back to life. Got up. Grabbed his wallet and phone. And left.

The past was behind him. Audre was his future. And he couldn't get to her fast enough.

•   •   •

Nitehawk Cinema, the cozy, retro-style movie theater, was only eight blocks away. So, Bash got there early. Walking up to the theater, he was surprised to see that Audre was already there, waiting for him under the red neon sign. Early. Twenty minutes early. She was just standing there, arms folded, not on her phone, not reading. She looked rattled. Damn, was she even blinking?

As he got nearer, he saw that her eyes were red and swollen.

His breath caught in his throat. And he sped up. Pulled out of her daze, she looked to her left and saw him jogging her way. And she attempted to smile.

It wasn't an Audre smile. It was artificial, overdone. The kind you make when you're trying to cheer someone up at a funeral.

"What's wrong?" he blurted out when he reached her. His impulse was to hug her, kiss her. But she stood rigid as a statue, unmoving.

"I'm great!" she said, her voice strained.

His heart rate began to speed up. "No, you're not. I know you. What happened? Was it the talk with your mom?"

She bit her bottom lip and shook her head rapidly. Was she fighting off tears? "You said you had some exciting news. What is it?"

"Audre..."

"Tell me your exciting news!" She raised her voice and then looked around to see if anyone was listening. Lowering her head a bit, she stepped closer to Bash and slipped her hand in his. "Tell me. I need to hear something good. Please."

Bash felt giddy. He was standing outside the movie theater at 2 PM on a Thursday, holding the hand of the girl he wanted more than anything in the world, and he felt a sense of doom so powerful, it was making him nauseous. But she asked for the news.

And, in the several weeks he'd known Audre Mercy-Moore, he hadn't been able to say no to her, once.

"I turned down the Myrtle Beach tattoo place. I'm staying in Brooklyn."

She blinked several times.

"For me?" she asked in a shaky whisper.

"For you," he said.

And then, she did cry. She fell against his chest and sobbed, gathering his T-shirt into her fists. Bash didn't know what to do, so he held her close, walking her to a quiet spot away from the entrance. He let her cry. Finally, she caught her breath. Almost angrily, she wiped her tear-streaked cheeks and looked him directly in the eye.

Bash knew what she was going to say before she said it. He flexed every muscle in his body, steeling himself for the emotional blow.

"We can't see each other anymore."

His eyes shuttered. The world went dark.

"Why?" he managed to ask, opening his eyes. "Your mom?"

She nodded, not looking at him. His mouth went dry. His heart imploded. Nearby, a dog-walker tried to steer five cockapoos from sprinting into the street. Somebody honked their car horn a million times. A blond kid whizzed by on a neon scooter. Normal Brooklyn shit was happening all around them. Life carried on, business as usual—while his world crumbled to dust.

"Audre . . . this can't be it. I can't lose you," he said, his voice cracking. His eyes reddened, blinking back tears. He was too flustered to do anything but beg. "Please. *Please.* I need you."

"I'm sorry," she whispered. "I'm sorry."

With that, she disentangled herself, pressed her lips against his cheek, and left him.

Hours later, his skin still smarted where she had pecked him. He felt the burn of it, just as vividly as if he'd been kissed by fire.

Chapter 36

Over the past five years, Audre had given tons of relationship advice. Decenter men! It's not love, it's adrenaline! Don't go back to an ex—if you see the same tree in the forest twice, you're lost!

Fine, but this advice was coming from a girl who'd never known the giddy high of finding her kindred spirit. A girl who'd never felt the addictive rush of finding a puzzle piece that slotted into hers perfectly. A girl who'd never melted from the sheer, intoxicating power of a single kiss. A girl who'd never felt all of this and had it ripped away from her.

The advice she'd given was logical. But it was also bullshit. Because there was nothing logical about falling for someone. It was sloppy, thirsty, embarrassing, uncool, irrational. All this time, she'd basically been advising people to put out a four-alarm fire with a water gun.

Turns out, Reshma was right, she thought. *I did need to experience real life to make me a better therapist.*

What were the chances that she'd meet her person at sixteen?

With all the bad hookups, misunderstandings, and failed crushes out there, the likelihood was slim. She researched it, actually. According to a 2017 study, mathematicians found that, on any given day, only one in 562 people has the chance of finding love.

One in 562 people. Roughly the number of students enrolled at Cheshire Prep. That's how special and rare it was. Despite scientific odds—and the fact that she wasn't even looking!—she'd found her person. Audre should've held on to him forever. If she'd had any balls she would've disobeyed her mother and done exactly that.

Audre had a boyfriend for less than a day. And now he was gone. And she was fucking *flattened* by the loss. Heartbreak was so all-consuming, it shocked her. *This* was what her clients had been feeling all these years? *This* was what she'd secretly dismissed as over-the-top drama? Well. The universe was paying her back.

For the first week after her mom brutally ended her only real chance at happiness, Audre stayed on the couch, buried under blankets. She cried racking, silent sobs for three days (until she gave herself a nosebleed from dehydration). Then the nightmares started. She never remembered any specifics, but she always woke up the same way—digging her nails into her palms like she was fighting to hold on to something that was slipping away. The next phase? Feverishly buying relationship self-help books on Kindle. She read *The Wisdom of a Broken Heart, The Breakup Bible,* and *Emotional Self-Care for Black Women,* and couldn't find a single detail on how to remove the section of her heart that *ached* for Bash Henry.

Losing him was excruciating. Hating her mom was almost as bad.

Audre couldn't look Eva in the face. During that bedridden hell week, her mom would nudge her lump of a body under the blankets, whispering words of encouragement—but no apology, curiously. Audre simply ignored her or responded with a one-word grunt. (Audre snapped at Shane, too, when he dared to speak. She wasn't mad at him. But he caught the smoke by association.) It just didn't make sense that her mom—the person she loved most in the world—had so carelessly stomped on her happiness. Eva had been her age once. She'd been in love with Shane! Yes, apparently, they were a disaster, but it was the real thing since they ended up together.

Audre and Bash weren't a disaster. They were good for each other. But her mom hadn't even bothered to hear her out. She couldn't see past her own teenage destructiveness.

Seven days after the breakup, Audre was done. She no longer wanted to rot on the living room couch, in the middle of the apartment, in front of an audience. Depression without a bedroom was mortifying. So she got up, swept her braids into a high pony, threw on black sweats (she was in mourning), and walked to the Central Library at Grand Army Plaza. Working on her book might distract her from the pain.

Once in the grand, almost museum-like building, she found a table tucked away in the Memoir section. With steely resolve, she sat down and opened a new Word doc entitled "What I Learned This Summer." The Stanford application process wouldn't stop just 'cause she was sad. Glumly, she stared at the blank screen for ages. Was her brain broken? She couldn't think past her sadness. Nothing came to her—until out of the corner of her eye, she spotted a framed poster nestled on a shelf to her left. It was a photo of a nondescript-looking, older white woman with mousy brown hair. Underneath, was a quote.

> Take your broken heart, make it into art.
> —Bestselling author
> and Star Wars actress Carrie Fisher

Audre had never heard of Carrie Fisher, and she wasn't a Star Wars person. But that quote ignited her like fireworks under her ass. It was A Sign.

I can do that, thought Audre. *She's not saying to ignore my sadness. She's saying to lean in, make something beautiful out of it.*

That was all the encouragement she needed. Without a moment's hesitation, she got to work.

WHAT I LEARNED THIS SUMMER
PROLOGUE

When I first started researching this book, I envisioned a guidebook with rules for living your best teen life. But I realized that I was thinking too broadly.

Everyone is different. Every teen, every client, every human. What I discovered this summer? Aside from "be a kind person" and "don't do murder," there are very few hard-and-fast, one-size-fits-all rules that apply to everyone. And though I'm a gifted therapist? I, sixteen-year-old Audre Zora Maya Toni Mercy-Moore, don't have all the answers.

My mom was an underage outlaw. My grandmother "dated" dangerous men to put food on the table. My great-grandmother lied about her race to escape racial terror, and my great-great-grandma was an (alleged) witch and an (actual) murderess. For better or worse, I come from a long line of rule-breakers. They'd probably die laughing at the idea that the secret to life is... more rules. I think it's more valuable to learn from your bumps in the road. Processing personal trauma. Figuring out how to survive.

Example? This summer, I met a boy who everyone said was a player. Someone to have fun with but not take seriously. Well, I fell for him so hard my head's still spinning. But we fell apart. And I can't shake the sadness. I've read every self-help book written on breakups, and none of the rules work for me. So, I'm done with them. Instead, I want to talk about lessons. The ones I learned this summer changed my life in immeasurable ways.

Stanford, I'm sure every psychology major applicant reads the same books and drops the same therapy buzzwords. Not me, though. On these pages, I'm drawing from the richness of my own experience instead. Read on, Stanford. Because I've learned a lot. And at your prestigious institution, I know I can polish my wisdom till it shines like gold.

The words spilled out of her. And soon, her daily writing sessions became a ritual. Every day she marched straight to the library, sat at her little table, and got to work. No veering off course. No talking to anyone. Just focusing on pouring truth from her fingertips. And with each new chapter, her mood lifted just a tiny bit.

And yet.

Audre kept her eyes cast downward on her walks. She was terrified of running into Bash. Despite her precautions, though, she thought she saw him everywhere—in every tall, lanky, deeply bronzed person within a two-mile radius. It always happened the same way. She'd see someone. Her breath would catch in her throat. Her stomach would burn with longing. Then she'd look closer—and it was never him. One time, Audre spotted a pair of pink Crocs walking through Grand Army Plaza and almost fainted. Until she noticed that the Crocs were attached to a statuesque pregnant woman.

Bittersweet relief. She wasn't ready to face him.

Actually, the day of the Crocs sighting, she was too rattled to go to the library. Instead, she walked past it and kept going until she ended up at Artist & Craftsman Supply. It was Middle School Audre's favorite store. Interesting. For so long, she thought her artist days were behind her. But maybe her feet knew something she didn't.

Being around Bash had inspired her to think about art again. Maybe it was time to just, you know, casually attempt a new painting. Even if it sucked, it'd be a perfect distraction. So, she brought a few canvases, oil paints, and supplies, and headed to

Prospect Park, where she set up a little art studio under her favorite tree. Without overthinking it, she began swirling paints onto the canvas. She didn't know it was going to be her mom's wedding present until she was finished.

It doesn't have to be a Museum of Modern Art masterpiece, she thought, letting her imagination take over. *Art therapy may not cure anxiety, but it definitely soothes and calms. It's cathartic. It's healing. It's . . .*

It's Reshma?

Audre looked up and there was her former best friend, framed by a brilliant, late summer sky. From her vantage point on the ground, Reshma looked larger than life.

"What are you doing here?" asked Audre, shielding her eyes from the sun with her palm.

"What are *you* doing here?" Reshma flashed a suspiciously wide smile. "Are you really painting in the park? It's very 2019 Audre."

She shrugged and went back to painting. "I'm honoring my inner child. I just read a book called *She's Still There: Rescuing the Girl in You*. Hopefully it'll help."

"Help with what?"

Without lifting her head, she muttered, "Help make me feel better. My mom made me break up with Bash."

"Break up? Wait. Wait, wait, wait. You were official?"

"For eighteen hours, yeah." Audre never once looked up from the canvas balanced on her knees. "So. Did you want something?"

"Noooo. Not really. Just . . . hanging out. So, uh, Eva and Shane's wedding's tomorrow. Am I still allowed to go?"

"They invited you; it has nothing to do with me," said Audre.

"Fair. Whatcha paintin'?" she asked in an aggressive Cockney accent. It used to make Audre giggle.

"Don't know yet. It's an abstract emotional expression."

"Okay, abstract queen!"

An aggravated sigh exploded out of Audre. Enough was enough. Gently, she set her canvas on the grass and then stood up to face Reshma. "What is this? Were you following me?"

She slid her sunglasses into her wild waves. Self-consciously, she took a step backward. "I saw your location on Snap Map."

"Jesus, Reshma." Audre bent down to gather her supplies. "I'm out."

"Come on, don't leave," begged Reshma in her raspy drawl. "How long are you going to ignore me? Please, just let me explain."

Audre stood back up in flustered anger, fists on her hips. "You don't have to explain. I'm a thousand percent clear on what happened. I asked you not to interfere in Clio and Bash's situation, and you broke your promise. And ended up embarrassing me and embarrassing yourself. The worst part, though? The very worst part is that you were so sure I couldn't get him without you butting in. Everything isn't always about you, Reshma. *God.* Sometimes it's exhausting being your friend!" She paused to catch her breath. "And guess what? I got him all on my own. And lost him just as fast. So you wasted your time trying to break up actual *siblings* for no reason."

With that, Audre stuffed her things in the shopping bag and tried to storm off. But Reshma was too fast, stepping in front of her and grabbing her wrist. The one with the raw, fresh tattoo.

"Ow, ow, ow!" exclaimed Audre.

"What?" Reshma snatched her hand back. "I didn't even grab you that hard. Wait." She gasped. "Is that . . . did you get a tattoo? I love it! IS THIS YOUR BADDIE ERA? Who even *are* you?"

"A lot's happened that you don't know about." Audre wiggled her hand, trying to shake off the burn. "Ugh, that really hurt."

"I know you hate me right now," she confessed. "I deserve it. I went behind your back. I lied. But I really thought I was helping. I did!"

Audre squinted, staring her down. "Tell the truth."

"I just . . . did?"

"You wanted to star in your own drama. You loved it. You were bored."

Reshma flinched in surprise. "Fine. Okay? That might be true. I'm not like you, Audre. I have nothing going on. I'm not good at a particular thing. I have no idea where I wanna go to college. My parents hate me. People at school are intimidated by me. And I'm all alone in that house. I'm lonely as hell. Maybe I did try to stir up drama. But ohhhh, I paid for it."

"You paid?" Audre raised her chin. "How?"

"Because now I think I'm in love with the coolest, hottest, sweetest girl, but she thinks I'm a crazy bitch."

Against her better judgment, her icy exterior melted just a bit. As long as Audre knew her, Reshma had never admitted to being in love. "Well. Because you are."

Reshma smiled softly. "You are."

"No, you."

With glistening eyes, she outstretched her arms. "I'm sorry, doll."

"I know," said Audre, leaning in for a fast hug. She wasn't ready to forgive Reshma completely. She still felt so betrayed—just a pawn in Reshma's game. But she wasn't speaking to her mom and wasn't *allowed* to speak to Bash. Honestly, Audre couldn't bear to lose anyone else. And in the end, Audre knew she wasn't trying to hurt her with those antics. Reshma just couldn't see beyond herself sometimes.

"How can I make it up to you?"

Audre looked up to the sky, mulling it over. The answer came to her in a flash. "Bring Clio to the wedding. As your plus-one. Then at least I'll know that some good came out of your antics."

Reshma grimaced, nervously flipping her hair to one side. "She'd never say yes. Clio has *principles*. I'm dead to her."

"You both tricked each other. Which means you're even. You can start over. Clean slate."

"Hmm. Not no." She pursed her lips, thinking about this. "You have a point."

"Duh. I'm a professional."

Reshma grinned at her. Audre grinned back. And then they linked arms, walking out of the park together. Audre hadn't forgiven her completely, yet. But she would.

When they stopped to let a group of rowdy tweens pass, her phone buzzed.

Ellison: 2 things. 1) i'm not apologizing anymore 2) keep your bf away from me 3) pls pls tell me if u told anyone? PLS

"On top of everything, the little bitch can't count," muttered Reshma, peering over Audre's shoulder.

Without pausing to think, Audre blocked his number. She should've done it months ago—but it always seemed pointless. What would be the point? Sure, Ellison wouldn't be able to contact her. But she'd still be stuck with the memory of prom night. Blocking him would've been a Band-Aid.

Today, though, Audre welcomed the Band-Aid.

Violence is never the answer, she thought. *But I can't deny that it was satisfying, watching Bash punch Ellison in his smug little face. If that makes me unevolved and shallow, then so be it. He did what I'd done in my head, in fantasies. In a way, it felt like the universe (i.e., Bash) had almost evened the score.*

Just then, Audre had a thought. She remembered a useful trick from years of watching horror movies with Eva. When confronted by a ghost, a poltergeist, or anything else that was haunting you, there was only one way to take the power out of it. Acknowledge its presence, make peace with it, and then let it go.

For better or worse, Bash punching him was the acknowledgment. Blocking Ellison would bring her peace. And she decided that, the following week, she'd finally talk to her therapist about prom. That'd be her way of letting the whole thing go.

Despite the nagging misery of missing Bash, Audre knew that she'd be okay. Not today or tomorrow. But hopefully soon. And then forever.

Chapter 37

"Raise your glasses, everyone! Toast time!" A drunk friend of Eva and Shane's was squawking into a microphone she'd swiped from the event planner. She was wearing a ballgown and somebody's tie knotted around her head. "Glasses up! A toast to Eva and Shane, the *only* novelist couple to have a healthy relationship in the history of book publishing! They're literal *unicorns*! Authors should never *date*, late alone get *married*, am I right? So much dysfunction, hahaha. But these two break the mold! They're gonna make it. Cheers! Woo-hooo!"

The toast was...dark, but the guests were too tanked to notice. A giddy "*WOOOO!*" rang out throughout the Prospect Park Picnic House grounds, followed by the clinking of roughly two hundred champagne glasses.

Weakly, Audre raised her glass of sparkling apple cider. She was sitting on a rustic picnic table on the outside of the action, balancing Baby Alice on her knee.

Toasts made Audre so uncomfortable. It gave her the same

squeamish feeling she had at hibachi restaurants—watching the chefs do tricks with butcher knives and fire. What if they messed up? What if they gave themselves a third-degree burn or took someone's eye out with a flying shrimp? Impossible to eat under such stressful conditions.

Audre was miserable.

But the wedding was pretty, she had to admit. The meadow surrounding Prospect Park's Picnic House had been turned into a dark academia wonderland for the big day. Piles of vintage books were used as cocktail tables. Typewriter planters held romantic lilac bouquets. Hanging lanterns lit up the night sky. And in the center of everything was a wooden dance floor, where Flip It and Reverse It—the band led by Clio's (ex?) boyfriend, Jake-Anthony—played throwback R&B. It was sort of amusing watching a bunch of sloshed adults wiggle around to "The Thong Song" in their black-tie finest. But other than that, Audre was in hell.

Oh, she was doing her job, though. As the "Bridesdaughter of Honor" (Baby Alice was the "Ringbaby"), she made sure to smile sweetly during the ceremony and be social during the reception. She'd posed for pictures with the happy couple and hugged and kissed them both. She helped her mom with her veil before the ceremony and danced at the reception with Shane for a song and a half. If this were school, she would've gotten a 100 percent plus extra credit for this wedding.

But her mask was starting to chip. She could feel the sadness rising in her, the tears burning behind her eyes. She was so tired of pretending that she wasn't missing Bash. Desperately. Being around all this love and celebration just reminded her that she'd lost her love. And had no reason to celebrate.

And, simmering at the bottom of everything was her anger at Eva. She *wanted* to forgive her, to get over it. Pretending things were fine—when they clearly weren't—was exhausting. But every time she looked at Eva, she saw the person who killed her chance at happiness. She didn't see her mom. She saw her enemy.

Audre decided to take a break from the festivities. Baby Alice was her excuse. And now she was sitting on that bench—all glammed-out in her lavender sweetheart-neckline gown, with lilacs pinned in her half-up hairdo—bottle-feeding a hungry baby. Looking down at her sister, she wondered what she'd be like as a teenager. Her life was going to be so different from Audre's. Growing up in a two-parent home. With a mom who probably wouldn't be so strict anymore. Studies showed that babies with older parents have an easier time because the parents mellow out with age.

Why couldn't I have gotten the mellow mom? thought Audre.

Baby Alice pushed the bottle away and gurgled a little. She smiled, showing off her four teeth. With a sigh, Audre sat her atop the picnic table and gave her a stern look. Baby Alice matched her expression, scowling for no reason. And then she grabbed the pacifier pinned to her tiny version of Audre's dress and popped it in her mouth.

"I have so much to tell you," started Audre, raising her voice over the music. (Behind her, Flip It and Reverse It was playing an Afrobeats version of Usher's "Yeah." It wasn't terrible, actually.) "You didn't ask for advice, but I'm giving it to you. Because

I wish someone had told me. As you grow up, you'll hear a lot about Mercy girls. Or, *Mercier* girls. Or...whoever the hell we are, I don't know. I'm sticking with Mercy. Mom's gonna tell you that 'Mercy girls do what can't be done.' She'll put pressure on you to be perfect. To strive for excellence at all times. Oh, and speaking of excellence? She named us after the most important Black female writers in *history*. I'm Audre Zora Maya Toni—for Audre Lorde, Zora Neale Hurston, Maya Angelou, and Toni Morrison. You're Alice Maya Octavia—for Alice Walker, Maya Angelou, and Octavia Butler. She set the bar too high for us from the day we were born.

"I was never strong enough to rebel. But I hope you will be. Because the thing is? Perfection ain't it.

"I always thought that if I behaved myself, took the right AP classes, and was the perfect leader at school, my life would work out. I thought excellence would save me. But I'm not saved. I'm not different, or special. I'm heartbroken. *I'm so fucking heartbroken.* Just like all my clients I secretly thought were silly because they didn't have my gift for good sense. Baby Alice, making the 'right' choices doesn't guarantee you a happy ending. So, follow your own path. Take chances, be wild, make mistakes, get messy, be colorful. Be true to whoever you are." She paused, squinting at her sister. "Who are you, I wonder?"

Baby Alice spit out her paci, pointed to Audre's chin, and announced, "SHIM."

"Chin." Audre pointed to her right eye. "What's this?"

"I!" she said.

Then Audre put her hand over her heart.

"HOT!"

Audre pointed at Baby Alice.

"OWISS!"

"That's right," said Audre. "I. Heart. Alice."

In the past few weeks, without anything fun to do, Audre had been teaching her sister some language. If they were going to be stuck in the house together, they might as well communicate. Unintentionally, they sort of bonded.

Then Baby Alice pointed just beyond Audre and said, "MAM."

She frowned. "Mam? What's that?"

Baby Alice kicked her chubby legs and kept pointing. "MAM. MAM!"

Confused, Audre turned around in her seat. And then she froze. And then she gasped so sharply and suddenly, she saw stars.

Not "mam." A *man*. Well, in several days, when he turned eighteen.

Bash.

Her Bash. At the wedding. Wearing a tuxedo. Looking like he was going to the Met Gala—but somehow still like himself. Deeply bronzed skin. Sun-kissed curls. Impossible height. He was the prince in every fairy-tale fantasy she'd ever dared to dream about.

A shy, slow grin spread across his face. "Hi, A."

"Hi, B." She let out a slow exhale, her heart slamming against her rib cage.

"C!" said Baby Alice, who knew the ABCs by heart.

Jolted from her trance, Audre grabbed the baby and plopped

her in the grass on a throw blanket. Baby Alice's massive eyes darted from Bash to Audre and back to Bash again.

"She's your sister? Pleased to meet you, Baby Alice! She has your dimples—it's *wild*."

Audre felt like she could hardly breathe. In a fever, she gathered her silk gown in her hand and rushed over to him. "What are you...why are you here? How did you get in? Did my mom and Shane see you?"

Bash blinked a few times, drinking her in. And then he took a step back. "They know I'm here. It's okay."

Audre took a step forward. "They *know* you're here?"

"Okay, you need to sit back down," he said through a nervous chuckle. "I need to tell you something. But I can't focus if you... when you're close to me. You smell so good and look so pretty and you're...so...so beautiful it hurts. You gotta sit over there."

If it were possible for humans to melt, Audre would've been a puddle. With a giddy smile she couldn't hide, she sat back on the bench. What was this all about?

Bash swallowed, hard. And then he pulled out a folded-up piece of paper from his pocket. "I handwrote this on real paper instead of my notes app. Shane said I'd feel more creative that way."

Audre thought she'd misheard him. "*Shane* said? Excuse me?"

He nodded, fiddling with his cufflinks. "Well, after we had to, you know, break up? I wasn't doing great. I missed you and just felt kinda lost. Pointless. Everything I was scared about happening—ruining another life, hurting you—it happened. Honestly, I just needed help. And Shane told me that if I ever wanted to talk to anyone, he had a mentorship group for dudes my age. So, I went to one of the meetings. And it was cool. It *is* cool. The other kids have issues like mine, broken families and whatever. And Shane just lets everybody talk. And there are doughnuts involved." He smiled.

Just then, she saw Shane and Eva rushing over (she'd gathered up her skirts in her hands, her white Jordans looking crispy as hell). When they reached Bash, Shane gave him a pound, and Eva hoisted Baby Alice up on her hip. And then she looked Bash up and down, nodding with approval.

"You clean up nice, Bash," said Eva, smiling. "Thanks for coming."

Am I having a stroke? thought Audre.

"What the hell is going on?" she demanded. "Mom, why are you suddenly cool with him?"

"I'm not suddenly cool. It took a while. When Shane told me Bash joined the group, I was resistant at first. But your stepdad told me I was being an asshole. And he was right. How can I say that I've accepted my past if I'm so haunted by it that I'm keeping you from enjoying your present? Bash isn't Shane, and you aren't me. It's a dangerous game, making you two pay for crimes Shane and I committed a thousand years ago." Eva raised her chin in Bash's direction, looking luminous in her wedding gown. "Last night I reached out to Bash and invited him to the wedding. Hardest surprise I think I've ever had to keep!"

"Eva doesn't get all the credit," said Shane. "I lent him the tux. Sharp, right?"

Bash smiled softly, watching the scene play out from the sidelines.

Stunned by what she was hearing, Audre turned to Shane. "I—I can't believe this. Shane, did you, like, hypnotize my mom? How did you convince her?"

"Easily. I'm the man of the house," joked Shane. (They all knew Eva ran the show.)

Still holding Alice, Eva pulled Audre into a one-armed hug. "I hate your tattoo. But I love you."

As Audre hugged her mom and Baby Alice, months of anguish seemed to melt away. She felt lighter somehow. And also more mature. And downright euphoric that Eva had accepted Bash. Over her mom's shoulder, she mouthed *thank you* to Shane. He responded with a nod and a wink, his eyes twinkling.

"Anyway, y'all talk," said Shane, grabbing Eva's hand and leading her away. "We're gonna pass Alice to the babysitter and get back to our party. When you're done here, can you ask Reshma and Clio to get a room, please?"

"It's upsetting the lead singer," said Eva, "and his vocals are pitchy enough as it is."

And they headed back into the rowdy, boisterous crowd, looking like wedding-cake toppers—and happier than ever. Audre turned to face Bash, who'd watched all that go down in respectful silence.

He was chewing on his bottom lip, looking both radiantly handsome... and nervous.

"Tell me what you wanted to say," said Audre softly as she sat down, her silk gown draping across the bench.

"Right. So, at Shane's mentorship group, he gave us all an assignment. We had to make a list of goals to accomplish by the end of the year. And I thought, this could be my own Experience

Challenge. And, if you're down, I'd like you to help me with it. You know, be my funsultant."

Audre blinked, a lump forming in her throat.

"Wanna hear the list?"

She nodded. "Badly."

"Okay." He unfolded the paper and cleared his throat.

1. Find a cheap apartment in Brooklyn. Bed-Stuy would be perfect, because that's where I'll be working, starting in September. King's Angel Tattoo Parlor. Hi, I'm Bash Henry, apprentice technician.'

Audre yelped with excitement and happiness, bursting into applause. "Oh my God, oh my God…"

"Please, no interrupting," said Bash.

"My bad. Go."

2. Work with the construction team to help Audre Mercy-Moore set up her bedroom. Shane and Eva's schedules are too crazy to do this, and time's up on the couch-surfing. Plus, working with your hands is good for depression. I learned that in group.

3. Practice my public speaking skills. Learning how to speak confidently about my

craft will come in handy for my new job. Hopefully, I can find someone with elite public speaking skills to teach me. Any suggestions?

With a sly smirk, he flicked his eyes from the paper to Audre, and she couldn't help but beam with happiness. Goofily, she raised her hand (like the teacher's pet she was).

4. Apologize to Farrow. Somehow, I led her on in that diner a few months ago. She's been wild in my DMs.

"Sorry, not to interrupt, but who's Farrow?"
"The girl I bought the bacon-egg-and-cheese for?"
"Ohhh. *Sparrow.*"
"Yeah, her!"
"Got it. Cool. Continue."

5. Tell the most important person in my life how I feel about her.

Bash folded the paper up and slid it back into his pocket. He bit his bottom lip, trying to hold back a smile. "Come here."

Audre flew off the bench and practically catapulted herself into his arms. With a happy laugh, he swept her into an embrace—holding on so tightly, it was as if he'd never let go.

Heart thundering, she pulled back from him a little. She

gazed into his eyes and felt dizzy with emotion. "How do you feel about the most important person in your life?" she whispered.

Bash brushed his nose against hers and said, "I love you, A."

"I love you, too, B."

To seal it, he kissed her sweetly, deliciously, his mouth lingering on hers—stealing her breath and her heart all at once. With that, it was official. Bash and Audre were definitely, absolutely, *not* just friends.

Acknowledgments

First things first, I'd like to thank you, the reader. I'm so honored that you allow me to tell you stories. And it's such a thrill when you get passionate about my characters! When I published *Seven Days in June*—a second-chance romance starring two writers, Shane and Eva—I quickly learned on social media that Eva's (then-twelve-year-old) daughter, Audre, was the fan favorite! Making her the star of her own book was truly a delight.

I graduated high school wayyy back in 199-(rhymes with knee). So, I did some focus group research to make Audre's world feel real. A massive thank-you to this genius crew who filled me in on the NYC high school experience: Jade, Lauryn, Rachel, Hanna, and Victory. Where would I be without your candid anecdotes and hilarious insights? I'm dazzled by each of you.

Huge thanks to my dear friend and Cali-girl, Shannon Mirabelli-Lopez, who decided that Bash was from Oakland. Now I can't imagine him being from anywhere else.

To my editorial team—Alvina Ling, Alexandra Hightower, and Crystal Castro—thank you for helping me shape Audre and Bash's story into rom-com deliciousness. I'm forever grateful for your instincts! And endless gratitude to Andi Porretta for her stunning cover illustration. How did you manage to perfectly capture what Audre and Bash looked like in my mind? And to my superstar book doula, dear friend, and literary agent, Cherise Fisher—"we the you-know-whats." Without you, ma'am? I'm just ideas and vibes.

As always, the biggest thank-you is reserved for my family, near and far. Especially my love/rock/cheerleader/husband, Francesco. And our perfect, brand-new baby boy, Aksel. But most notably, there'd be no Audre without my iconic, one-and-only daughter, Lina. Thank you for being my muse, my in-house romance expert, and my plot-brainstormer. (Aunt Devon's right, you should be a comedy writer.) I love you to the ends of the earth, ladybug. Finally, you're allowed to read one of my books!

Francesco Ferendeles

TIA WILLIAMS

is the award-winning, bestselling author of *The Accidental Diva, It Chicks,* and *The Perfect Find*—now a Netflix film starring Gabrielle Union. Her novel *Seven Days in June* was an instant *New York Times* bestseller and a Reese's Book Club pick. Her latest bestseller, *A Love Song for Ricki Wilde,* was named one of the year's best romances by the *New York Times* and Amazon. Tia lives with her daughter, son, and husband in Brooklyn, NY. She invites you to connect with her at tiawilliams.net.

READ THE NOVEL WHERE WE FIRST MEET AUDRE MERCY-MOORE!

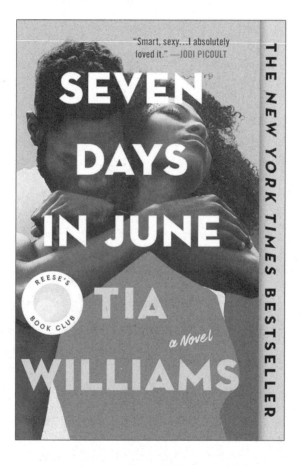

"I just could not stop turning the pages. It's so good."

—REESE WITHERSPOON